D0833051

BONES OF THE WITCH

EARTH MAGIC RISES, BOOK 1

A.L. KNORR

CR

Somerset County Library System
100 Collins Street
Crisfield, MD 21817
CRISFIELD BRANCH

Edited by

NICOLA AQUINO

Edited by

TERESA HULL

INTELLECTUALLY PROMISCUOUS PRESS

Copyright © 2019 by Intellectually Promiscuous Press

All rights reserved.

No part of this book may be reproduced in any form or by any electronic or mechanical means, including information storage and retrieval systems, without written permission from the author, except for the use of brief quotations in a book review.

❦ Created with Vellum

PROLOGUE

here's a billion-dollar industry built around getting rid of dirt...from our houses, our clothes, our skin, our hair. I get it, everyone likes to feel and look clean. As a child, one of my biggest pet peeves was having dirty feet, and you'd never catch me running about outdoors without shoes on.

Oh, how much can change in a year. Now I know that dirt is special beyond what most people realize. Did you know that a single teaspoon of healthy, nutrient-rich soil can contain up to a billion bacteria? A handful of the stuff holds more than fifty billion life forms. Having a relationship with it, especially while we're small, builds up our immune systems, feeds our vitality, and cleanses us in ways that scientists are only beginning to understand.

The ground is alive, it's full of magic, and we need it more than it needs us.

Last year something happened in me that unlocked that understanding and changed me forever.

I became a Wise.

CHAPTER ONE

*T*he smell of hops, smoke, and fried food hit me as I stepped inside *The Blackmouth Arms*. The din of laughter and conversation filled the small pub, the low ceiling and uneven flagstone floors amplifying the chaos. A fellow with a knit cap perched so high on his head it might slide off at any moment plucked at a fiddle, tuning it, alongside a fellow musician doing the same with a guitar. Several pairs of eyes glanced up at me as the door swung shut behind me. Thankfully, they were all friendly.

"Prop the door open, would you love?" hollered a rotund woman with red cheeks as she ran a rag over the bar. "There's a stone just outside the door."

I nodded and backed the door open, kicking the rock into place. It was a good call, as the place was as stuffy and humid as a cellar.

Scanning the heads for Jasher's dark hair, I spotted him deep in conversation at the far wall where the bar met the plaster. His back was to me, but I'd know that tall, broad-shouldered frame anywhere. I suppressed a surge of annoyance at him. Being frustrated with him wasn't how I wanted to start this adventure, but he'd sent a friend to pick me up at the train station rather than coming himself. If he'd been busy with work or unavailable for some good reason, I would have been fine with it, but when his friend pulled up in front of a pub and told me with a grunt and a jerk of her thumb that Jasher was inside, I had to admit, that hurt. He couldn't pick me up because he was out drinking?

I took a bracing breath and told myself he might have an unapparent but excellent reason and to restrain my ire so that I could give him a chance to explain. Shoving my luggage under a table where it wouldn't be underfoot, I sidled through the crowd in the direction of his back, trying not to bump my head on the incredibly low rafters.

Jasher looked to be in lively communion with a young fellow sporting an impressive foam moustache.

"Anything to drink, love?" the lady behind the bar called, raking wild curls away from her sweaty brow.

"Um." My mind scrambled for an answer. I didn't want to stay, but it was rude not to order something, especially since the beer making a pool on the bar at Jasher's elbow still had a lot left.

The lady was still waiting for my response.

I squeezed between the backs of two men bellied up at the bar. They projected enough heat to warm a small barn. No wonder this place was an oven. "Have you got apple cider?"

"Och, a tourist!" she bellowed with enthusiasm. "Where you from then, lass?"

"Canada, but I just arrived from Poland."

A few others overheard and peered at me with curiosity.

"Had a cousin went ter yer cold climes." The bar matron bustled to the other end and disappeared through a doorway that had to have given more than its fair share of goose-eggs in its lifetime. She reappeared with a glass and poured a fizzy brown liquid from a tap. "You picked a bad time o' year to visit, lass. Nothing but dire weather and unwashed locals in these parts until spring."

"You can count me among the number of the great unwashed. I've been on a train all day." I cocked my head as her words sank in. "And, I thought March *was* spring."

This statement was apparently naive enough to elicit laughter from the men on either side of me as well as the bartender.

"Come back in another six weeks if it's spring you're looking for." She set a dripping pint glass in front of me.

"Thanks. I'm not here for the weather, though. I'm visiting a friend." I picked up the glass and brought it to my lips when I caught the tang of alcohol. Whoops. I'd just made a tourist's mistake. I'd assumed apple cider here was the same as it was back home.

I dug some money out of my pocket and slapped it on the bar. Tilting a finger toward my oblivious friend, I said, "I've found him. Thanks for the cider."

She tipped me a wink and faced another patron who asked her for a Drambuie in a brogue so strong it sounded almost like a foreign language. The Scottish accent in the highlands was dramatically deeper than the lyrical lilt in Edinburgh.

Shuffling sideways through the crowd, I closed the distance between Jasher and me. In spite of my annoyance, some butterflies took flight in my stomach, brushing their soft wings against my insides. Jasher and I had had a rough start, but we'd become good friends. He'd been there when I'd inherited the earth magic, and that would always connect us. I was looking forward to being able to spend more time with him. At times, I still caught myself thinking about the kiss we'd shared in Ireland––the best one of my young life.

I set my glass of contraband on the bar just behind him

and tapped him on the shoulder. The musicians in the corner were getting loud, so I raised my voice. "Sorry to interrupt."

Jasher was just lifting his glass to his lips when he turned his head to see who had tapped him on the shoulder.

"Hello, Jasher," I said. *Nice of you to meet me at the station*, I mentally added. This was the burden of most Canadians, a detrimental level of politeness.

The myriad of expressions which played out on his features as recognition sank in was fascinating. His eyes widened, his lips parted, and his brows hiked up to his hairline. The expression of shock that stole over his face was so genuine that further words were startled right out of my throat.

Jasher's friend stared back and forth between us, his drink forgotten in his hand.

"Georjayna!" Jasher yelled it like a victory cry and startled both myself and his drinking buddy. Setting down his drink with a clack, he yanked me into a sweaty, almost violent hug. He smelled of beer and soap and wood. His body felt as lean and corded with muscle as I remembered. He pulled back to look at me, his face bright with excitement. "What are you doing here?"

Speechlessness afflicted me for the second time in fewer minutes. My mouth opened and closed as his question sank in. The sound of a highland jig struck up behind me and it was a surreal addition to Jasher's bizarre reaction.

"How much have you had to drink, Jash?" I finally asked.

I looked at his friend to see if there was some agreed upon ruse between them, but his companion only blinked at me with shallow, bovine interest.

My gaze swung back to Jasher. "I told you I'd be arriving today. I thought you were going to meet me at the station. Your friend dropped me off here. My bag is over there, by the door."

I thumbed over my shoulder, feeling strained from having to shout over the music.

This was a not so subtle hint. He'd had his fun, it was late. I was travel-weary and needed a shower and a bed.

Jasher's smile faltered and his eyes widened again. Surprise was quickly becoming the expression of the evening.

"You did?" He spoke with genuine shock and I found myself scrambling to recall the contents of the letters we'd exchanged. Yes, I was in the right country, and the right time, and he'd been here the whole time. This had been his idea.

I decided it had to be a joke. I rolled my eyes and laughed, directing another look at his friend, looking for a sign. He wore a green t-shirt that said––*Do good, die better*. I noted that he was blond, mid-twenties, and layered with as much muscle as Jasher. I wondered if he was a carpenter too.

"He's such a joker," I told his friend.

"Aye." Green t-shirt agreed, a twinkle flashing in his eye. "That's the first thing I realized when we started working together." He lifted his tumbler of ice cubes and the russet liquid sloshed. "That Jasher, he's something of a balloon."

Why did I get the feeling Green t-shirt was being sarcastic?

"Georjie." Jasher put a hand on my shoulder. "I don't know what you're on about, but this is truly an awesome surprise. I'm so glad you've come! How did you even know where to find me?" Earnestness. Authentic confusion.

"Jasher… your friend dropped me off here. The lady you sent to pick me up at Blackmouth's station." I combed for her name in my memory but was dismayed to find I couldn't recall it. Must be exhaustion. I normally had a pretty good memory for names.

Jasher gaped, his fine ruddy face a picture of bewilderment. I could practically see the gears turning. Frankly, it was getting old.

Finally, Jasher addressed Green t-shirt. "'Scuse me a minute, will you?" He blinked over at me and changed his mind. "No, actually…I think this'll have to be goodnight."

He swallowed the rest of his beer in four big gulps and pushed the empty glass to the back of the bar. Getting up, he gave Green t-shirt a parting nod. "See you in the morning."

"You going to leave without introducing me to your pretty friend?" Green t-shirt asked, then stuck out his bottom lip.

Jasher whacked his thigh, and a puff of sawdust clouded the air near his leg. Now that I was looking, his shirt was wrinkled and stained with oil spots. He must have come directly from work to the pub.

"Sorry mate." Jasher shook his head at himself. "She's got me all inside out and backwards. Will, this is Georjayna." He turned to me. "Georjie, this is Will. He works with me."

Will poked a finger into the brim of his baseball cap, making it sit a little higher on his head. "Family, are ye?" He looked hopeful.

"Not technically," Jasher and I replied at the same time, then laughed.

"Her mum and my adopted mum are sisters," Jasher explained as he liberated his wallet from a rear pocket and fished out some money. He winked at me and the dimples I had grown to love appeared. "We only met for the first time this past June, but we got on like a brushfire. Didn't we, Georjie?"

I crooked an eyebrow at him. We hadn't, actually.

"Adopted cousins, then." Will set his tumbler on the bar to shake my hand. "Welcome to the highlands."

"Smarter than you look," Jasher teased, tucking his wallet away again.

"Funny," Will said to me, jabbing a finger in Jasher's direction.

"He's a little crusty, but we like him," I replied. "Nice to meet you."

"See you round." Will smiled and picked up his drink. He settled his back against the wall and bobbed his head in time to the music.

As Jasher and I squeezed our way toward the door, one of the musicians yelled over the tune. "Are we that bad?"

"Aye, ye scare away the only tourist we've seen since October," crowed the woman behind the bar.

My cheeks warmed as the patrons watched us. I felt like we were bad kids sneaking out of class early. At the door, I bent to retrieve my bag.

"I'll get that." Jasher pulled the bag through the open door and I followed him.

"Thanks, Jash."

Jasher began to head downhill, the tires of my luggage making a racket on the cobbles. He stopped abruptly and looked around like he was lost. Sheepishly, he steered the bag around and headed uphill instead. "This way."

"Haven't you been here since the new year, Jasher? Blackmouth is even smaller than Anacullough. You expect me to believe you still don't know your way from the pub to the castle?"

He shushed me, holding a finger in front of his lips.

"Uh huh." I kept pace with him as we climbed the narrow, winding road, on which there was no traffic. The sky was a near starless layer of black over our heads, the clouds like a layer of wool. Tall stone walls divided a thick forest from the road. Pools of streetlight offered the only illumination leading up a hill so steep that whatever lived beyond it was invisible. "So, who was the lady you sent to pick me up? Friend of yours?"

When I'd stepped off the train, a middle-aged woman in a house-dress and a vacant smile had been waiting with my name scrawled on a piece of cardboard. She'd given me a name I couldn't now recall and told me she was to pick me up because Jasher wasn't able to, and bundled me into a small Fiat. Surprised because Jasher hadn't warned me ahead of time, and unable to call him because he'd long ago vowed never to own a personal cell phone, I elected to trust her. I'd gotten in the car and enjoyed the short, quiet drive through the village of Blackmouth.

Jasher glanced at me. "Our wires got crossed somewhere along the line. I didn't send anyone to pick you up, Georjie. Honest. I'm gobsmacked that you're even here."

I stopped walking at once and stared at him, well beyond laughing about it by now.

Jasher stopped walking as well. "Seriously. I've no idea what you're doing here, Georjie. But I'm so happy you came. What a great surprise!"

"Jasher." I closed my eyes briefly, asking for patience. "I'll speak slowly so you won't misunderstand. You wrote me a letter telling me all about your job at Blackmouth Castle and inviting me to come and stay for a while..."

The words died in my throat at his deer-in-the-headlights look.

Silence stretched out and a chill swept over me. Something very strange was going on here. Jasher didn't seem drunk, just a little tipsy, there was no way he'd had enough alcohol to have forgotten completely about the letter he'd written me.

"No, I didn't," he finally replied. "I mean... I did write you a letter, telling you about the job and where I was, but I didn't invite you to come." His face flushed. "Don't get me wrong, I would have, but it never occurred to me."

"But...you invited me." I was certain he had. There had

been a line in the letter welcoming me to Blackmouth since they were closed for the season and had plenty of spare rooms. Wasn't there? Jasher had to have forgotten. He simply had to. Either that or I was losing my mind.

He threw an arm over my shoulder and we continued walking up the hill. My mind raced like fingers over an old-fashioned rolodex. Had I misunderstood? No, I was sure I hadn't.

The distant clouds seemed to wheel for a moment. If Jasher didn't ask a friend to pick me up then who was the woman...wait, had it been a woman? Why couldn't I remember? The details of the person and the circumstance of my arrival at Blackmouth station now felt like a dream––the details of which were fading too fast to hold on to.

Doubts stalled as we crested the hill and a huge round-about led to a parking lot overlooked by a hulking black shape. The silhouettes of numerous turrets reached toward the clouds and I strained my eyes for a better look, wondering why there weren't more lights on.

Jasher was saying, "...important thing is that you're here now. Whatever's happened, it's a happy happening, and I hope you stay for a good long shift."

With this sweet but clumsy speech, he bumped against my hip and knocked me off course. I took him by the elbow and corrected his trajectory so we didn't walk into a mailbox.

"So, you haven't told Bonnie and Gavin that I'm coming." I could already feel the heat of embarrassment burning in my cheeks. If Jasher hadn't warned the castle's owners I was coming, it would make me an unwanted guest.

"No, but don't worry. They are the most hospitable folks you'll meet," Jasher replied with a squeeze around my shoulders. "I couldn't have found better people to work for."

I gave him a feeble smile as Blackmouth Castle loomed, blocking out the rest of the night sky.

Two motion lights bracketed the huge set of front doors, illuminating the brass knockers, one a stag's head and the other a boar's head. Condensation beaded on the glossy black lacquer. I instinctively headed for these massive doors, but Jasher led me to the side of the castle instead.

Gravel crunched under our feet as we passed by dark windows and leafless hedges. Another motion light illuminated a pathway of broad stone steps leading down another level. I caught a glimpse of yard lights in the rear of the castle as a dim glow around the corner, but we stopped at a side door before I got to see the source. A whiff of roses drifted by and I guessed a window must be open nearby, allowing some room fragrance to come outside. The scent was fresh and I took a big inhale, letting some of the day's tension drain out of my body.

I had Jasher's letter somewhere in my bag. I'd dig it out and show him just how forgetful beer made him. When his memory was refreshed, he'd tell Bonnie and Gavin of his mistake, and he'd remember the mysterious friend he'd sent to pick me up. A huge yawn stole over me, the jaw-cracking kind my friend Saxony called a 'cat-yawn.'

Tomorrow. I'd dig the letter out tomorrow.

Jasher opened the side entrance and gestured for me to go in ahead of him. He pulled my bag inside and closed the door. Flicking on the lights illuminated a pristinely kept hallway with clean white walls and a plaid carpet-runner. A narrow spiral staircase disappeared off to the left, and it was up these stairs Jasher heaved my luggage. At the next level up, he pushed through a doorway into another hallway lined with doors. It was chilly and painted in shades of gray, but a warm yellow light flickered from a sconce on the wall. There were too many closed doors to count. I admired paintings of horses, dogs, and highland landscapes and seascapes along the way, until Jasher tapped on a doorway as we passed it.

"I'm in here if you need me." He stopped at the next door and opened it on darkness. The smell of old wood and artificially fragranced drawer liners drifted out. "This room's free, but we can move you into a bigger room tomorrow if you like. I can ask Bonnie…"

I almost jumped down Jasher's throat. "No! I mean, please don't bother them, this room is great. It'll do fine." I grabbed my bag and wheeled it inside as Jasher flicked on the light.

Two single unmade beds in antique frames faced one another from opposite walls. The outer wall was stone while the side walls were papered with peach and mint colored flowers. A long set of double drawers served as bedside tables, and the only dressers in the room. A paint-chipped wardrobe against the wall opposite stood ajar, and a window with diamond-panes peeked from behind green paisley curtains. The space was both sparse and old-fashioned kitsch.

"There will be bedding in here, I think," Jasher said in a low voice as he hooked a finger in the wardrobe's door. He pulled out folded white sheets and set them on the bed while I pulled down a thick duvet.

A narrow door on the far side of the wardrobe caught my eye. "Is that a closet?"

"That'll be the loo." Jasher unfolded the sheets and set to making up one of the beds.

"There's a bathroom?" I dumped the duvet on the other bed and went to take a peek. "Do all these rooms have their own bathrooms?"

"Quite a few. The castle got plumbed and reno'ed in the sixties."

That explained the decor.

The bathroom was tiny and dated but sparkling clean. Pastel green porcelain and green candy-striped wallpaper greeted my eye. A pale peach shower curtain hid a box shower with a showerhead I'd be sure to bump my head on. I didn't care. It was utterly quaint: tiny wrapped soaps on the back of the toilet, clean fluffy towels in a matching shade of peach, and toilet paper dotted with peach colored roses.

Jasher's head appeared in the doorway. "It looks like Martha Stewart circa nineteen-sixty-five threw up in here." He shrugged and gave a crooked smile. "They had good intentions."

"I love it." I turned off the light. "How many people can say they've stayed in a medieval castle in the highlands? Even if the bathroom had peach and green stripes?"

We finished making the bed together and I put my bag on the unmade bed and opened it, digging for my toiletries.

"See you in the morning, Georjie," Jasher said, holding his arms open for a hug.

I stepped into them and closed my eyes, letting the relief of being finished with a long day of traveling wash over me.

"I'm up early for work," Jasher said as he released me, "but I'll let Ainslie, the housekeeper, know to expect you for breakfast around…eight?"

"Thanks. Will the owners be around?" The sooner I met them and cleared up how I ended up in their home without an invitation, the better I'd feel.

Jasher pinched my cheek between his knuckles. "Stop worrying. I'll introduce you. They'll be happy to have you, especially as you're a Sutherland. Gavin's a nut for the whole ancestry thing."

My brows pinched as I followed him to the door. "What difference does my last name make?"

"You're in the Sutherland region of Scotland, Georjie." He chuckled at my look of surprise. "I know. I didn't realize the Sutherlands were from Scotland either."

"We're not," I replied. "We're Irish."

Jasher waved a brown hand and shrugged. "Gavin will be

more than happy to debate with you on that. Count me out of it. I need to organize a demo, so I'll have my hands full."

"A demo...lition?"

He nodded.

"What's getting destroyed?"

"I don't know what it was. Some ruin off in the trees that hasn't served a purpose for God knows how many centuries. Gavin wants to build a cottage in its place, a kind of honeymooners' accommodation. You can see it tomorrow if you'd like."

"I'd love to." My eyes began to leak and I had another cat-yawn.

Jasher slipped out into the hall and looked back just before I closed the door. "I'm happy you came."

I gave him a smile and went to rummage in my bag for my toothbrush and pajamas. I took a quick shower and got ready for bed, slipping between clean sheets with the deep sigh of the bone-weary. My eyes closed and my body relaxed.

After several long seconds, my eyes popped open again.

Distantly, there was the almost imperceptible sound of rhythmic drumming. Or was I imagining it?

I sat up and cocked my head, straining my ears. No, I definitely wasn't imagining it. Someone was drumming, and if I wasn't mistaken, there were flutes, too. Who would be making music at this time of night?

I went to the door to listen, peeking into the hall. The hallway was in gloom, the sconces now dark. Diffused moonlight threw soft shadows across the carpet and walls from the small windows at the end.

The drumming sound was no louder in the hallway, but no quieter either. It was impossible to pinpoint where it was coming from. I glanced at Jasher's closed door, eyeing the crack at the floor. No light came from underneath. Probably already unconscious in a haze of beer-fog.

I padded down to the far end, peering through the darkness where the hall turned to the right. Another dark tunnel lined with doors, and still the drumming was no louder.

I stood there in my sleep pants and t-shirt, bare toes curling into the carpet, head cocked like a spaniel. I debated going farther down the halls in search of the source of the distant music, but I was too tired to go snooping. And what if I ran into Gavin or Bonnie or one of the staff?

Shrugging, I relegated the drumming to some insomniac in a distant suite listening to a recording and padded back to my room. It was barely audible, really. Nothing that would keep me awake. I returned to bed and burrowed under the covers like a denning animal.

CHAPTER TWO

The sound of men's laughter roused me from unconsciousness. I'd been dreaming I was still in Poland and thought maybe I'd wake to find myself in one of the Novak's luxurious beds. My eyes drifted open and I saw a mid-century dresser with the top drawer slid open. Blinking and disoriented, I sat up. The sight of my luggage, open and rifled through, brought back my memory. I was in the highlands and one of the voices outside the window was Jasher's.

My stomach gave a grumble as though chastising me for not getting up earlier. Grabbing my phone, I looked at the screen and gaped in disbelief. It was almost noon! The soft light coming in the window was deceptive; it was so dim it seemed like early morning.

Peeking out the window revealed smudges of green through warped glass. I opened the window farther and caught a glimpse of rolling treed hills and an expanse of blue-grey on the horizon––the North Sea. The clouds were thick and the color of gunmetal. I was surprised it wasn't raining already. The air smelled thick with ozone, rich earth and...yes, roses, unbelievably. I took a big inhale, sighing with pleasure. Scotland might be cold, but it certainly smelled lovely. It struck me as odd since it was now early March. What roses bloomed this early in the year, and this far north?

Scrambling for the shower, I hurriedly washed and dressed, throwing my long hair up in a topknot. Pulling on a pair of jeans and a plain cashmere sweater, I grabbed my running shoes and a rain slicker before finding my way to the stairwell Jasher had led me up the night before. Just before I got to the top of the stairs, I remembered that I wanted to find Jasher's letter, and skidded to a halt. Returning to my room, I dug in my luggage for where I kept paperwork. Retrieving a thin pile of documents, I rifled through until I found it.

"Aha!" I cried victoriously. Skimming the letter, I looked for the paragraph where Jasher invited me to come stay at Blackmouth. I read it over a second, and a third time, my stomach plummeting.

How could it not be there? I had read it; I would stake my life on it. I never would have come to Scotland without being invited. Feeling poleaxed, I sat on the floor with my back against the side of my bed, staring at the letter in my lap.

I didn't know how long I sat there like that, but when my butt began to hurt from sitting on the stone floor, I got up and tucked the letter back into my luggage. Totally bemused, I had to admit that I had misread the letter, but everything in me rebelled against it because I knew what I knew: I'd been invited. Either something very weird was going on, or I was going mad. Refusing to think too hard on that, I pushed it out of my mind. Letting my luggage drop closed, I left my room for the second time that morning, this time with a little humility in my step.

Women's voices in conversation drifted up the stairs. I slowed my pace and swallowed, wondering if Jasher had told the castle staff that I was here. Following the sounds of chatter, I came upon a ground-level kitchen where two women bustled about and two children sat at a long wooden table. The kitchen looked like something from a movie set if the film hadn't yet decided in which time period it was to be set.

A big iron soup vat sat over a deep stone fireplace. Copper cooking pots, pans, and utensils hung from the mantel. Dried herbs dangled from the thick beam overhead, making the room smell like rosemary and oregano. A mid-century gas stove with six burners sat opposite the fireplace, beside a squat fridge without any straight edges.

"Morning!" the more petite of the two women said as she retrieved a loaf of bread from a metal breadbox on the counter. "Sleep well?"

"Yes, thank you." I took the last couple of steps down to the flagstone floor. "I'm Georjie. Did Jasher..."

"That he did, lass, and you're welcome." The taller woman had a riot of frizzy red hair and a flushed but beaming face. She wore a gray poncho and reams of scarves. "You'll be hungry, no doubt?"

"Slept away the entire morning, you did," chimed in the one in the frilly apron with large gray eyes and soft cheeks.

I blushed. "I'm sorry, I guess I was tired from the journey."

The taller one flapped a hand. "Don't mind her, Ainslie's up at five every morning whether she's working or not. She's only jealous."

"It's true," admitted Ainslie as she set a sandwich with trimmed crust in front of a red-headed girl. "When you get older, sleeping in like a teenager is a thing of ages past. Have a seat beside Maisie, here."

I crossed the kitchen and made to sit beside Maisie, but she was seated at one long bench. Getting my ridiculously long legs gracefully over a bench with a narrow gap to the bottom of the table is near impossible.

"Och, she's a tall one." Ainslie cackled. "Take the chair, Georjie."

The girl's wide brown eyes followed me as I went around the table.

I smiled self-consciously at the little girl. "Nice to meet you, Maisie."

I turned to the boy. He too had inherited the same red hair as his sister, but looked like the older one. I opened my mouth to ask his name when he stretched a hand across the table.

"Lorne." He was as serious as death. "I understand you're a Sutherland?" He grasped my hand firmly and gave it one pump.

I laughed at his somber expression and mature way of talking, but he didn't laugh in return, so I bit my cheek. "That's right."

"We're Sutherlands, too. On Da's side," Lorne went on. "We're probably related." His brow pinched together as though the idea was a little disconcerting.

I didn't feel the need to go into the fact that I was planning to change my name to Sheehan––my mother's maiden name––and just hadn't gotten around to it yet. I didn't think I'd get support for rejecting the last name we shared from this lot.

"I'm Bonnie," declared the red-headed woman. "The mother with a capital 'M.'" She ruffled Lorne's hair. "And you'll both be late for your afternoon classes if you don't eat up."

Ainslie set a sandwich in front of me and I thanked her and took a bite. I took a cup from a stack in the middle of the table and poured myself some water, wishing for coffee but too shy to ask. I already felt like an imposition.

"Coffee?" Bonnie asked.

I gave her a grateful smile and said around my bite of sandwich. "Thank you, I'd love one."

She retrieved a stove-top espresso maker from a cupboard above the sink and I had to smile. It was identical to the one Targa had used in the trailer she and her mom lived in before it got destroyed in the storm.

Ainslie set a large roasting pan on the table and began to peel potatoes with the smooth, fast movements of someone who had been doing it since childhood. "So, you came in from Edinburgh?"

I nodded. "Last night. Again, I have to apologize for surprising you like this."

"Don't worry your head about it," Bonnie said as she snagged a coffee mug from where they hung on little hooks under the cupboard. "Any Sutherland is welcome here and we've plenty of room. Jasher says you're doing your last year of high school by correspondence?"

I nodded again, my mouth full of sandwich. Both Lorne and Maisie watched my every move, Lorne with the studiousness of a scientist and Maisie with her mouth hanging ajar. I winked at her and was rewarded when the corners of her mouth twitched.

"Have you always done school remotely?" Bonnie asked.

I shook my head, swallowing. "No, just this year. All my friends are abroad too, and I needed a break from my hometown."

"Can *I* do school remotely?" Lorne asked in his serious way, tilting his head back to look at his mother.

"Lorne, honey. You're eight."

"When I'm older, of course."

"Tell you what." Bonnie kissed his cheek and went to rescue the espresso maker from boiling over. "Let's have this conversation in another eight years."

Lorne frowned. "I'm more mature than other kids." He

appeared to be making a calculation in his head, one eye squinted closed. "Let's call it six years?"

I took another bite of my sandwich to hide my smile. I caught Ainslie laughing into her sleeve, potato peelings falling from her knife.

"We'll see." Bonnie poured espresso into my cup and told me to help myself if I wanted milk and sugar.

As I finished my sandwich, the kids were ushered from the kitchen, leaving me and Ainslie alone.

"She didn't say so directly," Ainslie said, keeping her eyes on the potato shedding its coat under her nimble grip, "but Bonnie Sinclair-Sutherland is the lady of the house."

I swallowed my last bite of sandwich and pulled my coffee closer. "Yes, Jasher told me a little about Bonnie and Gavin."

"Aye. Gavin, the laird, he'll be out back with the men, including your Jasher." Ainslie's eyes flicked to mine and I caught the question in her gaze. I realized that this petite and energetic housemaid likely made it her business to know every little thing that went on in the castle. I didn't miss the implication she'd made.

"Jasher and I aren't together," I offered.

"Ah." Ainslie relaxed and went back to her potato. "How long do you think you'll be staying in Blackmouth?"

It was a casual question, but the subtext felt thicker than honey on a cold day.

"I'm not sure," I replied, slowly. "When does my welcome run out?"

"You'll have to ask the lady," Ainslie said, "but Blackmouth is closed to tourists until May, so…if you're looking to make a little extra money, I could make use of a pair of hands from time to time."

I let out a sigh of relief. So that's what she was after. "Sure, I'd be happy to help when I'm not doing school work. I'm no pro at housework." At home we had a cleaning service, and my meal-making skills stopped at spaghetti. "But I'm a quick study."

I didn't need money, but I had sprung my presence on them without warning. It wouldn't feel right to turn down Ainslie's request right off the hop.

She dazzled me with a smile. "Wonderful."

I sipped my coffee but as the silence stretched out, I began to wonder whether she meant right now. Should I offer to help her peel potatoes? What I really wanted to do was go find Jasher and see the castle in the daylight. Maybe he'd have time to show me around. I got to my feet to signal my readiness to leave. Taking my empty plate over to the sink, I grabbed Maisie's and Lorne's plates as well. I didn't miss Ainslie's look of approval.

"Who was playing music last night?" I asked as I tossed uneaten bits of sandwich into the trash bin and began to wash the dishes.

Ainslie stopped peeling and looked up. Her spine straightened and her bosom swelled. "Music?" She tilted her head. "You heard music?"

"Yeah, I could hear drums in my room. Distantly."

Her look said that if anyone had been playing music late last night in the castle and she didn't know about it, there'd be hell to pay.

"Maybe the neighbors?" I guessed.

"The nearest neighbors are a quarter-mile down the hill. If they were playing music loud enough for you to hear it, they would have had a visit from the local bobby. Are you sure you weren't dreaming?"

I hadn't been; I'd been walking the halls, but I didn't want to get her riled. "Maybe."

The creases in her forehead relaxed.

"Where might I find Jasher?" I asked as I put the last dish into the drying rack.

"He'll be out back with Gavin most like," Ainslie replied, eyes returning to her growing pile of potatoes. "Go through the center path of the garden maze, follow it down the hill and into the trees. After that, things get a little prickly. Just follow the sounds of men making grand plans. Here." She set down her knife and went to the counter where she grabbed a fat aluminum Thermos and held it out. "Gavin likes a spot of tea in the midafternoon."

I took the Thermos and told her I'd deliver it.

"You tell those boys supper is at seven sharp. They have a tendency to get carried away and be late for meals." She pointed at me with the tip of her knife. "I don't slave all day over a working man's meal only to have it go cold afore he even sits down."

"Yes, ma'am." I saluted her. "I'll pass on the message." I went to the back door and found my jacket and boots.

Maybe the laird would be able to tell me who was playing drums here last night, since the housekeeper could not.

CHAPTER THREE

*L*eaving the castle by the side door, I continued down the stone steps along the side of the building. They flattened out and led me to the rear garden where I stopped dead in my tracks.

A beautifully manicured maze made of hedges, rose-bushes, and topiaries spread out before me. The humid air was heavy with the pungent aroma of roses in full bloom. A fountain burbled in the maze's center, and weatherworn statues of frolicking stags seemed to sprout from the greenery.

"Impossible," I whispered, staring at the sea of white roses and lush, thorny shrubs. The air was cold enough to condense into fog when I exhaled. It was too cold to be outside without a hat, gloves and a scarf, not to mention a thick pair of jeans...and yet this garden maze was in full bloom.

I went to the nearest rose bush and took a closer look. The blossoms were white threaded with green veins, and the base of each petal was a soft shade of coral. Similar colors to the bedroom I'd been given. Bending to take a whiff, I groaned with pleasure. It was these roses I'd been catching the scent of since I'd arrived. But how was it that they were in full bloom in the dead of winter?

Unable to stem my curiosity, I slipped my feet out of the rubber boots I was wearing and raked off my socks. The ground was so cold it made me cringe, but once I got used to it, it wasn't so bad. Laying the soles of my feet against the soil, I closed my eyes and tuned in to the roses.

It was extraordinary. The rest of the garden plants were dormant. The herbs, shrubs and other flowers were all in the right seasonal cycle…basically sleeping. The roses, however, throbbed and hummed with life. They were so vividly alive, they practically sang. I shook my head, amazed, and put my socks and boots back on, making a mental note to ask Bonnie or Ainslie about them.

Continuing through the garden, I passed two lichen-coated fountains of animals frolicking while spewing water joyfully overhead.

Following the sound of men's voices, I navigated a long downhill slope, slippery with mud and ending in a thicket of scrubby trees. The voices came from somewhere within the knotted woods so I continued on, trying not to slip. The kind of narrow path we referred to as a goat-track back home, wound through the woods. Brambles snatched at my clothes and the ground was littered with rotting leaves and soggy twigs. Winding my way through the dense underbrush led me to an open glade.

Jasher and another young man stood with an older man, gesturing as they discussed what looked to be a roiling mass of thorny bushes. Ainslie's claim that things got a bit prickly was an understatement.

I crossed the glade, noticing that within the impressive thicket of two-inch long thorns were several very thick, worn-down stone walls. The ruin Jasher had to demolish, I guessed.

The fellow with Jasher spotted my approach and lifted a hand. "We've got company."

"You found us!" Jasher beckoned me over. "Come, I'll introduce you."

The tall older man looked over his shoulder and smiled. He was wearing a kilt. His close-trimmed beard was giving its way over to silver. The corners of his eyes crinkled. "This must be your friend from Canada." Turning to face me, he held out a wide mitt for me to shake. "I'm Gavin, the laird o' these here lands and castle. Ye're welcome."

I shook his hand. "I'm sorry that my arrival is a bit of a surprise."

"It's no' a problem, lass," Gavin replied. "We've plenty o' empty rooms, but if you dinna watch Ainslie, she'll be offering to treat you to the joys o' peeling potatoes and cleanin' privies."

I laughed. "She's already done so. The potatoes part, not the…privies."

"And this is Lachlan." Jasher gestured to their other companion.

"Nice to meet ye, Georjayna. Welcome to Blackmouth." My heart tripped unexpectedly over his voice, which was warm and low, like a thick blanket. Lachlan's expression was open and earnest. Red shadow covered his jaw, and eyes the color of the sky before a storm sparkled from a wide, handsome face. He was almost as tall as Jasher, but broader and softer. Lachlan was the kind of guy you had to give a second glance to realize he was attractive, but once I saw it, I couldn't unsee it. He was lumber-jack hot, capable and trustworthy. His gaze kept a grip on mine and I felt somehow unable to look away until Gavin spoke again.

"Jasher tells me ye're a Sutherland?"

I nodded and smiled at how it had come up twice already today. "On my father's side."

"We'll be related then," Gavin said without any hint of doubt.

I had to laugh. "It's feeling a little déjà vu-ey around here this morning."

"A little what-ey?" Gavin's silver brows tightened. "Is that Canadian slang?"

"Déjà vu," I began, and decided against elaborating. "Your son, Lorne, he said the same thing at lunch. I'm sorry to disappoint, but my family is from Ireland."

Gavin's brown eyes widened and then he threw his head back and gave a belly laugh that was so infectious it had the rest of us laughing along, though I had no idea what was so funny.

"From Ireland, she says," Gavin said between bellows of mirth. "Lassie, do ye not know yer own heritage, then?"

"Of course," I replied, nonplussed. "My family has lived in Ireland for over two hundred years. I just spent part of the summer with my Aunt Faith there. Our house is full of family history."

Jasher nodded. "It's true. She's Irish on her mother's side. Her mum is my adopted mum's sister."

Gavin lifted a thick finger and beamed into my face as though he had some spectacular secret. "Tell you what, Miss Sutherland, ye're welcome to stay in Blackmouth Castle until she opens again for the season. Longer, if ye're up for some housekeepin' duties. But ye're going to spend some of that time in the library, learning 'bout yer own history. I'll no' have a relative of mine, distant or not, thinking they're *Irish*!" He broke into fresh gales of laughter, red spots blossoming on his cheeks.

I looked at Jasher, both of us laughing because when

Gavin laughed, it was simply not possible not to join in, but his look said, *I told you so.*

"I might be able to help you there," Lachlan said through a grin of his own. "I'm a bit of an amateur historian."

"Sounds like the perfect way to procrastinate from my schoolwork," I replied.

"Ye're standin' in the region of Sutherland, little miss," continued Gavin. "In these highlands, we're like royalty."

Lachlan nodded. "He's right. The reason there are Sutherlands in Ireland is because there was a migration in the seventeenth century. The Sutherlands that moved to Ireland never came back, and it'll be those that you've descended from."

I shared a startled look with Jasher. He just shrugged with that same look.

"I...did not know that." I felt mildly dazed.

"I understand if you feel more connected to Ireland than to Scotland, with over three hundred years of genealogy there." Lachlan shifted the pair of gardening shears I only just noticed he was holding, from one hand to another.

"Don't change that it's Scots bluid that's running through yer veins." Gavin thumped me on the back and I had to take a step forward so I didn't fall on my face.

I shrugged. "I feel connected here, too. It's so beautiful."

"Aye, the faeries keep it bonnie and green," said Gavin.

I shared another surprised look with Jasher, wondering if Gavin had meant the quip in a figurative way.

Jasher was the one who'd first introduced me to faerie cocoons. Most people couldn't see them. Not even my elemental friends could see the tiny, colorful spirits who hatched from tiny transparent cocoons. They happened when dappled sunlight penetrated fresh rainwater as it dripped from branches and leaves. According to Jasher, it used to occur a lot more often, but now faerie cocoons were so rare he almost never saw them anymore. I had to admit I hadn't seen any outside my own private garden back home, which I'd built just for the purpose. After I learned how fragile they were, I wanted to give them a safe place to hatch.

"Course, if the faeries have anything to do with these blasted thorn bushes, then I'd rather you evicted them." Lachlan hooked a thumb over his shoulder at the choked ruins behind us.

"Is this where you'll be building your cottage?" I took a few steps closer to the old foundation and broken-down walls.

"Aye." Gavin appeared beside me. "I've been wanting a wee house for guests who want their own private suite, a sort of honeymoon thing."

"What was it before?"

Gavin scratched at his chin, his eyes full of question marks. "Lachlan?"

"It was a game-keeper's home, something nearing five hundred years ago." Lachlan began to point out patches of land. "There was an old barn attached over there and a stable just there. There's a well here too. There was a fire at some point and the cottage fell into disrepair. I don't believe it was ever used for anything again after that, but"—he gave a shrug —"not everything was recorded in the history books, ye ken."

"That's quite a crop of brambles." I'd never seen a thicket of spikes nastier than the one choking the plot before us.

"Aye," Gavin grumbled, his tone darkening. "They've been a right pain in me arse. First thing we'll do is cut 'em back, find the roots and rip 'em up. Can't plan properly until we can see what's underneath 'em."

"I can round up some lads from the village," Lachlan suggested. "I have a cousin who could use a reason to keep out of mischief and it wouldn't hurt him to make a pound or two."

"I've got Will lined up to help pour the footings," Jasher added. "He won't mind coming a few days early to rip this mess up."

Jasher glanced at me and we shared a secret smile.

Well, maybe not so secret. I felt Lachlan's gaze on us. He hadn't missed the meaningful look that had passed between Jasher and me. Feeling the question in Lachlan's gaze, I looked away.

If anyone could be the most effective in convincing stubborn brambles to vacate the premises, it was me. I couldn't just go about snapping my fingers and making the thorns retreat back into the earth, though. If the men attacked the brambles today, then it was possible they wouldn't need my help. They might have them cleared by sundown. If not, I could find a stealthy way to help out that didn't make anyone's hair stand on end.

"Strange that they never spread, though," Gavin murmured, so quietly it seemed he was talking to himself. "All my life I lived on these lands. I played back here as a boy. Never in the thorns of course, they'd have made mincemeat of me. But we built a treehouse over that way," he gestured to the right, "and there's a little swimming hole down that way," he nodded to the left. "These brambles were always thick as Medusa's hair. My own father burned them once and they came back stronger than ever. But never have they grown beyond these ruins."

"Must be something in the soil here they like," I suggested.

"That makes sense, actually." Lachlan's eyebrows raised. He glanced from me to Gavin. "Maybe the lass has solved the mystery, and her being on the land only a few minutes. Something in the soil is feeding them."

"Maybe so," Gavin said thoughtfully. "Maybe so."

"Sounds like you have a green thumb." Lachlan raised his

garden shears and snipped away some branches. They fell away, leaving a window into a world of long, wicked-sharp thorns that looked positively villainous.

"Georjie's a genius when it comes to all the green things," Jasher said, dimpling.

"Are ye now?" Gavin turned to me. "Bonnie'd love to make use of yer talents. She's got it into her mind to re-landscape the maze and make a few changes to the gardens at the front. If ye're not too busy with yer schoolwork…"

"…or the potato peeling," Lachlan added with a grin.

"P'raps ye'll consider helping the lady. Ainslie's good, but Bonnie doesn't know a petunia from a pine tree."

"I'd be happy to help. You're being more than generous letting me stay in the first place."

"We'll no' be turning away a Sutherland," Gavin waved his mitt of a hand, "but help is always appreciated. We all have our talents."

"It would be a shame to change the maze too much, though. I love the roses and I've never seen any like them before. I hope Bonnie doesn't plan to get rid of them." Even now, this far away, the faint scent of rose could be detected.

Gavin gave a knowing chuckle. "No, she wouldn't dare. There's a story to them roses. You ask Ainslie."

"I'll do that." I suddenly remembered the Thermos. "Oh, and here's your tea. Ainslie says she'll string you up by your toes if you're…"

"…late for dinner," all three men said at once.

"Yeah, we know." Lachlan laughed.

I handed Gavin the Thermos. "Before I forget, was there a party nearby last night? I was wondering where the drums were coming from."

"Drums?" The laird looked blank and shook his head. "There'd be no one playing the drums around here."

"Well, it was more musical than just drums," I interjected. "It was fast, music to dance to. It sounded kind of pagan."

"Blackmouth Castle is quiet as the grave in the nights, Lassie." He went to where a pail was sitting on the ground and retrieved a pair of sharp-looking hedge clippers. He frowned at them. "I think we're going to have to recruit something a little more powerful to get this job done...like dynamite."

"You must have dreamed it," Jasher suggested. "My room is near yours and I didn't hear a thing."

"Huh." I chewed my cheek thoughtfully.

But it hadn't been a dream. It wasn't like the visions I'd had before I'd gotten my elemental powers. Those were vivid also, but afterward, I had been aware I'd been dreaming. But last night I'd been walking the halls, perfectly lucid, searching for the source. Then again, the music hadn't fluctuated the way music did; it had stayed constant, whether I'd been in my room, or down the hall and around the corner.

As the men went to work on the thorn bushes, I wandered back to the castle to start my schoolwork. But the reactions to my questions about the drums kept my thoughts coming back to it all day.

I hadn't dreamed the music. Of that, I was certain.

CHAPTER FOUR

"I didn't think I'd be back here so soon." I cupped my hands around a mug of steaming hot chocolate. "It appears *The Blackmouth Arms* has become your favorite hangout. You never spent time in pubs back in Anacullough."

"That's the beauty of no longer having to contend with the pesky undead." Jasher lifted his glass of ale and sipped it through a layer of foam. "One can enjoy the older haunts of the world unbothered and unencumbered. Cheers to you"—he clinked his pint jovially against my mug—"and your unusual gifts."

"What's got you so jolly?"

"Can't a man be jolly?" He took another sip, tongue peeking out to lick the cream off his upper lip.

"You remember how rude you were to me when we first met?" I said. "I was scared to be in the same room as you."

Even after Jasher had melted, he'd maintained a serious quality about him.

Jasher looked at the ceiling wistfully. "I was a righteous bear, wasn't I?"

"That's one way to put it."

Jasher hadn't warmed up to me until he realized I could see the faerie cocoons. Until then, he didn't know anyone else who could see them, not even my Aunt Faith, which was weird because she was a true believer. Once Jasher realized I had 'the sight,' his attitude totally changed toward me.

"Admit it, you thought I was a materialistic airhead." I poked him in the side.

"But a pretty one." He took another drink, his eyes darting off to a corner of the pub before giving me a sly look. "Hey, did you ever reread the letter I sent you?"

My face flushed and I looked away.

He set the pint down with purpose, then lay his elbow on the table and leaned forward, expression as inquisitive as a fawn's. "I see you have."

I nodded and took a sip of my drink. "You were right," I mumbled. "You never explicitly invited me."

Jasher nodded and I leaned forward on my elbows and whispered, "But you *did*! I know you did, I just can't...prove it."

"Maybe you just missed me so much, you imagined it," Jasher said with a smirk. His eyes darted to someone behind me again.

"You're so cocky, and who do you keep looking at?"

Glancing over my shoulder, I saw a dark sea of heads under the low beamed ceiling. Tartan curtains framed the small windows whose sills were deeper than my entire arm. A slender man in a fedora fiddled with a guitar in the corner.

"Is he going to sing?" I spun on my stool, angling my shoulders toward him.

"Aye. There's wailing here most nights," Jasher mumbled. He finished off his pint and lifted a finger to the bartender for another.

The fellow in the hat began to warm up his vocal chords and tune the guitar. The overall din of talk dwindled.

"Come on Garret, loose the thunder," somebody bellowed to a gale of laughter.

The musician revealed a set of oversized teeth. "Ye're just jealous, yeh old badger," he bellowed back between twanged chords. He threw his head back and with a full-throated wail––Jasher was right, there was no better word for it––let loose with a lively tune.

"Oh, ye cannae fling pieces oot a twenty-story flat…"

The singing was bad. Really, really bad. I glanced at Jasher, wide-eyed. Was this guy for real? Jasher almost spat his beer back into his pint glass.

"Seven hundred hungry weans'll testify to that," the singer belted atonally.

I hissed in Jasher's ear, "Is this a joke?"

"If it's butter, cheese or jeely, if the bread is plain or pan…"

"I'm afraid not. It's the best wee Blackmouth has at the moment," Jasher whispered back between dissonant phrases, wincing.

"The odds against it reaching earth are ninety-nine tae one." The warbling went badly off key then wandered adjacent to it.

"Oh my god." I put my forehead down on my arm. "I can't."

The singer hit a few wrong chords before picking up a fresh and painful new chorus.

Jasher didn't bother holding in his laughter anymore. The rest of the patrons were cracking up, too.

I mouthed, "My ears are bleeding."

Jasher nodded. "Why do you think I've taken up drinking?"

He wiped his mouth on his sleeve as he set his glass down. His eyes did another dart across the room.

"Who do you keep looking at?" I scanned the crowd.

"No one. Listen to Garret, don't be rude." Jasher gave me a stern look.

Cringing, along with everyone else in the room, I listened to the rest of the song, if you could call it that. Some people were crying with laughter, and the singer often broke into laughter himself. At least he knew he was awful.

He closed out the ditty with a flourish, to a gale of cheers and applause.

"Ye're stunned by my soulful talent, thank you. So kind." Garret swung an arm wide. "But big-hearted artists such as myself would be, well, just arrogant and self-centered, if they didna allow the dreamers, the little people, to practice their chords now and again." He put a hand over his heart and made a puppy-dog expression. "Ladies and gentlemen, would you please put your hands together for Blackmouth's newest talent, Jasher Sheehan!"

I turned and stared at Jasher, whose complexion flushed red.

He shook his head, but the crowd began to chant his name. I pulled him off his stool and pushed him toward Garret, who was holding out the guitar.

Jasher snatched up his pint glass and made his way to the small stage. Even his ears were blushing. Taking the guitar from Garret unleashed a fresh gale of cheers and whistles. Based on their reactions, it was not his first time singing in front of this crowd.

I'd heard Jasher play guitar and sing before. He was excellent. Just, at the time, I'd been distracted by the fact that he'd been singing for and talking to someone I hadn't been able to see.

Jasher struck up a minor chord and the crowd simmered down. The strains of Spanish guitar filled the small pub, raising the hair on my arms. Jasher's fingers flew over the strings, quick and delicate. He punctuated the song with drumbeats against the side of the wooden guitar. His eyes went soft and unfocused as the melody lifted. But as the song went on, those dark eyes narrowed on one point in the crowd and didn't shift from it for the remainder of the song.

I found the source of his attention. A young woman with dark, curly hair and a creamy complexion sat at a table with a group of young people. Her chin was crooked in her palm, and she gazed at Jasher with a dreamy expression.

At first, I couldn't tell if Jasher was looking at her or through her. But as the applause died down and he began a second tune, a Celtic ballad, I realized that they were looking at one another. It seemed as though Jasher was playing for her.

A shard of jealousy cut through my heart. Jasher and I had enjoyed a little romance in the summer, sure, but we weren't in a relationship. Jasher had been here for months already. Why shouldn't he have a highland fling? Unexpectedly, Lachlan's freckled face rose in my mind's eye. I was young, free, and Jasher was not the only coal in the fire. Just because we'd kissed didn't mean we had to pick up where we'd left off. Did it? The rationalizing came easily to my mind, but I had to admit, in my heart I was hurt.

The crowd was on their feet as Jasher finished. He stood and took a little bow before handing the guitar back to Garret. His eyes fell on the woman again and I watched as he jerked his head subtly toward the bar. She smiled and got to her feet, nodding.

Jasher picked his way over to me.

"You were just as amazing as I remembered you to be," I said. "Well done."

"Thanks, Georjie." He slid his empty glass to the bartender.

The dark-haired woman approached, her expression closed and shy. She was petite and possessed the kind of curves I could never hope for, a picture of femininity. Soft waves of hair framed her face, she had big doe eyes with long eye-lashes, and the small waist and wide hips possessed by fertility statues. I felt like a giraffe as I dropped my chin to smile at her when she stopped in front of me.

"You must be Georjie," she said in a soft voice. Her Scottish accent warmed my ears. "Jasher told me his cousin was here."

I shot Jasher a look of surprise. He never introduced me as his cousin to anyone. He liked this woman...a lot.

Jasher blushed again. "Georjie, this is Evelyn."

I shook her proffered hand. "Lovely to meet you," I said, and found that I genuinely meant it.

Evelyn's expression hardly changed, but the relief that flooded into her eyes melted my heart. It mattered to her that I liked her.

"I just arrived last night; when did you have a chance to tell Evelyn I was here?" I asked Jasher.

"Early this morning." Jasher blinked, but his eyelids were slow to move. "Evie and I met for coffee."

"Oh, how nice." I gave Jasher a concerned look. He was looking downright dopey.

"Jasher, luv." Evelyn lowered her voice. "How many drinks have you had?"

"A few." His voice was half an octave higher than normal.

"You have to work tomorrow." Evelyn glanced at the fine silver watch on her wrist. "Why don't we call it a night?"

I agreed. "I have to study for a physics exam, and I'm still feeling a little jetlagged." I smiled at Evelyn. "But it was great to meet you. I'll see you around?"

She opened her mouth to respond, but then looked taken aback as Jasher swung his head like it was on a string hanging from the ceiling. She took his hand. "Why don't I walk with you? I live close to the castle, on Strathvaich road. You pass right on the way."

"Perfect." I settled our bill as Jasher and Evelyn made their way to the door, arms around each other. Frowning, I noted Jasher leaning heavily on Evelyn. Why hadn't I noticed he'd had too much to drink? We'd only gone to one party while I was in Ireland. Jasher hadn't even finished his one bottle of beer, and we ran out after a bunch of spooks began to harass him.

They waited for me at the door as I snagged my jacket from the coat hook and pulled it on. We stepped out into a misty night. The air was biting. Jasher and Evelyn walked arm in arm toward the castle and I fell in step with them, zipping my jacket all the way up and bundling my scarf around my neck.

We walked in silence for a while. The sound of Jasher dragging his feet on the cobblestones was making me feel bad. I was thinking of a casual way I could ask Jasher about his new habit when Evelyn spoke.

"You're lucky you've come at this time of the year."

I shot her a surprised look. "Most people have told me the opposite."

"It's the season for spunkies." She smiled.

"What's that, a pastry?"

She laughed. "In other places they're called will-o-the-wisps. Some people think they're spirits that live in the woods."

"And what are they actually?"

"Oh, swamp gas for sure." She revealed a set of straight white teeth. "It's a very gassy area."

"Highland farts," Jasher added, and our peals of laughter filled the abandoned streets.

We walked until Evelyn stopped in front of an adorable thatched roof cottage, where we said goodnight. Evelyn kissed Jasher's cheek and we didn't move on until she was inside and the door was shut.

"She seems nice."

"Evie's the bomb."

"Uh huh." I glanced sideways at him. "Why didn't you mention her in your letters, Jash?"

He looked down as we walked for a while before answering. "I didn't want to hurt you. If I had known you were coming, I would have." He hooked an arm through mine, slurring his words a little. "Honest. I'm sorry."

I let out a sigh, still hurt but feeling a little better. "That's okay."

"Really?" In the glow of a passing streetlight, his face was soft with relief and his exhale sounded shaky. My own heart melted. He cared how I felt about Evelyn, which meant he knew that what we had shared back in Ireland had been special, even if it was temporary. I was glad.

"Of course."

He let out a sigh and squeezed my arm tight as we continued uphill toward the castle.

My phone alarm, turned very low so as not to wake Jasher in the next room, went off at three in the morning. Flicking it off, I perched on the edge of my bed, my brain coughing along at half-speed. Shucking my pajama top and reaching for a sweater, I paused. It wasn't likely I'd run into someone at this hour, but what if I did? Wouldn't it be better to be caught in my sleepwear than in day clothes? I could pretend to have been sleepwalking.

I looked longingly at where my parka peeked out from behind the wardrobe door but I pulled on the bathrobe instead. I stood at my door in a sleep-stupor, looking around for my slippers. Once they were found and donned, I made my way to the rear door. Leaving the door shut but unlocked behind me, I slipped down the steps and through the fragrant garden.

Feeling a little like a criminal, I threw a glance over my shoulder up at the castle. The many windows were dark, though several spotlights remained lit, casting large coins of light against the turrets, the leafless wisteria and the evergreen ivy. The wind tugged at my hair and blew through the fabric of my bathrobe, raising gooseflesh. Tugging the robe tighter, I shivered and continued on down the narrow path and through the woods.

The tangle of thorns looked like a jagged lump in the dim light of the grove. A thin cool shard of moonlight escaped through a rift in the clouds and illuminated the ruin momentarily. The men had made some progress in cutting back the thorns. Stumps of surprisingly thick trunks could be seen poking bluntly from the shadows. A silhouette suggesting the shape of a person materialized in the thorny shrub, as though someone had gotten trapped in the center of the bush and stood there waiting for rescue. My heart leaped, but a moment later the clouds moved and the shadow dissipated.

Kicking off my slippers and letting my bare soles press against the earth, I closed my eyes. Tuning in to the shrub, I realized it was a form of *berberis* called *stenophylla*. My eyes flew open in surprise. Stenophylla was an evergreen shrub and though it was spiny, this particular plant seemed to have spines in excess, and the thorns were longer, with a stronger connection to each branch than I would have expected. Stenophylla was used as a defensive hedge by some, because it was impenetrable, but it wasn't known for being more difficult to root out than other thorny bushes. Strange. Perhaps the thorn was sickly? Closing my eyes again, I searched the layers of earth, mentally sifting until I found the roots. Sensing a strange, stubborn resiliency but no illness, I shrugged.

Sending the stenophylla a command to retreat, I relaxed into the task, coaxing the shrub to shrink. Instead of taking energy and nourishment from the earth, it poured the energy back in. I could hear the subtle sounds of its growth reversing, its spines shrinking and retreating, its trunks thinning and weakening.

Reversing the stenophylla's growth was harder than I remembered it to be. I hadn't used my powers this way in several weeks, so perhaps I was just out of practice. Realizing I was shivering, I doubled down on the thorn bush. Its thick shadow was retreating across the ground, centering around the ruin. Rigid branches fell back like long wispy hands withdrawing from a cookie jar. The thorns softened and the fibers dwindled. Branches became nubs, and trunks became stems.

I couldn't get rid of the shrub altogether. That would be too noticeable. But I could make it a little easier for the men to clear it all away. Letting the reversal slow to an end when the shrub looked smaller but not alarmingly so, I sent the plant a comforting mental sign off, telling it to release its hold on this patch of earth without resistance.

That done, I took a deep breath, slipped my chilly, dirty feet back into the bath slippers, and picked my way back up to the castle in the dark. I was snuggled under the duvet a few minutes later with no one the wiser.

CHAPTER FIVE

*A*fter breakfast the next morning, I sat in the big second floor parlor, trying to keep focused on my physics lesson and failing. It was nearing ten. I had expected Jasher to poke his head in and pass along a secret thank you for making the job of removing the thorns a little easier. I told myself he was too busy removing the old walls and foundations of the ruin and couldn't get away. But once the thought entered my mind, I couldn't shake it. Finally, I packed up my laptop and deposited it in my room before trekking down to the site to check on the progress.

The mumble of male voices drifted through the trees as I passed through the narrow pathway. When I got to the clearing, I took a few steps back to keep my astonished face hidden while I absorbed what I was seeing.

The thorn bush was *larger* than it had been even before I had reversed its growth. I stood there, half hidden in the foliage, staring at the monstrous stenophylla, as shocked as I had ever been about anything in my young life. That included learning that my best friend Targa was a mermaid.

Lachlan, Jasher, Will, and one other man I hadn't seen

before were chopping away at the shrub with heavy-duty hedge clippers, each of them tackling a different side of the bush. Their mumbles and mutters were unhappy, and no wonder. Finally, I fixed my expression into something I thought might look neutral and emerged from the foliage.

"Hey, Georjie." Lachlan was the first to look up from his work. A large pile of cut-off branches lay within a stone's throw from him. Similar piles lay scattered throughout the glade.

Jasher and Will looked up and waved. Neither of them smiled.

The fourth man didn't even look up from his work but remained bent over with both hands on his clippers.

"Can you believe it?" Lachlan stepped away from the bush and took a kerchief from his back pocket. Mopping his brow with it, he stuffed it back into his pocket and stretched his spine. I could hear the snaps and pops from where I was standing.

"Take a break, guys." Jasher extricated his clothing from the grip of a few clingers. "Get some water."

The men slowly stretched their bodies and took turns pouring water from a large jug.

My mouth felt dry and the right words seemed so far away. What could I say? Great job? Not only had no progress been made, the shrub was bigger and nastier than the day before. Sorry my plan didn't work out? Nope. I finally settled for, "How's it going?"

Jasher handed the jug of water to Will. "This beast is unreal. We think the Mandela effect is at work here."

That gave me pause. "The what?"

"It's a pop term for group false memory," Lachlan explained, which didn't clarify things for me.

"The Mandela effect is just a name someone gave a weird phenomenon where a large group of people all remember something inaccurately." Will poured himself a second cup of water.

"Can you give me an example?"

"The name is the first clue," Lachlan said, plucking random spines from his pants. "A significant number of people remember Nelson Mandela dying in prison in the eighties."

The man I hadn't been introduced to yet blinked in surprise. "He did." He shot me a wave. "Thomas, by the way."

I gave him a smile. "Georjie."

Jasher was shaking his head at Thomas. "Nope. That's the effect talking. He passed away in twenty-thirteen from a respiratory illness."

I gave him a blank look. "Is there an example I might be familiar with?"

"Did your parents ever read you kids stories about a family of talking bears?" Lachlan leaned into one hip and stretched out his side.

I brightened and nodded. "Someone gave me a bunch as a birthday present when I was kid. They were supposed to be collectors' items but I actually loved the stories."

Lachlan nodded. "They were super popular. Do you remember the bears' last name?"

I snapped my fingers, my mind skipping on its wheels. "Bear-something. It's on the tip of my tongue. Bera… Berenstein!" I said triumphantly. "I haven't thought about those stories in years."

Lachlan nodded. "But they were never called Berenstein. They were always *The Berenstain Bears*."

"What? No, they weren't. I remember the name clearly. I would bet on it."

"Or do you?" Lachlan's eyebrow crooked and he stretched his other side. "Why don't you look it up and you let me know what you find? You're not the only one who swears that they were called Berenstein."

I got the point.

"Yeah, so anyway…" Jasher screwed the cap back on the jug. "We think the four of us are misremembering just how big this bloody thorn bush was. We could all swear that it grew overnight, and not just by a few inches, by…*a lot*." Jasher shot me a meaningful look. "And, not to change the subject, but might I have a word?"

I nodded. "Sure."

I wanted to talk to Jasher privately, too.

We stepped out of hearing range while the men went back to their work. Jasher put a soft grip on my elbow and leaned close, lowering his voice.

"I wasn't going to ask you this, but do you think you could do some of your magic and root out this shrub for us? I didn't build days into the schedule to deal with it, and Gavin is disappointed that we've fallen behind."

"That's the thing, Jasher." I dropped my voice to a whisper. "I *did*. Last night, while everyone was asleep, I came out here in my pj's and made it much smaller."

Jasher stared at me, unimpressed. "Did your powers break when you left Ireland or something? Because, I don't know if you've noticed, but it didn't work."

I gave him a withering glare. "Of course, I noticed. I stood in the trees in shock for like a full minute."

"So, what happened?"

"I don't know! I watched it shrink and then I went to bed. I was surprised when you didn't pop by while I was studying this morning to say thank you."

Jasher leaned back and gave a sarcastic laugh. "Thank you? Did you think it was opposite day?"

He was making light of it, but unease had wormed its way into my heart. "Jasher, it's not funny. Either something is

47

wrong with that bush, or there's something wrong with my powers. I swear, last night after I was done with it, it was half that size."

We heard Lachlan make a cry of pain and loose a stream of cusswords that made Will and Thomas both laugh.

Jasher and I stopped our conspiratorial whisper-fest to return to the glade.

"You okay?" I called.

Lachlan was cradling one hand but gave a dismissive nod. At least he had a kind of smile on his face. "I swear, the blasted thing reached out and stabbed me." A thin stream of blood dripped from his hand and onto the ground. He inspected the wound. "It's a deep one."

"Let me see." I picking my way around heaps of discarded thorny branches to Lachlan.

"It's nothing." But he held his hand out for me to see.

Dark blood welled from a thick, round hole in the fleshy mound of his thumb. "That really is deep. Let me run up to the castle and get you some antiseptic and a bandage."

"Dinna fash. It's just a wee cut. I'm fine. I always was a baby when it comes to pain." Lachlan's cheeks were bright with embarrassment and he glanced at the other guys and pulled his hand away. It was then that I realized that Jasher and Will were staring at us with smirks on their faces.

"It'll only take me a minute." I turned away to go back to the castle and rolled my eyes at Jasher. "You're so immature."

But it wasn't Lachlan's cut that was on my mind as I returned to Blackmouth Castle. My powers hadn't worked. It was worse than that. They'd backfired.

I tracked down Ainslie where she was rooting around under the stairs and filling a bucket with cleaning products and tools. She told me I could find the first aid kit in the cupboard over the fridge. Retrieving it, I scampered back down to the site.

The men barely looked up from their work as Lachlan set his clippers beside the water jug and held out his bloody hand for aid.

"Sweet of you," he murmured.

I smiled and took his hand and used peroxide to swab at the wound.

Lachlan watched quietly, his gaze on my face. He tilted his head close to mine. I looked up for a second and my breath caught at how close our faces were. I could see the flecks of green in his blue eyes.

I took my time cleaning and dressing the wound to give me time to tune in to the roots below me and the millions of compounds at my beck and call. Drawing on nature's healing power, I sent it into Lachlan's body, up through his legs and torso and down his arm to his hand, where the wound was now hidden under a bandage.

"It tingles a bit," Lachlan said, dreamily. "But it feels better already." He caught my eye again. "Thank you."

"Back to work, lovebird," Jasher teased.

Lachlan flushed and shot me an awkward smile as he retrieved his clippers and went back to work. I realized with a little hitch in my heart that I was growing fond of that blush.

Later that afternoon, I had just packed up my laptop and schoolwork and was heading to my room to deposit it when I heard Lachlan calling me.

"I'm here!" I raised my voice as I deposited my laptop on my bed and made my way to the stairs.

I found him standing in the foyer wearing boots caked in mud. He smelled of wood and soil and his face gleamed with a light sheen of sweat.

"What's wrong?" I asked.

"Nothing's wrong." Lachlan had his work hat crumpled in his hands. "We're finished up for the day."

"Good progress?"

"Some. That shrub is wicked resistant." His throat moved as he swallowed. "I just wanted to say thank you. Whatever you did, well, it worked like magic."

"Oh, you're welcome."

"Which—Fae or Wise?" he asked, his expression earnest.

My heart stopped. "Excuse me?"

His teeth flashed in a grin. "It's a local expression. We ask it as a joke when someone does something extraordinary." He bobbed his head. "As in––which one are you? A faerie or a witch?"

The skin on my entire body ran cold and the back of my neck prickled as the meaning behind the saying sank in.

"Wise is your word for witch?" Gooseflesh was crawling its way up my arms.

Lachlan nonchalantly put his cap back on his head. "Like I said, it's one of those local colloquialisms." His gaze grew studious as his eyes combed my face. "Are you all right, Georjie? Ye look like ye've seen a phantom."

"I'm fine," I replied weakly.

He relaxed. "Well, thanks again." He raised his bandaged hand, all five fingers splayed. "I can't even feel it anymore. Have a great night. I'll see you tomorrow."

"You're welcome. Sure. Tomorrow," I repeated, dazed.

The door closed behind him and I took a few wobbly steps back until I hit the stairs. Sinking onto the third step, I heaved a long exhale. Lachlan's words replayed in my mind like a peal of bells on Sunday.

Which one are you? A faerie or a witch?

CHAPTER SIX

I caught a whiff of floral perfume as someone entered the cafe and a gust of wind blew in. A low murmur of conversation hummed around me as I worked. When I'd moved from the parlor at the castle to a nearby cafe, my productivity had gone up. I liked the background noise.

Today there was also the sound of children chanting a kind of rhyme from the street. Craning my neck to look out the open door, I saw girls playing jump-rope in the park across the road. One of them was Maisie, I recognized her red hair. It was the same color as Bonnie's. I tried to catch the words of their chant as it kept time with the jumper.

"Bake her down, steal her magic and wear her crown," the girls sang. My blood froze as they took a pause and started again. *"Witch or Wise, loose your cries-"*

"Hello, Georjie," a soft voice said from beside me.

I jumped and did a quick half-turn to see a pair of familiar dark brown eyes.

"Hi, Evelyn." I glanced out the window at the girls but the words of their chant were lost to me as the door to the café closed. I made a note to ask Maisie about it when I saw her back at the castle.

"Sorry, I didn't mean to startle you," she said.

I cleared my throat and relaxed on my seat. "Coming in for a fix?"

"I'm a self-admitted addict." She perched on the empty stool beside me and peered at the screen. "Are you alright? You look a little pale."

I swallowed and gave her a smile. "I'm okay, thanks."

"What are you working on?"

"A history paper." My gaze caught on her unusual jacket. It was dark green with a high-to-low hem. The wool was cinched in at the waist with a belt emphasizing her tiny ribcage and the flare of her hips. "Cute jacket."

"Thanks." She leaned one elbow on the table, her brown curls swaying. "I've never seen you working here before."

"I needed a change from the castle. I like the energy, you know? The buzz of other people around me going about their day." I closed my laptop, hoping she'd take it as a signal to stay and chat for a few minutes. I had been all keen to research the French Revolution up until Lachlan had made that comment the night before. Now all I wanted to do was raid the library and internet for local 'colloquialisms.' I had promised myself I would once I got my history assignment finished.

"I know what you mean." Evelyn pulled the cloth bag hanging from her shoulder open, revealing the tablet inside. "I like coming to work here, too. My office feels like a vacuum. I like the hum of conversation, the endless supply of caffeine."

"What do you do?"

"I'm an architectural tech, which is not nearly as sexy as being an architect." She gave me a crafty look from under long lashes. "We do the grunt work and the architects get the glory, but you didn't hear that from me."

"Sounds very… mathy."

"Yeah, it is. But the job I'm on now isn't that complicated. I'm doing up the plans for Gavin's new holiday cottage."

My brows shot up. "That's cool. Is that how you and Jasher met?"

"Yes, actually." She assessed me. "Good guess."

I shot her a friendly side-eye. "You kids seem to fancy each other something fierce." To my initial horror, it came out with a heavy Scottish accent. I put my fingers to my lips as my face flushed, worried she might think I was poking fun at her. I didn't know her that well. "Ohmygosh, I'm sorry. I didn't mean that disrespectfully."

Evelyn loosed a peal of laughter that had a few other patrons looking up and smiling. "Relax, Georjie."

I smiled with relief. "We Canadians have a reputation for being exceedingly polite. They might not let me back into the country if I tarnish it."

She waved a hand. "To your question, I'm crazy about Jasher. I'll just put it right out there in open."

"Does he feel the same way about you?"

Her face took on a dreamy cast. "I think so, but sometimes I'm not sure. He can run a bit hot and cold, you know?"

"Yeah," I nodded. "I do. He froze me out for weeks when we met."

Her big brown eyes widened. She reminded me of a newborn filly, so alert, so attentive. "I'm glad to see he's stopped that nonsense. Especially after what you did for him."

The smile froze on my face. "What do you mean?"

"You know." She did the looking around thing again and lowered her voice. "After you helped him with the ghost thing."

The room tilted. I rubbed my fingers over my eyes to buy a second to figure out how to react. "He told you about that?"

"Sure, I mean…it's why he's here, isn't it?"

"It is?"

"Now that he's not worried about being haunted, he wants to travel the world."

I nodded slowly. "Yes." That was true. I was still spinning over the fact that Jasher had told her something so immensely personal, something most people wouldn't have even believed.

She was going on. "I can't imagine what life would have been like for him before, seeing spooks all over the place. It's no wonder he didn't want to leave home."

I gaped at her in wonder.

She finally noticed my shock. "What?"

I took a swig of my coffee to bolster my nerve. "It's just… Jasher is an intensely private person. He doesn't tell people about his past trauma."

"I know." She rolled her eyes with understanding. "I'm lucky he came out of his shell. The booze helped, if I'm really honest. Once he opened the tap, whoosh! I mean, the lad wouldn't shut up!"

Feeling cool, I fished my cardigan out of my bag and pulled it on. So I wasn't the only one who'd taken note. I hadn't said anything to Jasher about it because I wasn't sure what was normal any more. "Has it been a problem?"

"The drinking?" She considered the question. "He says he never drank while in Ireland. And here, it's like he's trying to play catch up. Like he's trying to reclaim some of his lost youth. I'm sure he'll grow tired of it. Maybe he just needs to have the freedom to get a few hangovers. They'll convince him it's not a wise activity for the long term."

"You think so?"

"I really do." She put a hand on my arm. "You worried?"

"Only a little. I never saw him drink, so I was surprised the other night." I caught her eye. "Shall we just agree to... watch him?" Recoiling a little at my own words, I added. "Sorry, that sounds a bit stalkery. I didn't mean it like that."

"I know, and yes. Let's just keep an eye." She set her bag on the counter and rubbed her shoulder where the strap had been. "I've got a few alkies in my family. Thankfully, Jasher doesn't show any signs of that."

"Alkies?"

"Alcoholics."

"Oh."

"The only defense an alcoholic has is to never take the first drink. Once they do that, they're doomed. They won't stop until they black out unless someone interferes. Jasher doesn't do that. He might have had a little too much from time to time, but I've never seen him get really sloppy, or pass out. My uncle drank himself to death. I swore I'd never let that happen to anyone else I loved."

I fell speechless after this monologue. There was so much there to unpack that I didn't know where to start. She'd spoken about her uncle like she was commenting on the view, and I had not missed the part where she essentially admitted to loving Jasher. The silence dragged as I searched for an appropriate response.

She saved me from having to come up with one. "What about your folks?"

I blinked at finding myself in the crosshairs. "*My* parents?"

"Yeah, are they around? You get along?"

I blew out a breath. Her earnest vulnerability had shattered my defenses. Part of me wanted to lay my head on her shoulder and cry at the way she'd divulged so much in so little time. This woman had no armoring, no emotional shields or guile. It was disarming, and I found myself warming to her because of it.

"I got along really well with my mom when I was little. But when my dad left and she got promoted, we grew apart. We're repairing things, but I doubt we'll ever be besties."

She put a hand over her heart. Her luminous eyes filled with sadness, shining with unshed tears. "I'm so sorry. When did your father leave?"

"I was five." I swallowed down a lump in my throat. Damn her empathy. It was like she was feeling all the emotions attached to my story and it was bringing stuff to the surface. "At first, he started canceling our play-dates. Eventually, he stopped coming around all together. Then one day..." I was surprised when my throat closed up as I fought back tears. I never cried over my father anymore. I never even thought about him anymore. Well, hardly ever.

"One day, what?" Evelyn gently prodded.

"One day he left a note. Just a scrap of paper. It had a phone number and, well..." I rifled through my bag for my phone. Showing her would say more than I ever could.

I plucked the folded scrap from a pocket inside my wallet and handed it to her. "I keep meaning to throw it out. I guess I keep it to remind myself that I had a dad once, but he was never worthy."

She took the note and gazed at it. "Oh, Georjie." She looked up and I felt like I was bathing in compassion as it poured from her eyes. "*For emergencies?*"

I nodded. "He might as well have written 'Don't call me' and not bothered giving us his new cell number."

She handed the note back to me. "Have you ever called it?"

A hot rush of indignation flushed my cheeks. "I wouldn't ask him for help if he was the last man on earth."

"Except that you haven't thrown it out," she replied softly.

Wanting not only to change the subject but tap into a local's knowledge, I asked on inspiration, "Do you know the saying: Which, Fae or Wise?"

She took a second. "So we're done talking about your dad, then? Sorry, just trying to keep up."

In answer I shoved the note into my pocket.

"Okay." She cleared her throat. "Yes, I have heard it. It's a way of complimenting someone when they've done something that's hard to do. Why? Did someone say it to you?"

I nodded. "Lachlan, after I bandaged a wound for him."

Concern wrinkled her brow. "Lachlan was hurt?"

I laughed. "It's nothing to worry about. Just a scratch from your not so friendly neighborhood thorn bush."

"Ah." She relaxed. "Well, in that case, he was just saying thank you."

"Any idea where the phrase originated?"

She shook her head. "I've no idea. It's been around for as long as I can remember. Could be hundreds of years old. Why?"

"Just curious." I tucked my hair behind my ear and looked away. "I thought I heard some kids chanting something similar across the street earlier, too. They were jumping rope to it."

"Really?" Evelyn looked bemused.

The café door opened again as a couple left and I glanced outside. "They're gone now. You never sang any songs about Wise when you were young?"

"Not that comes to mind. You could try the Blackmouth Castle archives. They have a lot of historical documents and stuff, but I don't think it would be easy to find something like that. It's just one of those things that's been passed down through the generations."

I nodded. "Yeah, you're probably right. It's just, that term—Wise—it's unusual."

"It's just another name for witch. Maybe it's unusual where you're from."

"Maybe." But the parallel sat uneasily with me. Was I a witch? I didn't feel very witchy, but then again, besides what I'd seen in movies and TV shows, I didn't know anything about real witches. Before last summer, I wouldn't have believed there were any.

"I'd better get my coffee and get some work done," Evelyn said. "It was really lovely talking with you, Georjayna."

"You too, Evelyn."

"Call me Evie."

"Call me Georjie."

She gave me a smile and went to the front counter to order herself a drink. I didn't notice when Evelyn left the cafe. I threw myself into my work and put the final touches on my history paper. Closing my laptop and pulling on my coat, I decided to take Evelyn's advice and check the Blackmouth Castle library about the colloquialism. Sliding my bag onto my shoulder, I zipped up my jacket and headed for the door, putting my hands in my pockets.

The feel of paper reminded me that I'd put my father's note in there. I pulled it out as I reached the door and my eye caught on the trash can sitting beside the coat rack. Holding the note out over the garbage, I paused. My hand trembled a little. Snatching my hand back, I tucked the note in my pocket again.

I'd throw it out some other time.

CHAPTER SEVEN

*B*etween my physics and history homework the following week, I stole a few hours to search the Blackmouth library, the way Gavin had invited me to do. Only I wasn't researching the exodus of Scottish people to Ireland. That was interesting, but it had taken a back seat. I was looking for the roots of local lingo, in particular the phrase Lachlan had uttered.

I found absolutely nothing.

Frustrated, I slammed shut the book I had in front of me, then got up and took it back to its place on the shelves. Letting out a long breath, I tugged at the neck of my shirt. It was hot and stuffy in the library. It was a circular room in one of the uppermost turrets of the castle, which meant heat traveled up from the lower floors and got trapped here. The room was charming, but not often used. It smelled of mildew and aged wood. I needed a breath of fresh air.

On my way outside, I popped into the kitchen for a drink of water and found Ainslie sitting at the table with her own steaming mug of something and fanning herself with a magazine. She looked up and smiled as I came in. Her face was a little on the pink side.

"How's our wee Canadian getting on? Schoolwork going well?"

"All good here, how about you? Looks like you had a busy morning."

"Every day is a busy day for me, but sometimes the 'change of life' gets the better of me." She laughed at the clueless look on my face. "Menopause. You too can look forward to feeling like someone set a flaming torch under yer arse."

"Ah. Sorry to hear that. I don't recommend hanging out in the library if you're hot, in that case."

Ainslie cackled like this was quite hilarious. "Come sit a spell. Have a cuppa geranium tea. It's supposed to balance the hormones." She poked at the squat ceramic pot sitting nearby. "Although, you won't have to worry about unbalanced hormones for a long while yet."

"I'm good with water, but actually there was something I wanted to ask you. Gavin told me you could tell me something about those extraordinary roses in the garden. I wasn't aware there were roses that could bloom in winter." I slid onto the bench across from her and took a sip of my water.

Ainslie's expression grew sly. "Aye, those are special roses and you won't find them anywhere else in the world. They're a hybrid that was crossbred after a dark time in Blackmouth's history, in celebration that the bad times were over." Ainslie settled onto her elbows, warming to her narrative. "Blackmouth was named such because at one time the villagers had a very bad habit of deceiving and lying to one another. Pranks and tricks were commonplace, and were not mere jokes but done out of true spite and a wish to harm one another. Children learned the behavior from their parents' bad attitudes and it went on for quite some time."

"How long ago was this?" I asked, my water glass pausing on its way to my lips.

Ainslie flapped a hand. "Och, a long way back. Hundreds of years. This would have been medieval times. Anyway, there was a 'cunning woman' in Blackmouth in those days, and she declined to get involved in the townspeople's petty spats."

"A cunning woman? Isn't that what they called a witch?"

"Too right." Ainslie nodded and paused to take a sip of her tea. "Her name has been lost to history, and a mythology has risen up to surround her story with exaggerations. But mark my words, she was real. As real as those roses out there." She pointed at the window behind me. "Many people went to her for help, and the stories of her healing abilities were legendary. But she grew tired of all the backbiting and bad behavior and the story goes that she created the rose and dubbed it *rós fírinn*––the truth rose. She claimed that the scent of them would inspire people to be truthful with one another."

The skin across my back prickled at the sincerity in Ainslie's eyes. "Did it work?"

"You bet yer bonny wee head it worked. After that, Blackmouth prospered and its people became real neighbors to one another, the way they remain today." Ainslie leaned forward. "And you know what else the myth would have you believe? That those roses are the very same crop that cunning woman started with." She nodded, eyes narrowing.

I cocked my head. "The same...what do you mean?"

"They don't die," she whispered. "In all my days working here, I've never had to pluck up an aged or sickly rose. Their heads never wither or drop off. They just close up tight and then reopen again. There's always heads in full blossom, rain or shine, dead of winter. Nothing can hold those roses back."

I took another drink of my water, wondering what to

think. If there was anything I had learned from having this new connection to the earth, it was that all living things lived and died in cycles. Then again... Targa claimed that sirens can live for several hundreds of years in a vital state of quasi-immortality. If a living being could have that attribute, why couldn't a plant? "What happened to the witch?"

Ainslie shrugged. "I wish I knew. Lost to the past, like so much of our history. There would have been people at that time who would want to shut up a woman like that, so sometimes I wonder what kind of end she came to. I'd thank her if I could. Those roses have seen us through some financially difficult times."

"How so?"

"Let me show you something." Ainslie got up from the bench, moving stiffly, and crossed the room to a hutch against the wall opposite the fireplace. Opening the uppermost cupboard revealed a row of binders. She pulled one out and returned to the table as she opened it and leafed through it. "Here we are."

She lay the binder open in front of me. I began to flip through the pamphlets and certificates of prizes won at gardening and agricultural shows from Edinburgh to Penzance.

"The rose has won prizes?"

"Aye, it's never lost any exhibit we've submitted it for. It wasn't easy in the beginning, because we had to request the judges come up here. Most shows expect you to bring your rosebush to their event, but we couldn't do that. So for a few years, our applications were rejected. But when we finally convinced a judge to come see the roses for herself, they made an exception for us. We can't compete in all the categories, but we sweep the ones we can register for."

I looked up in confusion. "Why couldn't you take the roses to them?"

"Because they die as soon as you take them out of Blackmouth."

My jaw drifted open. "They...die?"

Ainslie nodded sadly. "Can't tell you how many people have tried to plant them elsewhere. No one has ever been successful. This is the only place you'll ever find them."

I was completely speechless. My heartrate went up a notch. There was magic in those roses, and the cunning woman who bred them sounded like a Wise. If she was, it was no wonder the terms Wise and witch were interchangeable in Blackmouth.

Ainslie gathered up the binder and returned it to the cupboard. She closed the door and returned to the table to down the last of her tea.

"Back to work for me. You going to check on those boys?"

"Yes, that was where I was headed, actually." I took Ainslie's teacup and deposited it into the sink along with my drinking glass. "Thanks for sharing that story with me, Ainslie."

She nodded. "It's nice to have something happy to share with tourists when they come. Our history is so full of darkness and murder, it's refreshing that Blackmouth has something positive to contribute." She headed for the door. "See you at supper."

Setting the dishes to drip dry, I went to the back door and donned boots and a jacket. The day was fresh and there were even a few slivers of sunshine trying to make their way through the bank of clouds drifting slowly overhead. I took my time passing through the garden, appreciating the scent of the truth roses and their extraordinarily resilient beauty. Was I capable of manufacturing an immortal rose? If I was, I didn't have the know-how. And why did the roses die as soon as they were taken out of Blackmouth?

A nasty thought struck. What if some of the accused who

were burned during the witch trials, had actually been Wise? My heart bled at the thought.

Passing through the maze and toward where Jasher and the others were working, I heard the mix of concerned male voices. Entering the clearing, I saw that all work had ceased. Jasher was on the work phone he'd been given by Gavin, while Will and Lachlan stood nearby, muttering softly. They all looked serious.

"Look at the progress you've made," I said as I approached.

The thorns had been uprooted, finally, and the clippings and roots had been burned in a pit beyond the grove. With the ruins now exposed, I realized they were more extensive than first imagined. Crumbling stone walls as thick as two feet snaked about the grove at right angles to one another. Old stone floors were cracked and full of weeds as nature reclaimed her territory.

The men greeted me. Jasher looked up and gave me a nod, but he didn't smile. He went back to the conversation he was having on the work phone, his voice low and thoughtful.

"Progress stops once again," Lachlan said, "and you won't believe why this time."

"Why?" But no one needed to tell me. Once I was close enough to the ruin, I saw for myself.

There, within the thick stone and mortar of the ruin, lay an upright skeleton, with enough skin and muscle tissue remaining to cross over into mummy class.

"Whoa," I breathed. "Is that real?"

"Aye, we believe so. It's lucky it wasn't destroyed completely before we noticed it, because we were meant to demolish and remove all of the remaining walls today. When Jasher pulled away the stone covering its...face, he gave a frightful yell."

"Gavin should call the job off," Will said, uneasily. "If

those stupid thorn bushes were any sign, that thing doesn't want to be disturbed."

My insides gave a lurch of disquiet. I didn't know if Will was being serious, but I was a supernatural. His suggestion was completely within my realm of belief.

"Feeling a bit superstitious are you, Will?" Lachlan knocked him on the arm with a fist, but his smile was also troubled.

The skull stared out at us from hollow sockets. A line of wrinkled skin framed the bare teeth, leaving only a hideous grin. A long, tangled mat of fibers on either side of the skull suggested hair, and rotten cloth draped over the shoulders suggested clothes. Below the chest, the body was still trapped between layers of stone and cement, while the layer which had covered the face and neck had been pulled away. It sat there like a sleeping nightmare, trapped on all sides.

"I wonder who she was?" Lachlan murmured as we stared at the body.

Will's eyes darted up. "She?"

"Sure, look at the long hair."

"There have been times in history when men had long hair, too," Will pointed out.

"True." But Lachlan sounded doubtful.

I couldn't help but think about the story Ainslie had just told me about the cunning woman, how she wondered what kind of end she'd found. But just because the body was in close proximity to the roses didn't mean anything, and I was most likely linking the two because the story was fresh in my mind.

"Who is Jasher talking to?" I asked, my voice sounded paper dry.

"The police," replied Will. "That's a murder, right there."

"It's too old for the police to care about it," Lachlan shifted his weight from one foot to the other and lifted his

A.L. KNORR

spade to point. "That person would have been buried in the walls when they were first built, so it's been there for over three hundred years. There won't be a murder investigation. Whoever did it died ages ago."

Will had begun to pace, his hands tucked into his armpits. He threw disgusted glances at the skeleton, never allowing his gaze to linger for very long.

Jasher said goodbye and ended his call. "The Chief Inspector is on his way."

"Really?" Lachlan looked surprised. "They aren't going to send a constable?"

"Only because he's not far away and he's curious to see it for himself." Jasher gave me a tremulous smile and came to stand beside me.

We looked down at the skeleton, standing shoulder to shoulder with our backs to the others.

"Looks like the dead still have a way of finding me," he said quietly.

I took his hand and squeezed. I could feel his muscles trembling under my hand. "Sorry, Jasher. What a nasty find."

"It's all right. Just threw me for a bit of a loop, pulling a stone away and seeing that thing grinning up at me like a Halloween party decoration. Dealing with the remains is way better than dealing with the spirit. Though, I'd be able to tell her story if I was able to communicate with the dead still."

I didn't miss his reference to a female, and I had to admit, I was already thinking of the body as 'she.' "They'll have other ways of figuring out who she was."

Jasher nodded. "I'd better go out front and meet the inspector. He won't know how to find his way down here." He turned and disappeared into the trees.

We stood around in low conversation and in stretched-out silences until Jasher returned with a tall, pale man with red hair and a wide stomach. He was dressed in uniform and wore a serious expression to go along with it. He introduced himself as Chief Inspector Hamilton, not shaking hands but sparing each of us a nod. He wheezed a little as he knelt near the find. He took several photos and made notes.

"Are you going to investigate this as a murder?" Will asked.

Inspector Hamilton snapped his notebook shut and tucked it into his pocket, bracing a hand on the stone wall to help him rise.

"Of course not," he replied testily. "I'll have to call in a mortician to remove it. Once it's in the morgue, an osteoarcheologist will see what can be made of it." He made eye contact with each of us. "You've not disturbed it?"

Jasher shook his head. "Only when the stones in front of its face fell away, the head kind of fell to the side and stayed like you see it now. Otherwise, we haven't touched it."

"Good," the inspector replied. "Don't touch anything else until it's been removed."

"Are you sure we should remove it, Inspector?" Will's voice quavered a little. "I mean, disturbing the dead and all."

"What, you want to build your new cottage around it? Leave it for a good luck charm?" Inspector Hamilton gave a patronizing chuckle.

Will looked abashed. "It's bad luck to move it."

"Says who?" the inspector barked and Will looked down, embarrassed.

Jasher and I exchanged glances. I felt sorry for Will.

"We follow protocol," the inspector went on. "This is an archaeological find. It'll be documented, studied, and in this case"—the inspector swung his eyes to the skeleton again —"buried. There's no room for superstitious nonsense…"

"…in the law," Lachlan finished, sounding tired.

"That's right," the inspector said. "I'll make the appropriate calls. Like I said—"

"Don't touch anything," Jasher and Lachlan replied simultaneously.

"Yeah, we won't," Jasher finished.

Jasher left with the inspector while Will grabbed his stuff and gave Lachlan and me a hurried goodbye.

"Poor fellow," Lachlan said once Will had gone. "Whole thing has disturbed him a bit."

"Well, it is disturbing." I glanced uneasily at the skeleton. "She *was* murdered."

"Whatever happened here is part of Blackmouth's story. There'll be a way to learn who she was and why she was killed." Lachlan lowered his voice. "And I fancy Will was right. That bloody spook of a thorn bush had something to do with her."

"You think so?"

"Absolutely. I totally believe in supernatural stuff like that. Don't you?"

"Better not mention that to Inspector Hamilton."

Lachlan loosed a belly laugh. "That's an argument he and I have been keeping alive since I was ten."

I blinked at him. "Really?"

Lachlan shot me a wide grin. "He's my father."

"Oh!"

"He's a right dry old codger, too. Frustrated with me for not going into the service. But, he's right. There's no room for the supernatural in that line of work. I'd just feel hogtied. I'd rather investigate on my own."

"You like to investigate?"

"Sure, it's one of my passions. I've amassed quite a collection of documents and oddities over the years. Though I'll donate them to a museum at some point. She's got a story. There's a thread somewhere to be pulled at."

"How would you go about investigating her?" I asked.

He frowned thoughtfully at the remains. "Well, the

osteoarcheologist will be able to tell us when she died and how old she was. Roughly, anyway. From there, I'd look into the records of missing persons from the era, see if there's a description that might match her. Missing persons who were found in the end could be eliminated."

"Also, missing persons outside of her gender and age range," I added.

"Right. That would leave us with a smaller group. From there we'd have to see if we could find details about those people's lives." Lachlan rested a palm on the spade's handle and began to gesture. "The archaeologist might be able to give us something specific, like evidence on her body that shows she was a weaver, or had excessive calcium in her bones."

"What would that mean?"

"It might mean she lived closer to the ocean, ate more fish than those who lived in the highlands." Lachlan shrugged. "You never know what the tests might reveal."

I nodded. "What about the thorns? Do you agree with Will, that the two are linked?"

"That's harder to prove." Lachlan ruffled the hair under his cap. "We dug up as much of the shrub as we could, but it's impossible to remove every root and shoot. It would return before long if not kept in check."

"But your dad said they'd bury the body. If the thorns and the body are linked and they remove her..."

"Aye, if she's gone and the thorns *don't* resurface..." His gaze connected with mine. "Well, that might not mean anything. But..."

"If thorns start to grow around the burial site instead of here..."

Lachlan nodded. "Time will tell."

"Speaking of telling, has anyone told Gavin yet?" I asked.

"He's at meetings in Inverness today, but I'm sure Jasher

will call him right away."

"He won't be happy that progress has stalled," I said.

"On the contrary. Gavin will be thrilled." Lachlan began to laugh.

"Why?"

"Oh, you'll see. I know the laird well, and he'll be over the moon about this development. Trust me."

* * *

The osteoarcheologist arrived shortly after nine the next morning. We'd been instructed over the phone to cover the body with a tarp until he came. Waiting to greet him was quite the party. Jasher, Lachlan, Evelyn, Will and I stood around in the clearing as a team of two men and one woman were led to the site by Gavin himself. Lachlan had been right. When Jasher called to let him know what had been found on his property, he was as giddy as a boy with a new bike on Christmas morning.

"This place has all kinds of secrets," he said jovially, eyes twinkling, as the team set to work donning gloves and bibs. "Blackmouth has seen more than its fair share of morbid history." He said this with the glee of someone talking about winning a prize at the fair, rubbing his hands together. "I always knew that she'd start lifting her skirts, showing us her goods if we were here for long enough."

The osteoarcheologist cast Gavin an amused look. He was a slender fellow with thinning blond hair named Callum Gordon. He had an actual monocle dangling from his jacket on a chain.

"He's a mite too happy for someone who just discovered a murder victim on their property," Callum commented to the group in general. He finished pulling on his second latex glove. "We've amassed quite an audience today."

"With good reason." Lachlan stood at my right with his hands in the pockets of his jacket. "The last time a murder victim was discovered in Blackmouth, it was the year JFK was shot. We don't see much of that kind of action around here, thankfully."

"How interesting," Callum responded in a tone that said he didn't find 'modern' murders interesting at all. He gave instructions to his crew to work slowly and extremely carefully at removing the remaining rocks and mortar from around the skeleton. It took them so long to do this that Will, Jasher and Evie decided to go in for a coffee and one of Ainslie's biscuits. Only Lachlan and I stuck around long enough to watch the crew laboriously settle the remains into the plastic-lined box they'd brought for the purpose.

"So, Mr. Gordon," I said to the team leader.

"Call me Callum."

"Callum. How long will it take for you to do the autopsy?"

"It's not technically an autopsy as we hope not to damage the remains, and it's a completely different process than what's done with fresh victims." He chewed his lip thoughtfully. "I'm just a volunteer and might not be able to spare quite as much time as I'd like, initially…"

"You're a volunteer?"

"We all are," chimed the lady on Callum's team. "There's no budget for this kind of thing. It's too low-profile. No one really cares about some peasant who was stoned up in a wall to die."

Lachlan and I shared a look that telegraphed our disagreement with her.

Callum caught our expressions. "Well, sure. It's interesting in general. But Cathy means no one important in archaeology is interested in this kind of find. Unless she proves to be someone of noble descent, which is highly unlikely as we'd have record of such a thing being done to someone of consequence, she'll be documented and buried without fanfare."

Lachlan and I shared a borderline desperate look as the team wrapped the skeleton up and closed the lid on the box. They began to sift through the rubble where she was found, making sure that they hadn't missed anything important, but they were almost finished here.

"Would it be all right if we called on you when the investigation is done?" Lachlan asked. "I'm an amateur historian, I love this kind of thing. And she," he gestured to me, "is just drawn to the macabre."

He said the last bit in a teasing tone and I thwacked him on the arm.

"Certainly, I'd be happy to let you know what I've found. I'm warning you, it's likely to be very dull," Callum said, taking off his latex gear and apron.

Lachlan gave him a patronizing smile. "She was buried in a wall. That's not something that highlanders did to one another, at least not often."

"She could be a victim of a clan war, couldn't she?" I asked as the team began to move out of the grove with the find. "I've come across stories of what the clans did to one another. They were brutal."

Callum shrugged. "Maybe. But maybe she just cheated on her husband and he went overboard."

"She might have stayed alive in there for quite some time, mightn't she?" I fell into step between Lachlan and Callum. "She might have dehydrated to death over a course of days."

"To your point," Callum said calmly, "it's not likely––if she was put into the wall alive––that she survived more than a few minutes. Given the state of preservation and how tightly mortared those stones were, I'd theorize there wasn't much oxygen left to survive on."

We'd arrived at the parking lot and the team began

loading up the vehicle, sliding the body into the trunk. The box looked like it was made for a child.

Gavin came striding out the front door as Callum shut the trunk.

Callum addressed the laird. "I'll let you know when the investigation is complete."

The archaeologist got into his vehicle and the engine coughed to life.

When the vehicle had left the parking lot, Gavin turned to me and Lachlan. "I'll be sure to relay the findings. You crazy kids seem to love this stuff as much as I do."

"But for different reasons," replied Lachlan.

I cocked my head at Gavin. "What's *your* reason?"

Gavin put a heavy hand on my shoulder. "Bookings, my girl."

"This find will be good for business?"

"Absolutely." Gavin gave that booming laugh of his. "Every ghost-hunter and spook-ninny will come from miles around––even out of country––to spend a night or two in the cottage built on the site of this find!"

Lachlan was laughing on my other side. "You watch, Georjayna. The moment Gavin puts the story of a body found in the walls on his website and pushes it out in his newsletter, they'll be falling over themselves to book a room next season."

"It's brilliant, couldn't have worked out better than if I'd planned it myself," Gavin added as he reached into his pocket and pulled out a set of keys. He said goodbye to us, got into his Land Rover, and left the property.

"Too bad we have to wait so long to learn more about the body," Lachlan said as we wandered from the parking lot back to the castle.

"Yeah," I agreed, but couldn't help smiling to myself. I didn't have to wait for anything, and I didn't plan to.

CHAPTER EIGHT

*J*asher agreed to come with me on a Wise trip down memory lane, as long as I agreed to describe what I was seeing as I was seeing it.

"I don't want to stand there all shivery while you stare off into oblivion for ten minutes, or longer," he said when I'd asked him in a quiet corner after dinner. "Besides, it'll be more accurate that way. Whatever you see, you describe in detail as it happens."

"I don't have a problem with that," I replied.

"Good, then let's meet at the entrance to the maze at one." He waggled his eyebrows conspiratorially. "A little midnight sleuthing mission."

I gave him a bored look.

"What?"

"Our rooms are next door to one another. Why don't we just meet in the hall?"

"Oh. Right." He looked sheepish.

I patted him on the shoulder and went into the parlor. Maisie sat on the window seat reading a book. Lorne sat on a sofa, looking through a book about space exploration. The kids always read in the parlor before going to bed.

"What are you reading, Maisie?" I sat down beside her.

She looked up as I sat down but she didn't answer. She closed the book to show me the cover.

"The Illustrated Black Beauty," I read aloud. "You like horses?"

She nodded and looked down.

"You know, I saw you the other day playing jump rope with some friends and singing. Across from the café. You're good at skipping."

Maisie nodded but didn't look up.

"I was hoping you could teach me the song you were singing?" I asked, gently. "I guess it was more like a chant than a song."

Maisie shook her head.

Lorne glanced up from his book. "She's shy."

"I was wondering where you learned it. You wouldn't help me learn it?"

Maisie kept her head down. She wasn't taking the bait, and I was beginning to feel bad for disturbing her.

"Do you know the song, Lorne?" I asked.

He wrinkled his nose. "That's girlie stuff."

Maisie bumped me with her elbow as she looked at her brother. She stuck her tongue out at him then looked at me. She pushed the book into my lap. "Read to me?"

It was the first real olive branch she'd handed me. "Of course." I took the book and began to read aloud, letting go of the questions about the chant for now.

At eight-thirty Bonnie came in to take the kids to bed. Maisie thanked me for reading to her before she left the parlor. I considered it progress.

At one, I pulled on a thick wool sweater and jeans and

met Jasher in the hall. He gave me an exaggerated 'be quiet' face, his finger smooshing his lips.

Amused, I wondered if it was Evelyn who made Jasher so happy. Jasher had never been this goofy while we'd hung out in Ireland. Granted, after he'd lost the ability to communicate with the dead, I'd gone home. So maybe this was the real Jasher.

The real Jasher shooed me down the hall. In the foyer, we pulled on our shoes and Jasher grabbed a flashlight and a small umbrella. Sneaking out the back door, we crept down the side steps and out through the maze. The moon was a cold, white rind hugged by dark clouds, but there was enough light that we didn't need the flashlight.

"It's really not a very maze-y maze," Jasher whispered. "I mean, how difficult can a maze be when there's a straight line running all the way through it?"

"I think it's actually two mazes." I grinned in the dark. "Plus, it's for kids." We passed the end of the maze and entered the thick copse of trees.

"Oh, well that makes more sense." His voice was so close behind me it made me jump. "But you know what would make it better?"

"What?" I held aside a thick branch for him so it didn't whack him in the face.

"Thanks." He took the branch and then let it fly behind him. "Clowns."

"What?"

"Yeah, don't you think a maze would be a lot more fun if there was a scary clown chasing you through it?"

"Yeah, if the point of the maze is to terrify children."

"A happy clown then."

"Still terrifying."

We emerged from the forest into the moon-dusted glade.

I rubbed my hands together to warm them. Our breath misted in front of our faces.

"Are you going to need me to light the show?" Jasher asked as we looked at the remains of the ruin.

"I don't know. I'll let you know, okay?"

"Okay. Ready when you are."

I squatted and pressed my fingers into the damp soil, thankful I didn't need to take off my boots in this cold. Retrieving a clump of earth, I stood and cast my gaze onto the ruin.

The grove filled with an ethereal gray mist. Darker smudges coalesced into moving human shapes. I took in a breath as two humans materialized from the fog, their forms visible as grainy shades of gray.

"See something?" Jasher's voice sounded distant, dreamy.

"There are two people coming from over there," I pointed past the ruin and into the trees beyond. "A man and a woman. They're dragging something." The figures approached and the details cleared. "No, he's pushing a wheelbarrow." My stomach dropped. "There is a body in the wheelbarrow. I can see a dress, an arm, and the top of a bonnet."

"What year do you think it is?" Jasher's disembodied voice drifted dissonantly through the grove. I felt like I was dreaming, and he was speaking from the real world.

I almost laughed. "I have no idea. My best guess is medieval. The man and woman are dressed like peasants. She's wearing a shawl crossed over her torso, and he's wearing a kilt and one of those lopsided hats, a...beret."

"It's called a tam o' shanter." I felt Jasher step closer, and he lowered his voice. "What are they doing now?"

"They've stopped pushing the wheelbarrow."

"Is the woman in it alive?"

"If she is, she's unconscious. She looks richer than the other two. There's lace on her skirt, but the hem is filthy."

"Is there a building?"

"Just the start of one, but it looks like they were planning this."

"What makes you say that?"

"There's a pile of rocks and a bucket with a hand-held spade on the ground next to it. There's a half-built wall, and what looks like a couple of buckets of mortar." I covered my mouth with my hand as the residual man and woman picked up the woman from the wheelbarrow ungracefully. "They're not careful with her at all."

"Why would they be? They're about to kill her, if they haven't already."

"Good point." I cringed and wanted to look away. "They just dumped her against the stones."

"Can you describe her face?"

"Her head is bent so I can't make it out. Just her lips, which are full. She has long hair. I can't tell what color, but I would guess light brown or maybe red."

"How old?"

"Young. Her skin looks smooth and pale. They're…"

"What?" I felt Jasher tug at my elbow.

"They're building the wall around her now, stone by stone. I don't think I need to see any more." I turned my hand over to drop the earth.

"Wait, there might be something else, some other clue," Jasher caught my hand and kept my fingers closed around the dirt. "Don't stop yet."

Stomach squirming, I held the earth and watched as the couple walled up the woman I really hoped was dead by then. Sympathy tugged at my heart. She was so young. Where was her family? Why were these people condemning her to such an awful end? The couple weren't in any rush and built the wall with care, using a lot of mortar and not stopping until the man laid a thick wooden beam over the stones where the body was hidden. Now it looked as though they were getting ready to put in a window. My feet felt cold by the time the residual reached this point, and Jasher was shifting impatiently beside me.

"Now what's happening?" he asked.

"They're finished. They're putting the bucket and spade into the wheelbarrow. Wait. They've stopped. They're talking. The woman put her face against his chest. I think she's crying. He's put his arms around her."

"Lovers?"

"Maybe. They're talking and holding each other." I gazed at the two people, looking for all the world like this was a husband who'd just met a beloved wife at the ship's docks after a long separation. The two pulled apart and looked meaningfully at one another.

I cleared my voice. "The man looks like he is comforting her. She looks pretty upset."

The man took the woman's face tenderly by the chin. He kissed each cheek, then the two turned away from me. He released the woman to pick up the wheelbarrow and she stayed close to his side.

"They're leaving the way they came."

The woman looked back over her shoulder once, glancing at the wall. Her expression was laced with a complexity of emotion. Fear, relief, grief, weariness, and a touch of smugness.

"Now can I drop the soil?" My heart thudded with sadness after watching the whole scene. It was much more impactful than watching a film. This was real; it had happened right here where we were standing.

"Just a moment longer," Jasher replied. "Let's see if they come back."

"I'm tired, Jasher." And I really was. After watching the long, tedious exercise in covert medieval murder, I was exhausted.

"A minute longer, then we'll go. They might come back, offer some clue we'll be happy we didn't miss. You said the residual blinks out and resets itself when it's done, right?"

"Yes."

"Well, has it started over?"

"No." I was still watching the couple navigate the woods, but they were growing smaller and difficult to make out. "Nothing else is happening, Jasher."

"Okay." He sounded ready to give up, finally. It was cold and dark out here, and I was feeling spooked.

I was about to drop the earth when something moved. I gasped and took a step back. Every hair on my body stood on end.

"What is it?"

"I don't know. It's…it's a…" But I was lost for words.

It was a shadow, really. But it was more than a shadow. It was a roughly human shape, with unusually long limbs. It was hunched over and the head was thin and stretched long, giving it an oblong profile.

"It's like a ghost," I said, unwilling to look away. "But not a ghost. There's no details, it's just a black shape."

"Moving?"

"Yeah, moving around the house, like it's looking for something…or maybe dancing." I felt mesmerized, watching the wisp of thick shadow move. Its arms and legs curled and uncurled, its long hands crooked and flexed. "It's so graceful."

I felt Jasher tug on my jacket. "Does it have a face?"

"No face. It's just a dark shape. It's circling the house, stopping now and then. It almost looks like it's…sniffing."

"Maybe it's looking for the woman?"

"Maybe. That's a good guess. Why else would it turn up right after she'd been walled up?"

The shape had gone still. It was bent at the waist, its spine a long 'c' shape. Its oval head hung out by its thin neck, crooked at a curious angle. Its long arms and legs were all bent. The long fingers at the ends of its hands were thin, with little curls at the end of each digit that seemed to dance and move, like candle flames, only they were void of all light. The thing was spectral, unearthly.

"So creepy," I whispered.

The thing's head turned as I spoke and my body went cold. It looked as though––if it had a face, if it had eyes––they would be narrowed in on me.

I took a step back.

"It can see me," I choked on the words, reaching my hands out blindly for Jasher, the fingers of one hand gripped tightly around the dirt. Jasher grabbed my free hand and I saw his form in my periphery, but I couldn't tear my eyes away from the apparition. Panic rushed up my throat. "It can see me!"

I took another step back and the thing took a step toward me.

A scream was rising in my chest.

Jasher was there, squeezing my hand, an arm circling my waist. Distantly, I heard him say my name, saying it wasn't possible. He sounded so far away, like an echo.

Throwing down the soil as though it had become a writhing mass of worms, I staggered backward, heart pounding.

But the residual didn't fade and the specter was still coming for me. The scream expanded, my lips opened, my heart felt as though it was going to explode with fear. A hand clamped over my mouth. I tore at it, trying to back up, get away.

The long black shape floated over the ground on footless

legs. Where its feet should be were black candle flames, smoking and flickering.

"It can't hurt you," I heard Jasher whisper fiercely in my ear.

But it could, and it was going to. Clawing at his hand, I struggled. He put his arms around me in a great bear hug, holding me steady. The specter was upon me and the world blinked out, and it was gone. It had passed through me.

The residual was over.

Panting, and with my heart sprinting at a frantic pace under my ribs, I grasped at Jasher's arms. I couldn't find words. My legs trembled and then failed me.

"Georjie," Jasher said, alarmed, as he took my full weight and we sank slowly to the ground. "Are you okay? Hey?"

He turned my face toward him. His face came into view, solid, in living color, real. I put my hands on his cheeks, leaving dirt on his face.

"I thought it was coming for me, Jasher. That awful thing."

"You're all right, Georjie." He pulled me to him and squeezed me. I could feel his own pulse throbbing in his neck. "I promise. It can't get you."

My mouth felt dry and pasty, my hands were clammy. I pulled back and tugged at the neck of my jacket, thirsty for big gulps of air. We sat there on the wet ground, Jasher's arms around me, until my breathing returned to normal.

"I'm sorry if I scared you," I said when I'd recovered a sense of safety. My voice cracked. "That was one of the most frightening things I've ever seen. It moved like it was made of candlelight, only it was totally black. Its limbs and hands flickered like small flames in a breeze. It was so...eldritch." Come to think of it, that was the perfect word for it.

Jasher's face was all serious shadows as he listened. "How tall?"

"Taller than you, but thin. So thin. With long arms and legs, always bent, never straight. Its back, too. It was always curved over, like it had something heavy hanging from its neck."

A millstone, I thought. *Like it had a millstone looped over its neck and it was dragging it around.*

"What else?" Jasher brushed some hair away from my eyes.

I sat up straighter, using my hands to show him. "It had a long face. Like its chin was down here," I held my hand four inches from my chin, "and its forehead was up here." I held my other hand four inches from my own brow. "And its cheeks were only this wide." I held my palms facing one another, only about five inches apart. "It looked right at me, right *through* me." My heart skipped a beat at the memory. "And it had cheekbones."

Jasher's shadowed face went still. "Really?"

"Yes, because it turned its head and I saw its quarter profile for a second before it looked right at me."

"That's when you started backing up?"

I nodded and made to stand. Jasher helped me up.

"Yes." I straightened and faced Jasher. "I could have sworn it knew I was watching it. Even through the centuries."

"But that's impossible," Jasher said. "Whatever that thing was, it's part of the past."

"Yes. It was silly of me to think it could get me." Now that the residual was over, I felt embarrassed. "Sorry, Jasher. I must have scared you."

"Don't worry about me. Are you going to be able to sleep after that?" He put an arm around me as we headed into the trees. The air was biting and my dirty hand felt coated in ice. Off in the distance, a crow gave a hoarse cry and took to the air.

83

"I'm totally shattered, actually. Sleep is exactly what I need."

He planted a peck on my forehead and we walked back to the maze in silence. We'd just passed by the fountain in the center of the maze when he asked, "Do you think the thing had something to do with the body in the wall?"

"I don't know. We could ask Lachlan or Evelyn if there's anything in the local myths about a specter like the one I saw."

"Like it was made of candle-flame," Jasher muttered.

"Even the wraith I faced in Ireland didn't scare me like that thing did."

Jasher paused with his hand on the back door. He looked down at me. "Are you sure you're okay? You know that thing can't hurt you, right?"

I nodded. "I know."

"Good. But I'm just next door if you can't sleep or if you need a cuddle-buddy." Jasher winked at me in the moonlight. "It's not like we haven't done it before."

I laughed. "What about Evelyn?"

"She'd understand. She's not the jealous type." Jasher turned away and opened the door, holding it wide for me.

At another time I might have flirted back, but my mind was already running back to the image of that thing. A creepy, stealthy, phantom made of nightmares. But there was something else. Using only negative adjectives to describe the thing wasn't entirely fair.

Because it had beauty, too.

CHAPTER NINE

*L*ife fell into a comfortable routine. While Jasher and the team worked on the cottage, I buried myself in the library. I tried asking Maisie about the chant again but she wouldn't talk and I didn't want to keep harassing her about it. I went to the café often, hoping to catch the girls skipping rope again. So far, no luck. Between my classes and assignments, and brief sprinting stints around the castle's extensive yard to keep myself awake, I perused every book I could find in Blackmouth Castle's library about the myths and legends of Scotland. When I'd exhausted Gavin and Bonnie's meager collection on that subject (they were more interested in collecting books on the true history of Scotland and real events), I migrated to the library in town.

The amount of bright unfiltered sunlight Blackmouth experienced in one year could be counted in mere days. It rained every day for at least a few hours as the highland winter crawled slowly toward spring. Pellets of what sounded like ice against the thin glass, but I knew was only rain, hammered the window near the long wooden table I'd parked myself at. I'd learned a lot about the Loch Ness Monster, the Loathly Lady, Magic Mist, redcaps, and kelpies. The Scots loved their myths, but nowhere in the dozens of beautifully illustrated and poetically written books on the subject did I come across a Wise, or a creature that fit the description of the flickering shadow-creature I'd seen in the residual. I'd taken to calling it 'the eldritch thing' until a better identifier could be used. I felt like the odds of defining it were rapidly running out as I scanned the pile of encyclopedic tomes. If it were a recognized thing in mythology, surely I would have found it by now.

The smacks of heavy wet soles on the hardwood drew my attention up.

"Well spotted." Lachlan stood between two narrow bookshelves, dripping on the floor from his raingear. He pushed the hood of his jacket back. His eyelashes were wet, making his blue eyes look wider and sweeter. "Jasher said you've been burying yourself in your schoolwork. I was hoping you might drop by the project every once in a while so I could say hello."

I closed the book and batted my own eyelashes at him. "Did you come here just to find me?"

"Sure." He raked a hand over his unruly hair. "Gavin gave us the afternoon off. The tarp doesn't do much against sideways rain." He glanced out the blurry window and its cold gray light.

"So that's how you've been managing." They'd constructed a tarp over the worksite. "Clever. How's the project going?"

He hooked a toe around the leg of the chair across from me and pulled it smoothly from the table. "Footings and framing are done."

"No more problems with thorns?"

"So far, so good."

"Will has stopped complaining that the body shouldn't have been removed?"

"Aye, he's over it." Lachlan's eyes fell to my pile of research, sifting through the titles. "Is one of your subjects mythology?"

"More of a personal interest." I eyed him thoughtfully. "Hey, you've never heard of a creature that looks like it's made out of flames, have you? Black flames, no face, kind of flickery when it moves?"

"Like a ghost?" he offered doubtfully.

"Different from a ghost. Longer limbed and thinner."

I flipped open my notebook and showed him a drawing Jasher had done for me as I'd described the creature.

"Kind of like this." I pushed the drawing toward him.

He gazed at it, forehead creasing. He pushed it back, sans expression of enlightenment. "The ghost of a starved elf?"

I laughed. "Never mind. I'll take that as a no." I closed the notebook.

"Why? Where did you come across a creature like that?"

Time for some artful dodging. "It's all your fault, really."

He blinked. "Do tell."

"It all started the day you said that thing: Which, Fae or Wise? I got to wondering what a Wise was and looking for that just kind of sparked my interest, I guess. I haven't found anything about Wise, but Evelyn suggested that it's the same as a witch."

"Unless the saying is 'Witch, Fae, or Wise.'" Lachlan leaned back in his chair. "In which case, witches and Wise are not the same thing."

I stared at him. "Fair point." Why hadn't I thought of that?

His gaze held mine and the corners of his mouth twitched up. "Nice way to procrastinate from your schoolwork."

We sat there smiling at one another for a minute, the

sound of water dripping from his clothing punctuating the silence.

Those eyes, they were so naked and transparent with his attraction to me. When I looked into them, I felt like he was baring his soul and asking me if I was up for doing the same. I cleared my throat and gestured to the gathering pool of rainwater. "You might catch hell from the librarian shortly."

He looked down and made a face. "Mrs. Heron isn't one to mess around." He got up and brushed the water off the chair before putting it back. "I came to find you for a reason. You haven't left Blackmouth since you arrived, and there are other beautiful seaside towns nearby. Jasher and Evelyn are up for an outing tomorrow. The rain is supposed to let up in the afternoon. Can I interest you in a little adventure?"

I brightened. "Yeah, you can. What did you have in mind?"

He put up a hand. "Nothing fancy. There's a network of trails south of here that run parallel to the coast. We could go for a hike and then drive into Inverness for dinner. There's a charming three-hundred-year-old pub I think you'd love."

"Count me in." I began to stack the books. "Jasher and Evelyn will come, too?"

I was about to tease him about it looking like a double date when he said, "Like a double date." He followed this with a shameless grin and his eyes sparkled. "Are you okay with that? Best to say no if ye're not interested. I wouldna want to waste your time."

I grinned in answer, suddenly needing a big glass of water and a breath of fresh air.

His impish smile didn't diminish, but his eyes had gone soft. "You're the bonniest lass I've ever seen, Georjayna Sutherland." He said it with a sincerity that took my breath away.

"Wow." I swallowed. "You go straight for the jugular."

"Wouldn't want my intentions misread," he continued in that same serious tone. "I intend to kiss you one day soon, too."

My jaw dropped as a cloud of tiny butterflies battered featherlight wings against my insides.

He tipped me a wink and strode away before I could say anything else.

* * *

Lachlan's bald statement of intention gave me something else to think about over the rest of the week besides mythology and eldritch shadow creatures. I hadn't been self-conscious around Lachlan before, but as Saturday approached, I found myself distracted by a more superficial problem: what I should wear. Not that I had a lot of material to work with. I had only packed one dress, and given that we were hiking, it wouldn't be appropriate. I'd have to settle for a lined rain jacket, a warm sweater, jeans, and waterproof boots...again.

Jasher and I met Evelyn and Lachlan in front of Black-mouth Castle shortly after noon on Saturday. Lachlan was driving his Jeep Renegade and had picked up Evie on the way. Jasher insisted I take the front seat while he shared the small rear seat with Evelyn.

"I thought you said the rain was supposed to let up, Lockie?" Jasher said as he poked his head between the two front seats.

"Lockie?" I glanced at Lachlan.

"An unfortunate nickname I mean to eradicate." Lachlan shot a mock glare at Jasher.

"Good luck with that." Evelyn laughed as we pulled away from the castle and made our way to the highway which skirted the coast. "He's been known as Lockie since he was a baby."

"It's not raining," Lachlan said in a loud voice, before adding to me in a much softer one, "see that clever change of subject?"

"But would you look at those thunderheads." Jasher gave a low whistle as he settled back in his seat and peered out the window. They'd begun to fog up and Lachlan turned up the air.

"What's our plan B?" Evelyn asked from behind me.

Lachlan looked properly horrified. "There is no plan B. We made a plan to go hiking and hiking we shall go." He held up an authoritative finger. "We are due at least two solid hours of sunlight this afternoon."

Speckles of water began to spatter the windscreen. I shot Lachlan a look.

"What? You doubt me?"

I leveled a finger at the glass.

"Just a fine mist," Lachlan said, "mark my words. It'll clear up by the time we reach the trailhead."

Thunder boomed from somewhere out over the sea, and the speckles of rain didn't let up. Twenty minutes later, Lachlan steered the Jeep into a vacant gravel parking lot bordered with trees. Jasher's face appeared between the front seats as he squinted at the signpost beside the trailhead.

"What does the sign say? I can't read it through all the water pouring down the windscreen."

Lachlan turned the car off. "I'll have you know, this is Dornoch's finest..." His words were lost as thunder crashed overhead and the rain became a downpour.

"You were saying?" I had to raise my voice over the sound of big drops hammering the car. I actually felt the vehicle rock a little from side to side.

Lachlan, his hand still on the key, stared dumbfounded out the front window before dropping his face toward his lap. His shoulders slumped. He took a breath and popped his head up again, plastered with a big carnival grin. "Who's up for a pint?"

Jasher and Evelyn cheered from the backseat.

Lachlan turned his fake, frozen grin toward me. "Sorry, Georjie."

"Hey, I don't know about you, but the three-hundred-year-old pub was the part I was looking the most forward to. We can hike next…in the spring."

Lachlan muttered something about March being almost over, but started the car again and piloted us back onto the highway and toward Inverness. By the time we arrived in the capital of the highlands, Evelyn and Jasher were singing some bawdy song about a bare-breasted maiden flashing ships from a castle wall. Lachlan steered the car into a parking lot near a tall stone wall choked with dripping ivy. He looked over at me as he turned off the car once more and jerked his head at the silly couple in the backseat.

Before I could respond, Jasher and Evelyn were out of the car. We could hear them giggling as they ran through the rain to the doorway of the pub. I had to admit that it warmed me through to hear Jasher laughing like a little kid.

"It's like they've already had their pints and then some."

I laughed and grabbed my rainhat. "We have some catching up to do in that case, but if you're expecting me to sing, you're S.O.L."

"S.O.L? Is that a Canadian saying?" Lachlan unbuckled his seatbelt.

"Yes. Yes, it is." I gave him a closed mouth smile that said he'd have to look it up for himself and got out of the car.

Lachlan and I dashed through the pouring rain and bolted through the pub's doors. Water was dripping down the back of my neck, making me shiver. Jasher and Evie were already seated at a table near the fireplace where a man in a bar apron knelt and erected a little stack of kindling.

"Oh, good. Fire," Lachlan hung my coat for me and I rubbed my hands together to warm them.

The pub was everything one could want from a centuries-old establishment. Warm side-lighting, thick beams, ancient looking books and old maps, floorboards with worn pathways crisscrossing all over. We ordered bowls of the special, a beef stew, and a jumbo serving of triple-cooked chips to share. The fire had begun to crackle in earnest, throwing its welcome warmth over us as we were delivered our drinks.

When my eye fell on two men who came in, one of them familiar, I bumped Lachlan with my shoulder. "Look, it's Callum."

He looked over to the door where the osteoarcheologist had dropped his umbrella into the bucket provided to contain the mess of rainwater, and was now stripping off his jacket.

"Oi! Mr. Gordon," Lachlan called.

Jasher and Evelyn broke off their conversation to look up.

Callum's face lit up with recognition. He said a few words to his companion and came over to our table. "Out to enjoy our fine Scottish weather, are ye?"

Lachlan gestured to the empty spaces at our benches. "Would you and your friend care to join us?"

"Thank you for the kind offer, but we've got a meeting to prepare for."

"We were wondering," I leaned forward on my elbows, "have you completed the investigation on the body?"

"Nearly," he replied. "I can tell you that it was indeed a woman, and a young one at that. No older than thirty. She came to her untimely demise sometime in the early seventeenth-century."

"What was the cause of death?" Evelyn asked, and I

noticed that the fingers of her left hand were entwined with Jasher's right.

"That bit's still uncertain," Callum replied, but his eye was on his colleague where he sat waiting at a table near the door. "Sorry, I should get back to my business. Nice seeing you again."

Callum went over to his table and sat down just as our food arrived.

"Interesting," Lachlan said, not paying attention to the mouthwatering smells of the stew and fries. My stomach was growling like an angry leopard.

I picked up my spoon. "What's interesting?"

"In the early seventeenth century, a lot of young women lost their lives. Not just young women but older ones, and a few men too. A dreadful thing was taking place in the highlands at that time, as well as in many other places around Europe."

I knew what he was talking about. "The witch trials."

"Aye." He picked up his spoon. "But they didn't bury witches in walls. Mostly they burned them at the stake. I wonder how this unfortunate lass found herself with a different fate."

My mind drifted back to the story Ainslie had told me about the roses and the cunning woman who had created them. Ainslie hadn't given me a year, but she had said that the witch trials had started after the rose was created and the cunning woman had disappeared to history. No one knew what had happened to her. There were no solid ties yet to tether Ainslie's story to the body in the wall, but now we knew for sure it was a woman, and we knew the era she'd died. We didn't have much, but at least we had a direction to look in.

* * *

The following Monday, Ainslie had me dusting the frames of the artwork in the hallway and along the stairs. At six feet tall, she claimed I would only need the ladder half the time. In truth, I spent over an hour teetering from an aluminum double ladder, trying not to knock anything off the walls.

The portraits lining the main staircase were mostly of distant family. Cherubic babies frowned from under fluffy white bonnets, and vampiric looking children perched morosely on velvet chairs, feet dangling. The older set were far better at looking noble. Women posed with strapless gowns dripping from their shoulders while feather head-pieces arched aristocratically over perfectly coiffed curls. Men in hunting tartans dominated carcasses, or jumped furrows on horseback in pursuit of a distant red blur with a fox tail. But it was the massive still life paintings depicting artfully arranged dead animals that had my shoulders and neck aching.

As I leaned over with the duster, movement from outside the window caught my eye. Their shapes were blurred by the wet glass, but I recognized Jasher and Lachlan as they stood near Lachlan's Jeep. They looked deep in conversation. My aching muscles demanded a break, so I climbed down the ladder, left my duster sitting on the top of it, and went down to say hello. Heaving open one of the heavy wooden front doors pulled a rush of fresh air into the front lobby.

Lachlan looked up immediately as I stepped outside. He held up a hand, his eyes wide. "Georjie! Your timing is perfect." He beckoned me over.

I crossed the wet gravel. The Jeep's door was open and Lachlan's elbow was resting on top. Jasher had a blade of grass protruding from his teeth. He had a workmen's tool belt slung low over his hips and his cheeks were flushed pink.

"I heard Ainslie's got you polishing the pride of the Black-mouth?" Jasher teased.

I rotated my shoulders, wincing. "Something like that. She has suggested that dusting is my destiny." I looked at Lachlan. "What's up?"

"I was just telling Jasher what I found."

"Something about the body in the wall?"

"It's mysterious," Jasher admitted, "but there's no solid link. It could be a coincidence."

"Link between what?"

Lachlan pulled out his phone, activated the screen and pulled up a photograph of an aged document covered with barely discernible writing. He held it out so I could see.

"That looks like a photo of a photo of a photo." I squinted at it. "Is that Gaelic?"

"It is. I couldn't take the book out, it's too old, but they let me look through the digital copy and take a photo of this page." Lachlan turned his phone off and tucked it away. "I took GME for eight years in school."

"What's that?"

"Gaelic Medium Education. It was an immersion school and my first language of study for a while. The Gaelic here," he patted his phone through his pocket, "is pretty different from the Gaelic I learned, but I had enough to translate it, with a little help from a lady at the library in Inverness."

"You went to Inverness to find that?" Jasher gave a low whistle. "You *are* obsessed."

Lachlan's eyes were on mine. "It's a missing persons document. The only one for a woman in this area between sixteen-hundred and sixteen-fifty. Her name was Daracha Goithra, which is weird. She was—"

"Wait." I stopped him, not wanting to miss anything. "Why is the name weird?"

"Goithra is the old version of Guthrie, which is a lowland

95

name." He rolled his eyes to make a concession. "Well, it's low to us. It's from the Angus region, down near Dundee."

"But Daracha went missing up here near Blackmouth?"

"Exactly," Lachlan nodded. "She was young, only twenty-seven, and unmarried."

"As fascinating as all this is," Jasher said, spitting out the grass he'd chewed up, "we have work to do. We need to get those stones split."

Lachlan nodded and gave me a smile as the two men began to move across the parking lot. I fell into step beside Lachlan, tightening my sweater around me against the breeze. At least it wasn't raining.

Lachlan went on. "It's unusual that an unwed young woman would be found so far from her clan. They didn't move around unless they were being married off. There's nothing else to be found about a Daracha Goithra in the local archives, but there might be something about her down in Dundee."

Jasher gave a dry laugh. "Too bad there isn't some amazing interconnected digital web of information that would allow you to look up Dundee family histories from here."

Lachlan chuckled. "Yes, a lot of information is available online, but there's a lot yet to be archived. Do you have any idea how many medieval records there are moldering away in attics and basements?"

"Looks like a trip to Dundee might be in order?" I ventured hopefully.

"It's a three-and-a-half-hour journey by car, if the weather is good," Lachlan replied as I followed them down the side steps. He looked over his shoulder, appearing pained. "I haven't got time for a long trip like that anytime soon."

"Trains are faster, aren't they?" I asked.

Lachlan stopped at the bottom of the stairs. "Not likely, but you could check."

Jasher kept walking and didn't look back. "I'll be warming up the maul."

"Be right there," Lachlan called, then lowered his voice. "There's something else weird that came up with this missing person case, Georjie. You remember I was telling you that this woman was murdered during the same time as most of Europe was in the grip of witch hunts? Well, Daracha's name came up as one of the accused."

My jaw dropped. "They thought she was a witch?"

"Someone did. She was thrown in jail to await trial. Here's the weirdest thing of all." He stepped close enough that I could make out those bright flecks in his eyes. "Daracha Goithra spent less than a week in jail before she went missing. An article I found claims that she escaped prison and there was no evidence of how she did it. The cell was locked, there were no windows, no foul play. Her escape must have convinced them she really *was* a witch."

I frowned. "If she was able to escape jail so cleverly, how did she end up murdered and stuck in a wall?"

"I don't know." Lachlan's thick shoulders gave a shrug. "There's no further record of her after she went missing. Maybe someone outside the law caught her and took things into their own hands?"

The image of the man and woman from the residual sprang to mind, hugging after they'd done the deed. Lachlan might be closer to the truth than he even realized. "It could have been scared townspeople taking the law into their own hands," I suggested, my mind racing with images and possibilities, "only to be caught, and instead of turning her in to the lawmen, they did away with her themselves. Maybe they were worried she'd be found innocent."

"Maybe." Lachlan looked doubtful. "The fact that she was

walled up is the part that's tripping me up more than anything else. If they really thought she was a witch, they would have burned her. That was the legal punishment in those days."

I nodded and in the space of silence, we heard Jasher calling for some help.

"You'd better go," I said. "Thanks for sharing what you found. We have more threads to pull on."

"I'll let you know if I can swing a trip to Dundee, but it wouldn't be for a couple of weeks. I'm committed here until the frame is finished."

"Okay." I watched as he walked away, then called out to him again.

He paused and turned back.

"What are they doing with the body now, do you know?"

"Callum will finish up his investigation, and you never know, we might get some other interesting tidbit from that. But they'll bury the body soon."

"If you told them what you found, do you think they would return her to Dundee?"

He shook his head. "I doubt it. There's no proof that the body is Daracha's. Even if I did tell them, there's no pains taken for a death this old. They'll bury her here in Blackmouth's cemetery. Close to where she died."

"Won't they want a name for the grave?"

He nodded. "I'll mention to Callum what I've found."

Lachlan and I said goodbye and as the men went back to work, I returned to my dusting.

So, we had something, even if it was small. But what Lachlan had learned only raised more questions. If the body was Daracha Goithra's, why was she so far from home? How did she end up on trial for witchcraft? How did she escape— or did someone let her out? She'd just gotten her freedom, only to end up walled up in someone's cottage. What if she was the cunning woman from Ainslie's story? The fact that they'd accused her of witchcraft leant some credence to the possibility.

I felt bad for the woman, whether she was the truth rose's creator or not, and yearned to give the body and the spirit the rest she deserved.

CHAPTER TEN

$\mathcal{I}$ came awake with my hair standing on end as a dog's howl split the silence of the highland night. Lurching up to sitting, I opened my eyes wide as I listened. The wail was joined by a second distant howl. As the first two ended, two more canine voices rose to fill the gap, and a moment later, what sounded like the yowl of a frightened cat made my body shiver.

Throwing back the covers, I got out of bed and went to the door. Snagging my robe and pulling it on, I poked my head out into the hall and saw that Jasher was already headed toward the stairs.

"Jasher," I hissed.

He jumped and whirled. "Jaysus, Georjayna!" He was wearing a pair of baggy boxer shorts and a long-sleeved t-shirt.

"Sorry." I tightened my robe and joined him. The sound of howling dogs seemed to permeate the whole building. "What a racket," I whispered. "It's a wonder everyone isn't up."

"They probably are. What the hell is wrong with all those animals?"

We crossed the shadowed second-story parlor to the large bay window that overlooked the vast front lawns and peered outside. Dark columns between the outside lights crisscrossed over the lawn and roundabout, and beyond that, the lights of the town glimmered. Dogs continued to howl, more voices joining the chorus by the minute.

"So creepy." I shuddered and looked at the dark sky. "It's not even raining. I thought at first a storm had them freaked."

We listened as the howling continued, glancing at one another uneasily.

"Do you think we should go into town?" I asked. "Maybe there's trouble? A fire, or something?"

Jasher considered it. "Give it five more minutes. If they're still howling, then yeah, maybe we should. Someone might need help."

I perched on the edge of the window seat while Jasher stood leaning his shoulder against the frame. We could hear the distant angry yells of people bellowing at their pets to shut up, in both English and Gaelic. I cringed when there were a few yelps added to the din.

A heavy sound drew our attention to the doorway, where a large, dark shape appeared.

"I see you've been rousted from yer beds as well," said the laird as he crept into the parlor to join us at the window. "What an almighty racket."

"Has this ever happened before?" I asked, tightening the knot at my waist with a shiver. The howling was making me feel colder than anything else. The dogs sounded positively panicked.

"Sometimes the local dogs will get one another going, but..." Gavin shook his bearded head, his hair sticking up like a hedgehog's. "This is something else. Those pups are spooked."

"And they're not letting up." Jasher looked at the laird. "We were thinking someone might be in trouble, or maybe there's a fire. Should we take a drive into town?"

Gavin's dark eyes roamed the skies and the distant twinkle of the village lights. "There's no visible firelight, but it's not a bad idea. Better to be forewarned if something's gone amiss."

After a few more minutes of listening to the town's dogs wailing their poor brains out, Gavin nodded. "Right then. Ye two coming?"

Wide awake now, I stood and headed for my room. "I'll put on some clothes and meet you downstairs."

We convened in the parking lot where Jasher and I waited, listening to the continuous mournful noise, while the laird pulled a car out from the garage behind the castle. Piling in to the front bench seat of the old car, Gavin waited for us to buckle before driving us down the main road toward town.

The noise was much louder in town as more than half of the residents had dogs and many of those were still outside, yowling from back yards and from on tops of dog houses.

"It's enough to bring the dead to life," Gavin shuddered from behind the wheel. "I've never heard anything like it."

The laird slowed the car to a crawl as we peered out the windows, looking for anything amiss. People could be seen looking out of upper floor windows, and trying to comfort their dogs in their yards. Gavin stopped the car when an elderly man on the sidewalk lifted a hand to him. The man came slowly to the driver's side window and Gavin rolled the window down.

"Ernest," Gavin said, "yeh were out communing with the dead again? Or perhaps the local wolf pack just moved through town."

I gave Jasher a look of alarm and he mouthed, "He's kidding."

Ernest gave a raspy chuckle. "Mighty strange, isna?" He had to raise his voice to be heard over the dogs. He bent at the waist and peered in at Jasher and me, giving us a friendly nod. "All of Blackmouth'll be complaining of a poor sleep tomorrow. I wouldna worry about it. They'll wear themselves out in short order, I should think."

Gavin nodded. "I hope so. G'night, Ernie."

"Night." Ernest gave the hood a tap and we drove on.

"No fires, no wild animals, just a bunch of frightened pooches." Gavin turned us down another narrow street where we witnessed and heard more of the same. "Nothing to be done."

"Ernie is right, they'll get tired soon," Jasher said, his jaw cracking wide with a yawn.

"Aye."

Gavin piloted the car down a narrow alley and the town graveyard came into view on the left-hand side. Crooked, worn headstones scattered across the gentle hills like bad teeth.

"Is this where they'll bury the body we found?" I asked Gavin, watching the wrought iron fencing go by.

"Aye. Already dug the hole, I b'lieve."

"Will there be any...ceremony, or anything?" I asked, feeling a little foolish.

Gavin laughed. "Why, you want to pay your respects?"

"Sort of," I mumbled.

Gavin stopped smiling and he shot me a look of what might have been respect. "That's sweet of ye, Georjie."

My face flushed with heat. "I just think it's sad. I mean, her family never knew what happened to her. She died all alone." I added silently that there was a possibility she'd been the creator of a very special and exquisite kind of rose.

"There won't be anything official." Gavin raised his voice to be heard over a fresh wave of howls and yelps. "But there's nothing wrong with going to visit the graves of the nameless dead. There'll be more than one of them in this here graveyard."

But she wasn't nameless. In my gut, I felt that the young woman had to be Daracha. I wondered if there was a way it could be proven, and if so, whether they might consider making a proper headstone for her.

The dogs finally did quiet down, but it wasn't until well after we'd retired to our rooms to salvage what was left of the night.

Lunch hour the next day found me drooping over a bowl of soup in the kitchen and listening to Ainslie and Bonnie plan Bonnie's business trip to Edinburgh for a hospitality conference. The kids had already come and gone.

"You look like death warmed over," Ainslie said as my chin slipped off my hand and my head bobbed for the third time. "Why don't ye take an afternoon nap?"

"I have an art history exam to study for," I replied.

"Twenty minutes'll do you a wonder." She reached over to pat my hand. "I plan to catch a few winks myself before tackling the laundry. Those dogs were a terror last night."

"At least the whole village will be feeling it," I mumbled. "I went down to the cafe to work this morning and the staff and patrons had all been replaced with zombies."

"For my part," added Bonnie, looking far too sprightly as her spine straightened, "I find a stroll and some fresh air does me more good than a nap."

"I like that idea." I set down my spoon and picked up my soup bowl. "I'll take my textbook and sit in the park. At least it's not raining." I tilted the bowl and drained it.

"I like a girl who's not afraid to show she likes my cooking," Ainslie said with a chuckle.

I swallowed the last of the soup and set the bowl down. "Sorry, that was rude."

Bonnie tsked. "This is the highlands, missy, not the queen's parlor."

I washed my dishes and said goodbye to Bonnie and Ainslie. Grabbing my textbook, I layered up with a rain jacket, hat, and scarf and left the castle through the front door.

Jasher was standing on the gravel at the top of the steps leading to the back yard, work phone to his ear. He gave me a nod but didn't smile.

I began to head across the driveway when he called to me. "Have you spoken to Evelyn today, Georjie?"

I turned. "No, why?"

"She's usually quick with her replies, but I haven't gotten any response back yet today. Just wondering if you'd heard from her."

"I haven't seen her since the hiking fiasco, sorry." Come to think of it, it was weird she hadn't popped into the cafe this morning.

Jasher nodded. "Thanks anyway."

"Sure." Carrying on, I began to walk down the hill and into Blackmouth, headed for one of the larger parks. It would be easy to stop by Evelyn's house on my way. I noted and appreciated the lack of barking dogs as I turned down Evelyn's street. Her house was the only thatched roof cottage on her road. I crossed the road and opened her front gate.

Her cottage was everything you'd want an old Scottish home to be. Winding wisteria trunks, old and gnarled, curled up both sides of the rounded door and arched overtop. Most of the leaves had fallen off, but there were remnants of the dangling blooms still hanging on. Two large windows with small diamond-shaped panes hugged the front porch, and within the door sat a round, stained glass window depicting a red rose.

I reached for the knocker, a black wrought-iron greyhound, but my hand paused. The door was ajar. Just barely, with an inch of space between the door and the jamb. With a fingertip, I pushed on the door. It swung open silently, revealing a cozy and welcoming hallway.

"Evelyn?" I called. "Are you here?"

No answer.

The hall was lined with a carpet runner decorated with the same rose motif as the stained-glass window. An antique table sat to one side and a round mirror with key hooks was fixed just above. The key hooks held several sets, one of which I recognized as the keys to her little Fiat. So, her car was still in the garage.

Taking a step on the mat, I called out, "The door is open, I'm coming in."

I felt dumb talking to no one. The house had an empty feel, but what if it wasn't empty? What if Evelyn had fallen and hit her head? She said she lived alone since her last roommate had moved out and she hadn't yet advertised for a new one.

After toeing off my sneakers, I padded down the hall, poking my head into the living room and the small kitchen at the back of the cottage. A quick glance through a window over the sink showed no one in the back yard. I left the kitchen and took the short hallway leading to the two bedrooms and bathroom. Everything was neat and tidy, no signs of an accident, or of leaving the house quickly. The only thing that was messed up was her bed. The duvet was thrown back and there was a dent on the pillow. A pair of slippers poked out from beneath the bed like a pair of bunny noses. A dark red robe was draped over the footboard.

Feeling a little guilty, I backed out of the room and

returned to my shoes. As I slipped my sneakers on, I noted the full shoe rack. Boots, galoshes, two pairs of sneakers, a pair of ballet flats. I'd seen Evelyn wear the boots and both pairs of sneakers. But the fact that they were neatly lined up on the shoe rack wasn't necessarily a sign of anything weird, right? I mean, who knew how many pairs of shoes she had, and where she kept them all?

I put on my shoes and went to close the door when I heard a buzzing sound coming from the coatrack. Fishing in the jacket pocket of Evelyn's raincoat, the same one she'd worn to Inverness, I retrieved her phone. My blood cooled and slowed as I recognized Blackmouth Castle's number. I knew who it was instinctively.

I pressed the talk button. "Jasher?"

"Oh, thank God…" he started, then stopped. "Georjie?"

"Yeah, it's me. I'm at Evelyn's place."

"Is she with you?" I could hear his breath speed up.

"No. She's not here. Her door was unlocked and open. All her shoes and outdoor stuff is here. Her car keys, too. I didn't get freaked out until I heard her phone buzzing."

Jasher let out a quick breath. "I'm going to call the police."

He hung up the phone before I could reply, leaving me standing in Evelyn's hallway staring at her phone and wondering what to do. Finally, I pocketed her phone, closed her door, and headed up the hill to the castle as fast as I could manage.

I arrived to find Jasher, Ainslie, Bonnie, Gavin, and Lachlan standing in the front foyer with Inspector Hamilton. They all turned to look at me as I came in. No one was smiling.

"Hi, Inspector Hamilton," I said.

He didn't waste his breath with a greeting. "I need to know the last time you saw or spoke with Evelyn Munro."

"Saturday. I was with Lachlan and Jasher. We went into Inverness together."

Lachlan and Jasher both nodded in agreement.

The inspector said grimly: "That's what I thought."

"Tell him what you told me," Jasher prompted, his arms crossed tightly over his chest.

"I went by her house and the door was unlocked and open." I told him about her shoes and her jackets, her car keys, and I gave him her phone.

He took it and woke it up, frowning at the locked screen.

I said, "I wasn't too worried until I found her phone. It looks like a..."

"Kidnapping?" the inspector interrupted.

I nodded. I felt Lachlan move to stand behind me. He put his hand gently on the small of my back and I felt grateful for the subtle support.

"We won't jump to that conclusion just yet," Inspector Hamilton said. "It's been less than twenty-four hours since she's been seen, but her parents are worried because she hasn't been answering her calls. She had dinner with them last night and was meant to drop by their house this morning to return something she'd borrowed. It's too soon to file a formal missing persons report, but the sooner we act, the better."

Jasher was chewing a thumbnail now, and nodded. "She's always been fast to reply. It's out of character. I knew something was wrong. I could feel it."

"We're forming a volunteer search party. Can I expect all of you to be part of it?" The inspector eyeballed the group.

"Of course," Gavin replied. "Just tell us where to meet and when."

"We'll muster at the station in an hour." The inspector finally found a reassuring smile, though it was more of a grimace than anything. "More than likely, there's a perfectly reasonable explanation for where she is and why no one has heard from her. We haven't had an actual missing persons case in…well, ever."

I didn't mention Daracha Goithra, figuring he wouldn't appreciate me bringing up a case that was centuries before our time.

We said goodbye to the inspector and stood in the hallway chatting for a few more minutes.

"It's been exciting around here lately," Gavin said, his eyes taking on that mischievous twinkle. "Bodies in the ruins, ladies galivanting about mysteriously."

Bonnie whacked him on the arm and I didn't miss the daggers Jasher sent his way. Lachlan glanced at me with an apologetic look, embarrassed by Gavin's cavalier words.

"It's not funny, Gavin," Bonnie said. "What if something's happened to the poor woman?"

Gavin waved a big hand. "Nothing's happened to her. Nothing ever happens around here. Blackmouth went to sleep after the Falklands incidents and never woke up again. We haven't had a donkey's fart o' trouble. Mark my words, she'll be sleeping in her own bed tonight."

Gavin, Bonnie, and Ainslie left the foyer to prepare to join the search party.

I wrapped an arm around Jasher. "He doesn't mean to be an arse," I said. "She'll turn up. You'll see."

Lachlan spoke in a quiet tone. "Gavin is worried too. This is just how he handles it. I'll run home and change. See you guys at the station." He closed the door behind him.

Jasher turned to me, clutching my hands tightly between his. "You can see what happened, Georjie."

"Only if it happened on soil. There's no soil in her house or in her front yard. There's pavement everywhere. Even the wisteria has gravel right up to its base. The closest dirt is well up the road. It's too far away."

Jasher's eyes closed but his hands tightened on mine, almost hurting me. The look on his face sliced my heart to ribbons.

"You know I'll do whatever it takes, but I need dirt to see, Jash." I squeezed his hands back. "Listen to me. People are mobilizing as we speak. The inspector will have a search party out within the hour. If we don't find Evelyn, we're bound to find a clue, and that clue might be enough to tell me where to look next. Okay?"

Jasher looked me in the eyes and the expectation I saw there frightened me. He was putting all of his hope and trust in me to find her.

What if I couldn't?

CHAPTER ELEVEN

A group of forty-three volunteers convened at the muster station, where the police broke us up into eight parties, each responsible for searching their own section. Three of the groups––those with experience on the water––joined up with the Maritime and Coastguard Agency to search the North Sea. The rest of us were assigned a captain and issued a section.

Lachlan, Jasher, Will, and I were shuffled into the group slated to search the queen's parkland to the north. This was the least populated and most remote section of the 'pie' and meant we had to do much of our searching on foot.

The North Sea edged the village to the east where rolling green hills boasted patches of thick old-growth forest. The queen's park to the north and west played host to a myriad of deer, foxes, pheasants, and other highland animals. Farmland and a few large manors with extensive yards and forests of their own speckled the south. Royal land began just beyond the outermost suburb of Blackmouth, and it was there we were dropped off.

111

Equipped with rubber boots and raingear, tactical flashlights, and small handheld radios, seven of us spread across the land in a line, each responsible for combing a width of fifteen meters.

With Lachlan on my far left and Jasher on my far right, we began the long and arduous stalk across the park. The midafternoon light was pale and heavily filtered through a low bank of near impenetrable clouds. The ground was mossy, uneven, and saturated. Each step resulted in an unpleasant squelching sound. We'd been instructed to watch for footprints, telltale residue on trees and bushes like hair or fabric, and of course, any sign of Evelyn herself.

The forest was a strange blend of huge old oaks, gnarled and twisting into the sky with their thick, furry arms, and thin, scrubby underbrush. Streams wound their way through the landscape like veins and arteries, adding their own trickling music to the occasional calls of Evelyn's name.

As I continuously scanned the semi-circle in front of me, I thought how unlikely it was that we'd be the group to find her. This land was reserved for wildlife. It was inhospitable to hikers unless you kept to the thin trails, which were mostly overgrown and mucky. Hikers preferred the trails along the sea or on higher ground where their hard work could be rewarded with beautiful views. Down here, it was a disorienting landscape of branches, undergrowth, mud, and moss-riddled rocks.

We'd been instructed to search until we reached an old military road marked as B9012 on the map. We were to be picked up there by one of the constables. The search was projected to take us just until nightfall, but the going was agonizingly slow.

Several hours and a soggy tuna sandwich later, I was climbing over a bank of stones shot through with roots when something caught my ear. Pausing, my hand gripping at a wet root, I listened.

Drums.

It was a fast, almost celebratory rhythm, but very muted; it sounded far away. Like my first night in Blackmouth, the drums sounded like they were coming from everywhere and nowhere. Hauling myself up over the edge of the bank, I straightened, my ears straining. I was not imagining them. The drums were there, and I thought they were even punctuated sometimes by a cheerful flute.

"Lachlan?" I called across my zone. "Jasher?"

"Find something?" Lachlan called back.

Jasher answered from somewhere in the trees. Neither of them was visible.

"I haven't found anything, but do you hear those drums?"

No answer as they listened. The unmistakable sound of a primitive drumbeat came filtering through the trees. Anyone with decent hearing should have been able to detect it.

Then, from Lachlan, "Nope, sorry."

"No drums for me either," Jasher added.

"Seriously? Are you both deaf?" I mumbled.

"I heard that so, no." Lachlan chuckled. "Beware the spunkies, Georjie. Maybe they're trying to lure you into the swamp."

I couldn't bring myself to banter in return. It was frustrating to be the only one to hear the music. Who would be banging on drums out here in the middle of the wilderness? Why could I hear it out here when I'd also heard it from my little room in Blackmouth Castle? And why wasn't the music any louder out here than it was when I'd heard it from inside those thick stone walls? A screw of unease drilled itself lazily into my midsection and I couldn't bring myself to move for a time. I stood there, listening, my every sense trying to pinpoint the origins of the drums.

Determining finally that it was coming from the west, I took a step in that direction, then stopped. I was expected to monitor my section of the search area. I couldn't just go running after some mysterious drum music and abandon my team. I let out a frustrated huff.

"Torches on," called one of the team members from far to my right.

I realized with a start that it was a good call. The forest had grown dim. Reaching into the pocket of my jacket, I pulled out a flashlight and the headlamp I'd been given. Fixing the headlamp in place on my forehead, I flicked the on switch. A bright white beam of light illuminated the underbrush ahead of me. Depressing the switch on the torch in my hand added a second beam of bright light. Beyond me to the right, Jasher's beams came on in the distance—little glowing streams broken up by branches. To my left, Lachlan's two beams swung and bobbed behind the trees.

Forget the drums, I told myself. Don't let your team down, let alone Evelyn. But the thought of Evelyn redoubled my concern. What if Evelyn had heard the drums, too? There was something compelling about them. Distant music was a draw in any scenario, walking the old cobblestone streets of a medieval town, or just crossing a park in Saltford during a music festival. Music was magnetic, but this music was more than magnetic. It was beginning to demand that I find its source. Was it my own curiosity so urgently asking me to follow those drums, or was it something bigger, compelling me?

The more I thought about it as I followed the bobbing beam from my headlamp, the more certain I became that the drums had something to do with Evelyn's disappearance. It was too strange otherwise. Why would she leave her car, her house with its door ajar, even her shoes and jackets? True, I didn't know for certain she'd left her house without footwear or outdoor clothing; she might have taken something from her bedroom rather than her hall entrance. But I couldn't shake the feeling that there was something supernatural going on here, and the drums had something to do with it.

"Hello, there."

I gave a startled scream and nearly tripped over a tussock. My headlamp slid down my forehead to cover one eye, and I dropped the torch. My heart was throbbing like I'd sprinted up a hill. Scrabbling at my face, I yanked the headlamp off my brow and directed its beam in the direction of the voice.

"Easy," said the slender man standing near a fat oak, his hand raised to ward off the light.

I directed the glare over his shoulder, so I could make out his features without blinding him. As I took him in, I lost all my words.

He was tall and possessed slightly too-large eyes and pointed features. Bushy, wild hair gleamed in the artificial light like burnished copper. Little ears poked from the mane of rough-chopped curls, too sharp at the tips to be normal.

A wheeze issued from my throat as I took in his ears and his upturned eyes, bright and mischievous. His face was boyish, charming, and devilishly handsome, but his body was all man. Broad at the shoulder and narrow at the waist. Thick, well-muscled legs filled out what appeared to be leather pants that ended just below the knee. He was barefoot and bare-chested; not even a vest encased his upper body. He didn't even appear to be cold. He stood with a lithe, natural grace and gave the impression of being lighter than he looked, like he had anti-gravity powers. I didn't miss the knife hanging in a scabbard from his waist.

He gazed at me calmly, patiently, as though waiting for my shock to pass before introducing himself.

"Did I startle you?" he asked with a strange accent. It was lyrical like a Scottish brogue, but much softer on the t's. A smile crept across his face, revealing straight white teeth and lines bracketing his mouth, which led me to believe he wasn't as young as I'd first thought.

"I hope so," he admitted. "You were so intent on your own thoughts, it was too tempting to let you wander by."

Staring at him as I was, barely blinking, I found my mind grasping to categorize this being. I'd seen faery creatures before, but they'd manifested as small bright lights with tiny, humanoid, near-transparent bodies. But this man was taller than me, without wings, and had a distinctly dangerous air about him.

The music. I took in a sharp breath. The music was louder now and clearly coming from behind me and to the east, in the direction of home.

"Who…" I shifted my stance, straightened, and cleared my voice. "Who are you?"

"Laec." He made a small mocking bow and held his hands out to the sides. His hair fell over his shoulders and I got a good view of the slightly too-pointed eye-teeth as he grinned. He straightened, eyeing me with that same calm, mildly amused look. He took a few steps toward me.

"Don't come any closer," I said, holding out my palm. "I have friends nearby."

He cocked his head, lifting one pointed ear, catlike. "What friends?"

I swept my gaze to the left and right, where I'd seen the light from my friends' torches only moments before. All was quiet. All was dark. I called casually to Lachlan and Jasher. No response. I began to sweat despite the cold.

Laec gave a smirk that brought a flush to my cheeks.

"We're alone." He took another step closer.

I stepped back and slipped on the slick earth. Righting

myself, I held out a finger. I vaguely registered that the air felt warm, or was it just me? I had begun to sweat under my rain gear. "That's close enough. Who are you?"

"I told you."

"What are you doing out here?" I could hear my heart pounding in my ears.

"I live here," he replied softly. "I should be asking what *you* are doing here."

While my rational mind was working to convince me that this was just a human, a weird human, dressed up and occupying his own make-believe world out here in the queen's forest, my heart knew otherwise. This man was fae.

My pulse began to slow, my breathing began to regulate. I was a Wise. I belonged in the realm of fairytales, just like this Laec did...if this wasn't some sick joke. My muscles refused to relax, though.

"Why so nervous?" Laec's voice was low and gentle. "You're at home too. Aren't you?"

"I...I'm wondering where you came from, and why I can't see my friends," I said, my lips feeling numb.

"Ah." A look of understanding crossed his face. "You were born 'without.' I should have guessed based on your ugly clothes." He swept a hand toward my rain jacket and down to my boots. "Explains why I've never seen you before. I know everyone." His brows stitched together over his dark eyes.

"I'm looking for a friend of mine who's gone missing," I explained, sounding a bit more like myself. I could appear as though I was under control, but if he took any more steps closer to me or went for that knife, I'd have the earth swallow him up so fast he wouldn't know what hit him.

His fine brows arched high over tilted eyes. "There, was that so difficult? What's your friend's name?"

"Evelyn Munro."

"Ah, well. You won't find her here." He gestured to my gear and outfit. "Not like *this*."

"Excuse me?"

He let out an almost impatient sigh, like I was stupid and he was growing bored. "You have the power to find her, little Wise. What are you waiting for?"

I took a step back as though he'd hit me in the gut. The hair on my legs and arms spindled to standing.

"It never occurred to you to look where she was last seen?" He said this in such a patronizing way that it sliced through the shock of him addressing me as 'little Wise.'

"Of course it occurred to me," I snapped. "But I don't know where to start and her yard is nothing but pavement." My mind reeled. Why was I standing here debating with this person? And how did he know what I was? Only my best friends knew what I was. I looked no different than any other human on the outside.

Laec laughed with genuine humor and surprise. "You are so ignorant?"

Stung, my mouth dropped open.

My expression seemed to make him realize that my distress was genuine. He put his hands on his hips and rolled his eyes. "Use bentonite clay. Failing the presence of clay, asphalatus will do."

"Asphalatus?" I parroted weakly.

"Before you draw the residual," he said impatiently. "Honestly, you *without* are like lost souls."

"Without?"

He waved a hand through the air. Someone grabbed me by the shoulders and whirled me around to face the direction which I'd come, only there was no one there, no one holding me, even though I could feel fingers pressing into the flesh of my shoulders.

"Go on then," Laec said, and the invisible hands shoved

me forward, though I knew he was not close enough to touch me. "I tire of this game."

I staggered forward, arrested myself and turned, fury rising in my chest. How dare he shove me around like that?

But he was gone.

CHAPTER TWELVE

*B*eams of white light bounced and flashed through the trees in the darkness beyond where I stood. Neither Jasher nor Lachlan had noticed my interaction with Laec.

I put my palm over my heart, feeling its frantic pace. Closing my eyes, I took a few deep breaths. There might be a logical, rational explanation for Laec's sudden appearance, and the Georjie of a year ago would accept nothing less, but the Georjie of today…she'd seen tiny fae birthing from little transparent cocoons, she'd been covered by them, named by them. She'd seen a wraith suck the life from a man, a wraith who'd once been a Wise herself. Mysteries abounded in my new reality, but the realm of possibility was much broader than it had ever been.

My fingers grazed the edge of a hawthorn tree and the uses and powers of it tingled in my blood and strengthened my heart. If I could draw the healing power of plants in only a touch, then I could believe there might be fae beyond the tiny, ethereal creatures I'd already seen.

I picked up my flashlight and walked on, keeping the fact

that I'd met Laec to myself for now, and scanning the darkness with my lights for Evelyn or signs of her. We emerged on the road well after dark where we were met by a constable and returned to Blackmouth. Another shift of searchers was to begin as we retired.

When Lachlan said goodnight to me, I found a smile for him, but was secretly thankful I would now have some time on my own. During the remainder of the sweep through the queen's land, I had stewed over what Laec had said. If he was right--and surely this would prove his authenticity more than anything else could--then either bentonite clay or asphalatus would help me to see Evelyn's residual, even through pavement.

So, when the castle took on the restful silence of sleeping inhabitants, I slipped out the back door and walked down the hill and into town. Making my way to Evelyn's road, I stopped on the pavement near a small patch of grass. Kicking off my shoes and tucking my socks inside them, I stepped on the tiny piece of bare land and tuned in.

I couldn't find any nearby bentonite, but through the whispering of countless other species, asphalatus answered my call. Growing beyond the park in a thin strip of brush, its nature echoed through my bones and made my feet and legs tingle. Drawing the plant's essence in my body, my frame grew warm, my eyes and ears tingled, and my hands flexed with a new, raw energy. I bent and dug my fingers into the earth, retrieving a lump of it.

Opening my eyes, I walked toward Evelyn's house--now closed up tight and locked, her curtains drawn and the house giving off an abandoned feel--my feet bare and cold against the bitumin. I gasped as I saw the residual was already there, waiting for me.

Evelyn stood in the doorway of her cottage. Her feet were bare on the carpet runner and her ghostly white nightgown fluttered against her knees. A shawl was draped over her shoulders. Her eyes were wide, vacant, and unblinking. Her curly hair drifted around her face as she stared forward. One pale hand rested on her door handle as she stood there, gazing down her front walk and out onto the street beyond.

At first, I thought she was really there, so clear was her image. Any residuals I'd seen up until this point had been grainy, like old silent films. But Evelyn was as clear as if she was right in front of me, only colorless. In the dim nighttime light, she might have appeared colorless anyway, but then she stepped forward and I knew. This was the Evelyn of the past. Under the light of the lamp over her doorway, her hair did not glimmer brown, but in tones of black and gray.

In my periphery, something moved. Something dark and flickering.

Turning to look, I gave another gasp and nearly lost my footing.

The eldritch thing danced at the end of her walkway, just beyond her gate. Bent and curved, its flickering fingertips beckoned to Evelyn. Its long head wavered back and forth in a serpentine sway, and its hands curled and called.

Evelyn stepped forward, her eyes fixed on the shadow.

My mouth went dry as I watched this scene unfold. The thing had been there when I'd seen the body buried in the wall, over three hundred years ago. It was here now. So it was an immortal thing.

What did it want with Evelyn?

I swallowed hard and resisted the urge to call out to Evelyn to ignore the dancing shape. Evelyn strode forward slowly. She momentarily gripped the door handle and then released it. Her door swung nearly shut, stopping only and inch from the frame...the way it had been when I'd visited her house.

Evelyn strolled down her walkway, her stride slow and

smooth, her face expressionless. Her eyes were dark and shadowed, focused on the too-thin-to-be-human dancing shape as it beckoned her.

The cold earth held fast in my hand, I waited until the eldritch thing passed me, thankful it seemed unaware of me this time. Then Evelyn wandered by, a sad sight, thin and pale in her nightdress, her hair mussed and with dark circles under her eyes. She looked like an orphaned child sleep-walking in the streets.

When her back was to me, I followed the residual Evelyn as she wandered after the luring creature. My heart ached with sorrow, feeling that this could not possibly have a happy ending, but my blood also surged with energy, as I felt on the verge of the answer to where our missing friend had ended up. If the creature murdered her, tricked her into some awful demise...I choked back a little sob as I strolled down the middle of the empty street, my eyes on the scene before me.

Fighting back panic by telling myself to be patient, I realized that the eldritch thing was now swinging toward a copse of trees. On the other side of the little grove was the graveyard. My skin swept with a chill. Was that where we were headed?

Evelyn slipped into the trees, her white nightdress giving its own near-otherworldly glow. The eldritch thing nearly disappeared in the woods, a shadow among shadows, a vacuum within the dense underbrush. As the eldritch thing emerged and ascended the little hill leading up to the front gate of the graveyard, Evelyn's back flickered and fuzzed out for a moment, before refocusing.

I was losing the asphalatus in my system, but at least now, Evelyn was on the soil again. The herb had done its trick. I dropped the soil in my hand and the residual blinked out. Scraping together a new lump of earth, I straightened.

Evelyn reappeared with the graininess of former residuals, dim and in poor quality. Evelyn followed the dancing shadow through the narrow archway and toward the dark hills dotted with headstones. Picking up the pace, I narrowed the gap between us and fell into step with Evelyn. Peering at her face, I saw that nothing had changed. She was still open-eyed and unfocused.

The dancing shadow stopped and my hand flew to cover my mouth when I realized where the dark flaming thing had taken her.

To a freshly dug grave.

The ground yawned with a rectangular hole. A pile of dirt sat on a nearby tarp. No headstone had been erected and the grave was in an empty, distant part of the graveyard. I fought the urge to scream as the eldritch shape beckoned to Evelyn with its curling, flickering fingers.

Evelyn stepped forward to the edge of the hole. Her hands came slowly up to the shawl draped over her shoulders. Taking it off, she held the shawl out in front of her.

The eldritch thing lifted its own long hands and with a swirling motion, the shawl was lifted into the air on a ghostly wind. It wound its way around Evelyn, at first with a soft swirl, and then tighter and tighter - now so tight I could see the shape of her body through the fabric. It seemed to expand as it wrapped over her face and head, covering her completely from head to toe.

"Oh, Evelyn," I moaned, choking on another sob. Tears poured down my face and blurred my vision. I swiped them away with my clean hand.

With a flick of its wrist, the shadow gave Evelyn one last instruction. She stepped forward, and fell into the grave.

A scream tore from my throat and I threw down the soil. Sprinting to the edge of the grave, I skidded to a halt at its edge and looked down. There she was—a shape wrapped in a white shawl, laying completely still.

"Oh, please don't be dead. Please don't be dead," I murmured over and over as I knelt down and dropped into the grave beside her. My skin crawling with fear and my hands shaking, I found the hole in the fabric at the top of her head. Hooking my fingers into it, I pulled the shawl away from Evelyn's face. Jamming my fingers under her chin, I closed my eyes and held my breath. I let out a big breath of air when I felt the weak pulse under my fingertips. She was alive!

"Evelyn?" I took her by the shoulders. "Evie, honey. Wake up! Please wake up!"

Planting the soles of my feet against the dirt on either side of her shoulders, I stood over her with my hands on her face. Closing my eyes, I drew every good and strengthening thing the earth had to offer and poured it into Evelyn. My limbs and torso buzzed with life and vitality as I let the magic of the flora around me run through me and into her.

Evelyn's body warmed, her cheeks flushed, her breathing steadied and her heartbeat gave a powerful throb. I opened my eyes, my own heart fluttering with hope and excitement.

"Evelyn?"

She did not open her eyes.

Swearing silently, I got my feet to one side of her and bent over her awkwardly, trying not to fall on her in the small space. I got one arm under her neck and shoulders and the other under her knees.

Drawing fortifying power into myself from the soil, I gave a grunt and lifted Evelyn's body up. Taking a break for a moment to breathe, I stood there, the top of my head level with the grass. I'd never have the strength to lift Evelyn's dead weight up on to the lawn without my elemental powers. Calling to the nearest tree, I bade it bend.

Long wispy branches appeared overhead, coming toward me, coming to take Evelyn. I lifted her body up to my shoulders, sucking in air, and gave her frame up to the ash tree. The branches slipped beneath her body, curling around her legs and torso, and bore her up out of the hole. The ash tree deposited Evelyn on the grass as I heaved myself up out of the grave.

Kneeling beside her and panting, I gazed at Evelyn's still form and caught my breath. The ash tree returned to standing and swayed in the breeze as though nothing had happened.

What now? She was in a coma. She needed medical care. My own powers had strengthened her vital signs but hadn't been enough to wake her. I had no cell phone with me, I never took it on these little Wise excursions because the signals were toxic and might interfere, the way they interfered with faerie cocoons. The hospital was too far for me to carry her, even with reinforcements from the earth, because Blackmouth's clinic was on the other side of town. It would take me at least an hour to walk there, but she needed help now. And what about Inspector Hamilton? He needed to know right away that she'd been found.

"I don't want to leave you, Evelyn," I whispered to her, "but I have to go get help."

Getting to my feet, I took off at a sprint in the direction of the closest help––the police station.

CHAPTER THIRTEEN

*G*asping for breath, I halted at the police station, one hand on the door. I hadn't stopped running except for the seconds required to stop and put on my shoes when I'd reached them. The building was a gray stone box with small windows. Wrenching open the door I went inside and yelled for help. There was no one in the small front lobby, but a petite woman in uniform appeared in the doorway behind the desk, eyes wide and coffee-bright.

"Steady on there, miss." She came forward. "What can I do for you?"

"I've found the missing woman," I said between gasps, one hand on my pounding heart. Gym class no longer had a role in my life and this was the first moment I regretted that. "I've found Evelyn. She needs medical attention right away."

Quick as a brake-light, the officer produced a radio and sent the message through to the inspector. She paused to ask, "Where is she?"

"She's in the graveyard." I noted the absence of surprise. She might be young, but she must have seen a few odd things already. Surprising, in the sleepy town of Blackmouth.

She passed the message on, giving the inspector the particulars on where exactly in the graveyard Evelyn was as I fed them to her.

I turned to leave and she said, "Where are you going?"

I shot her a desperate look. "Back to Evelyn. She's a friend of mine, I'd really like to be there for her. She might wake up, and it would be good for her to see a friendly face."

The officer pinched her lips together. "The ambulance will get there before you will. It's best if you don't get underfoot. I've requested an officer to return here to sit with you, but if you like, I can have him escort you to the hospital."

I blinked at her in surprise. "Why do I need an escort?"

"Inspector Hamilton will want to take your statement. We don't want to lose track of the one who found her." Seeing my consternation, she added, "Don't worry, it's only a formality. He'll just want to hear how you found her."

The sound of a motor outside drew our attention to the window.

"That'll be Constable Sheldon now. He'll take you to the hospital."

Not wanting to waste any more time, I thanked her and left the station.

Constable Sheldon, a silver-haired man with a neatly trimmed beard, was just getting out of the car when I went for the passenger side.

"I'm Georjayna, I found Evelyn. The"—I realized I'd not asked the officer's name—"officer inside the station said you'd take me to the hospital. Evelyn's a friend of mine. I'd like to meet her at the hospital."

He bobbed his head once and retreated back into the driver's seat. I hopped in beside him and he piloted the car into the road and toward the small Blackmouth hospital.

"Nice to have a bit of good news," Constable Sheldon said

in a gruff tone. Glancing briefly at me as he steered the car he asked, "How did you find our missing lady?"

My stomach gave a lurch when I realized that of course I'd be asked this. I hadn't thought up a story yet. Whatever Constable Sheldon asked, Inspector Hamilton would also ask. I needed to keep my head and my story straight.

"I was part of the search team which passed through the queen's land earlier tonight." I gripped the door handle tightly as I scrambled to come up with a simple lie, one I wouldn't get snagged in later.

"Aye," replied the constable, "but ye found her in the graveyard?"

"Yes." My mouth felt like it was lined with carpet. I'd never been great at lying, not the way my friend Saxony was. She could produce an elaborate story on a moment's notice. "I couldn't sleep after my search party's shift was over, so I went for a walk."

He shot me another side-eye. "In the graveyard?"

I just nodded.

Pulling into the hospital parking lot, blinking red lights could be seen reflecting off parked car windows in the side parking lot.

"Ambulance is already here," the Constable said, pulling the car to a stop and putting it in park.

Unclipping my seatbelt, I opened the door and got out.

"Just a moment, Miss," the constable said as he undid his own belt. "I'll need to take you in."

Irritated, I waited for him to get out of the car and lock it. Moving like refrigerated honey, or so it seemed to me in my impatience, he made his way toward the hospital entrance.

Once inside, we registered with the receptionist and were told to wait in the seating area. I wished desperately for my cell phone. Jasher would be upset with me for not at least trying to contact him. In order to do that, I needed to call the castle. It was possible no one would answer at this hour, but at least I could say I tried. Getting out of the hard vinyl chair, I told the constable, who was seated across from me and typing into his phone, that I wanted to let another of Evelyn's friends know she'd been found. He nodded without looking up.

Passing through the lobby to the receptionist's desk, I smiled down at the lady working there. "Would you mind if I used your phone?" I asked. "I need to let my friends know that Evelyn's been found."

"Of course, dear." She picked up the industrial office phone and gently tugged at its cord before setting it up on the counter in front of me.

"I need one more favor," I added sheepishly. "I need to call Blackmouth Castle, but I don't have the number. That's where my friend and I are staying."

She looked up in unmistakable delight. "Ach, you must be the Canadian lassie they've got there helping out for the closed season. Ainslie and I are old friends. She told me all about you at our last book club meeting. Of course, I'll get you the number."

I let out a relieved sigh. "Thank you."

The receptionist retrieved the number from her computer and typed it in for me. I listened to the ringtone with bated breath, but when a recording answered and began to list tourist information about the upcoming season, I hung up.

The receptionist saw that the call hadn't gone through. "I could call Ainslie and she could wake your friend up. She won't mind."

I shot her a grateful look. She nodded and waved me back over to the seating area. "I'll take care of it." The phone's headset was already at her ear when she paused. "What's your friend's name?"

"Jasher, but Gavin and Bonnie will want to know Evelyn has been found as well."

She waved me away but I was hesitant to go, wanting to get Ainslie's reaction. When she waved me away a second time, I went, but slowly.

Sitting across from the constable, I watched the top of the receptionist's head as she murmured into the phone. She looked up once and went back to her conversation for a few more moments. Then she ended the call and gave me the 'a-okay' sign.

Not sure what that meant, I leapt up and went back to the desk. "What's happening?"

"Ainslie will wake the laird and lady and let your friend know. They'll be down here as soon as they can come."

"All of them?"

She shrugged. "We'll see who turns up, but probably. People care about one another in this wee village."

I thanked her and sat down again. What felt like an eternity passed before anyone else entered the waiting area. Unfortunately, it wasn't Jasher or the laird or lady. It was Inspector Hamilton, and he looked grim.

I got to my feet the moment he appeared from the hallway leading to the rear of the hospital. "How is she?"

His eyes were tired and heavy looking. I didn't like the look of him and I liked the look he gave me even less. "She's alive but unresponsive."

The pit in my stomach grew. "That's the way she was when I found her." It was almost the truth. Actually, she'd seemed on death's door when I'd found her, with a weak pulse and waxy complexion. My powers had put some color back into her cheeks and made her heartbeat and breathing stronger. "Do they know what's wrong with her?"

A darkness settled into his stony gaze which further frayed my already frazzled nerves. "I'll be the one to ask questions, Miss Sutherland. I'd like you to accompany me to the station to relay the events leading up to your discovering Miss Munro in a hole in the graveyard."

"Am I under suspicion?" I crossed my arms over my chest, wondering why they'd air condition the clinic in the middle of winter..

"No, but it's important I understand the facts," Inspector Hamilton replied with none of the warmth his son had in spades. I wondered how such a hard man had raised Lachlan.

"Can I tell you everything here? I'm waiting for a few more of Evelyn's friends to come. Jasher, Gavin and Bonnie are on their way. I'd like to be here when they arrive."

He gave a stiff nod and led me to a couple of the upholstered chairs in the corner under a TV mounted to the wall. He took out his cell phone and interacted with the screen.

"With your permission, I'll record this."

"Sure." My hands knotted together in my lap. I wasn't guilty of anything, but his behavior was making me feel nauseated.

"State your name for the record," he prompted, and set the phone on the coffee table at our knees.

I said my name.

"How do you know Evelyn Munro?"

"I met her through a friend of mine," I replied. "They're dating. I first met Evelyn at a pub here in town. *The Blackmouth Arms.*"

He rested his elbows on his knees and leaned forward, penetrating gaze drilling me in the forehead. "How was it you came to find her?"

I cleared my throat and took a moment to inhale. "As you know, I was one of the volunteers who searched the queen's land yesterday afternoon. We searched until well after dark but didn't find anything. When our shift ended and we returned to Blackmouth, I couldn't sleep. I was wired from the search and a bit upset. So, I went for a walk."

"What time did you arrive at the castle after your shift?"

"Around ten, or shortly after."

"And when did you go out for your walk?"

"I'm not sure. Maybe just before midnight."

He shifted in his seat and folded his hands together. He was watching me the way a hungry dog watches the nearest human in possession of food. "Continue."

"I went to Evelyn's house first," I explained, "in case she'd shown up at home. But the house was locked and still empty, so I kept walking. I went up the hill toward the graveyard. I was thinking about the body we found on the castle grounds. You know, the one in the wall?"

The inspector made a sound in the back of his throat that was probably meant to assure me he knew what I was talking about.

"Someone had told me that a grave had already been dug for the body. Since I was going that way anyway, I thought I'd see if I could find it."

He gestured for me to continue then sat back and began to stroke his chin. I could hear the sound of his whiskers rasping against his fingers.

"There was a mound of dirt visible near the top of one of the hills so I went toward it, thinking it might be the grave." I realized I was hugging my stomach tightly and told myself to relax. "When I looked into the hole, it wasn't empty. It was Evelyn." My voice cracked on her name and I felt my eyes mist up. Good, maybe the inspector would see my distress and ease up a little. I brushed at my eyes and looked to the sliding doors, hoping to see Jasher stroll through them. I wanted an end to this interrogation.

"Could you see her face?" The inspector began to pick at a nail absently, gaze still on my eyes.

I swore to myself silently. He probably knew Evelyn's head and face had been covered up because she didn't have dirt in her hair.

"No, the body was wrapped up." But I stopped there, feeling the bonds of my story tightening around me like a boa constrictor.

"Then how did you know it was Evelyn?"

"I...well." I gave a nervous laugh. "I had some kind of premonition, I guess. I could see that it wasn't the mummy, because that body was tiny and emaciated." I felt like a small animal sitting frozen in the underbrush as a larger, very toothy predator stalked by. "This body was bigger and the wrappings looked so white and fresh. The shape looked feminine and she was the right size to be Evelyn."

He made a grunt in his throat which I interpreted as, '*Ok, that's a bit of logic, but I still suspect you of something unsavory.*'

Emboldened, I added another detail that would help me to look less crazy. "I thought I could see the body breathing."

"In the dark?"

I nodded. "I have good night vision and the wrappings were white so it wasn't hard to see them move. At first I thought I was seeing things, but when I realized I wasn't, I got into the grave with her. Just to be sure. When I pulled away the fabric covering her face and felt her pulse, I lifted her out of the grave and then ran to the police station as fast as I could."

"So, let me understand." Inspector Hamilton shifted forward in his seat. His teeth glinted and the suspicion had not fully vacated his eyes. "You found a wrapped body in a grave, thought it might be alive, and actually *went into* the hole to check?"

I felt myself wilt. When he said it like that, it did sound a bit crazy. But what would a non-crazy reaction have been, I'd like to have asked. Instead I just said, "Yes."

"And when you realized it was Evelyn, you lifted her dead weight out of a six-foot-deep grave all by yourself?"

I nodded, not looking away from his penetrating gaze.

He stared at me, letting the silence drag on, probably hoping I'd add something to damn myself, or just break and admit it was all a batch of lies.

I said nothing, and stared back and wondered what he thought had *actually* happened. He surprised me with his next question.

"How tall are you?"

"Six foot even," I answered steadily. It was the first time I'd ever answered this question truthfully. I'd been sensitive about my height for as long as I could remember. I always said five-foot-eleven.

He stared at me thoughtfully. "Could you demonstrate for me?"

"What?" I straightened sharply.

"Could you get into a hole in the ground and lift the dead weight of an unconscious body up over your head and out onto the ground?"

I stared at him in disbelief.

He stared back, unblinking.

"What is it you suspect me of, Inspector?" The first flares of righteous anger went off in my chest and I let it harden my voice for the first time.

"Nothing, yet," he replied smoothly. "But you have to admit, your story sounds pretty strange."

"It's the truth," I snapped back. "I found her and reported it as soon as I could."

"I understand Evelyn is dating your friend, Jasher?"

I narrowed my eyes at him. "So what?"

"I understand also that you used to be an item with Jasher yourself?"

I felt as though he'd thrown a bucket of freezing water

into my face. Words fled and my jaw dropped in as the implication slowly stepped forward out of the shadows.

"What are you implying?" I finally asked, beginning to feel a tremble in my knees. It's a good thing I was sitting down.

"Were you jealous of Jasher's relationship?" the inspector asked as casually as if he'd asked for a tissue.

"Of course not!" I wanted to scream that if he paid attention to his family he would have realized by now that it was his own son I had an interest in, not Jasher.

Three people rushed in through the sliding doors. Gavin, Bonnie and Jasher made a beeline for the front desk, not seeing me and the inspector.

I made to get up when Inspector Hamilton said, "We're not finished here."

I stood and glared down at him, firing ice-bullets with my eyes. "If you think I had anything to do with what happened to Evelyn, besides *rescuing* her, then arrest me." My voice was trembling with anger. "If not, then leave me alone."

Without waiting for a reply, I got up and went to join my friends in the lobby. The inspector didn't follow me but I felt his gaze stabbing into my back as I left the waiting area.

CHAPTER FOURTEEN

The doctor had just appeared from the emergency hallway when an older couple came rushing in through the front sliding doors. One look at the woman's petite frame and wild curly hair told me these were Evelyn's parents. After quick introductions, the doctor explained to the group of concerned faces pressing in on her that Evelyn was in a coma but that she'd sustained no visible injuries. There were no apparent internal injuries either. The doctor suggested that Evelyn might have sustained some psychological trauma that resulted in her loss of consciousness. The moment she finished talking with us, she took Evelyn's parents aside to discuss a course of action.

Gavin and Bonnie were in conversation with one another so I took the opportunity to pull Jasher to a quiet corner where we wouldn't be overheard. With a glance toward the waiting room, I saw that Inspector Hamilton and the constable had both vacated it.

By the time we were in the waiting area, Jasher was pulling me more than I was pulling him. "What did you see?"

"It was the eldritch thing," I muttered with an uneasy

glance at the camera mounted high in the corner of the room. Shuffling him off to the side and out of its range, I wondered too late if it only served to make us look suspicious. "The shadow that scared me so badly when we went to the ruin that night. It did this to Evelyn."

Jasher's normally ruddy complexion washed out and his eyes stretched wide. "But, it was in a memory that's hundreds of years old…"

I nodded. "Whatever it is, it's immortal. I'm wondering if it orchestrated the whole thing with the woman who was walled up, and now it orchestrated this." My voice hitched. "Jasher, it was awful."

Jasher's hands gripped my arms as he pulled me down into a chair. "Start from the beginning. Don't leave anything out."

With a glance over at the rest of our party, I saw that Gavin and Bonnie were hugging Evelyn's parents. "Not here. It'll take too long and it won't look good. When we get home, I'll tell you everything."

I straightened as I saw Gavin, Bonnie, and Evelyn's parents heading our way. Evelyn's mother opened her arms wide as she headed straight for me, tears streaming down her face. I stood and let her enfold me in a hug that smelled like cloves.

"Thank you," she whispered into my hair.

Evelyn's father stood nearby and patted my shoulder awkwardly while his wife leaked tears onto my neck. My heart ached for them.

"I'm only sorry she wasn't found sooner," I said as Evie's mother released me.

"What possessed you to go walking through the graveyard alone in the middle of the night?" Evie's dad asked, shaking his head. But his expression wasn't condescending or suspicious; his eyes were soft with gratitude.

I gave them the story I told the inspector, and no one seemed to think that I should be implicated in a crime, which made me feel better. When I came to the part about wanting to see the mummy's grave as my reason for going to the graveyard in the first place, Gavin was nodding and said to Evelyn's father, "She wanted to pay her respects. Big softie, this one."

Evelyn's parents explained that the doctors had put Evie on an IV and were monitoring her vitals. She could breathe on her own but she had minimal brain activity and would receive a brain scan as soon as she was properly hydrated.

"They're concerned about brain damage," Evelyn's mother said and her face crumpled. Her husband wrapped an arm around her.

"Don't let's make any assumptions," he murmured with a loving tone. "Come on, let's allow these good people to get some rest."

Evelyn's parents moved arm in arm through the lobby and disappeared down a hallway to the left.

"Are they going to stay with her?" I asked Bonnie.

Bonnie nodded. "Normally, there are no overnight visitors, but they're making an exception for them, just for tonight."

"What a weird night," Gavin said, rubbing the top of his head and making his hair bush out. "You must be exhausted, Georjie. Come on, let's go home."

In the car, Jasher reached across the back seat and took my hand, squeezing it gently all the way back to Blackmouth Castle.

"Did anyone call Lachlan?" I asked as Gavin pulled the car into the parking lot.

"There wasn't time," Jasher replied as he released my hand and unbuckled his seatbelt. "When Ainslie woke us, all we could think to do was get down to the hospital as fast as we could."

"Lad will be sleeping anyway, Georjie," Bonnie threw over her shoulder, the shadows under her eyes as deep as I'd ever seen them. "Call him in the morning."

We got out of the car and headed into the castle. Murmuring goodnight and giving hugs all around, we headed to our respective quarters. Jasher trailed me to my room and closed my door softly behind us before we each sat on a different bed, facing one another.

Jasher's work-roughened hands twisted together in his lap. Little bags of exhaustion had sprouted below his eyes. For the first time since I'd met him, he looked much older than his years.

"I wouldn't have known where to look or even how to see Evie if it wasn't for what happened during the search party earlier tonight," I began.

Jasher's brows tightened. "During the search?"

I nodded. "I was walking along between you and Lachlan, I could see the light from your headlamps and flashlights through the trees on either side of me. Out of nowhere, a man was just...there. He didn't walk out of the gloom or drop out of a tree; he was not there and then he was there. He had—" I took a shaky breath, reminding me that this was Jasher I was talking to. A friend who could see faery cocoons and used to be able to talk to the dead.

"He had no shirt on, only a pair of pants that looked homemade, and bare feet."

Jasher recoiled with surprise. "A random crazy?"

"No. He had *pointed ears*, Jasher. He looked a lot like a faery, only he had no wings and he was as big as we are. Everything about him screamed magic, not the least of which was the fact that your lights totally disappeared, then reappeared when he went away. I even called for you when he was there, because I was frightened. But you didn't answer."

Jasher looked pale. "I never heard a thing."

"I know. It was like there was something between us for a few minutes, a veil or something. He said his name was Laec, and he said that I was from *without*."

Jasher shook his head, his nose wrinkling with confusion. "Without what?"

"Just, without. And," I leaned forward to emphasize this part, "he *knew what I was*. He called me 'little Wise.'"

Jasher's mouth opened but no words came out. He looked, well…like he'd begun seeing ghosts again.

I went on. "He asked me what I was doing and I told him I was looking for a friend. I told him about not being able to see residuals over pavement. He scoffed and told me I was basically an idiot not to know that I just needed to use a certain plant."

Jasher closed his mouth finally and processed what I was saying.

"Did you feel threatened?"

"A little, at first. He was a bit aggressive, but in the end he was right. The advice he gave me led me to find Evelyn."

Jasher rubbed his fingers across his brow as though he was fighting a headache.

"You remember how I asked if you heard drum music?"

Jasher nodded. "Not for the first time."

"I heard it while we were searching, and when Laec appeared, it got louder. Before I saw him, it just sounded muffled and distant, but not coming from any one direction. Just from everywhere. But when he was there, it seemed like it was coming from the southeast."

"Southeast from where you were…" Jasher calculated thoughtfully, "as in back toward the castle?"

"Yes. And when Laec disappeared, the music went dim again. And your torchlights reappeared."

"Why didn't you tell me as soon as we got back to Blackmouth?"

"Everyone was so tired. I couldn't sleep and I went out not knowing if his advice was going to work. Besides," I added with a touch of bitterness, twisting the edge of my pillowcase in my fingers, "the inspector acted like he suspects me of something. It's better that I was alone."

Jasher looked aghast and moved over to sit beside me. "What do you mean he *suspects* you? Of what?"

"I don't know." I raked my fingers through my hair, frustrated. "It doesn't matter, I think he was just being a jerk. He's got no evidence of any foul play; if he did, he would have arrested me. But Jasher," I turned toward him, "most importantly, the advice Laec gave me *worked.* I was able to see Evie's residual, and that's when I saw the shadow-man."

I described for him in detail everything that happened after I'd left Evelyn's house up until we all met at the hospital. He listened in horrified silence, gripping my hand. When I finished, we sat there ruminating for a while before he spoke.

"You've only ever seen the eldritch thing in a residual," Jasher said, getting up and walking to the door and back again. "But you saw it lure Evie from her house, that means that thing is here, now, in Blackmouth somewhere. And if you can see it in a residual, that suggests that it should be visible to the naked eye in real-time. We have to find it, make it fix whatever it did to Evie."

"We don't even know what the bloody thing is." I got to my feet, my arms hugging my waist. I felt cold at the thought of confronting the weird dancing shadow. "We don't know how to call it, how to fight it. It has magic."

"You have magic, too."

"Yeah, but it's like a spirit, not fully there. It doesn't look like it has a solid body. What can I do against a wraith…" But my words trailed off. I *had* destroyed a wraith once before.

As though he could read my mind, Jasher said, "Actually, you've proven quite handy when going up against a spirit before."

"But I'd wanted to destroy it. In this case, we need to know what it did to Evelyn, see if she can be awakened."

Jasher and I stared at one another and I knew he was thinking the same thing I was.

"Laec."

Jasher nodded. "Do you think you could find him again?"

"I don't know." But my mind was racing. "We could go back to the woods? Maybe if we go to the same place as before?"

Jasher nodded. "Can you hear the drums now?"

I paused, listening, then shook my head. "Nope." But I knew where he was going. "I'll tell you the minute I do."

Jasher nodded, his expression hopeful. "I'll drop whatever I'm doing and we'll head into the woods. Odds are good that if you hear the drums, he's close."

I nodded and tried to ignore the doubt roiling in my gut. There was one big flaw with this plan. It meant we had to wait until I heard the drums before we could act. I didn't want to wait, and what if I never heard the drums again?

CHAPTER FIFTEEN

Staggering in the rear door of Blackmouth Castle, Jasher and I collapsed on the floor and the bench against the wall respectively. After I'd heard the drums again, Jasher begged off work early and we'd spent the late afternoon and evening searching fruitlessly for Laec in the wilderness.

"My feet are wet and numb," I groaned, reaching down to untie the soggy laces of my hiking boots.

Jasher lay on his back on the carpet runner, rainhat drooping over one eye, arms and legs splayed out. "If your feet are numb, how can you tell they're wet?"

I turned my hiking shoe upside down over his face and a few droplets of mud and pine needles landed on his cheek. "Wise ass."

He rolled his head to the side but otherwise moved nothing else. "Thank you for that."

"You're welcome." I began to untie my other shoe.

"I'd wipe away the mud you so kindly deposited on my face, only I'm too tired to lift my arms."

Toeing off my other hiking shoe, I slumped against the

wall and let my head tilt back against the wall. An itch brought my fingers to the back of my neck where I found a little nest of bumps. "I have midge bites in places midges are unwelcome."

Jasher rolled his head to look up at me with the one eye not hidden by his hat. "Is there a place midges *are* welcome to bite?"

"How are they even alive at this time of the year? It's freezing out there. I won't be warm again until I have a hot bath."

Jasher let out a long sigh. "Me too. I can't believe we spent the entire afternoon and evening out there and have nothing to show for it except blisters and bug bites. Are you sure you heard the drums?"

"I heard them." Pulling my rain hat off, I tugged at my hair elastic. It snapped against my thumb. "Ow." My damp hair poofed out in a wavy mess. I frowned and ran my fingers against my scalp. "I was so sure he'd appear."

"Maybe he's shy of men." Jasher gave a yawn that nearly split his face in two. Laboriously, he pulled himself up to sitting to take off his shoes.

I chewed my cheek and wondered if Jasher had a point. Maybe it had been a mistake to let him come with me.

Putting his wet boots on the drying rack, Jasher tugged at his zipper and wormed his way out of his wet coat, still sitting on the carpet runner. "I'm shattered. We didn't conquer those woods, they conquered us."

I grunted and began to strip off my own wet outerwear. My body itched in multiple places now. I was about to issue more complaints when Jasher said something that chased all thoughts of bug bites from my mind.

"Do you think that the little tiny fairies can grow into really big ones?"

Why hadn't I put the two together before? Laec had

pointed ears and too-large eyes, just like the little fairies did. There was one big difference though. "Laec didn't have wings," I said.

"Maybe he just didn't let you see them. You said he looks the same, only bigger." Jasher shrugged. "It's a logical conclusion."

I chewed my lip thoughtfully. "If they do, then that means he wasn't carried in a womb and born, but hatched."

Jasher's nose wrinkled up. "If that's the case, then I wouldn't want to be whatever he is."

"Why not?"

Jasher eyed me. "No sex." Faery cocoons were created when dappled sunlight penetrated fresh rainwater as it dripped from leaves and branches, the small twinkling creatures had no copulation that we were aware of. Of course, who knew what happened in the secretive fae world.

"Well, they might be able to," I ventured. "For pleasure rather than procreation."

Jasher grunted and rubbed his face vigorously. "I'd explore this theory further but right now I have the IQ of a carpet tack. I need to go to bed."

I got to my feet feeling weary in every little bone of my body. "Thanks for searching with me, Jasher. I'm going to fall asleep in the bathtub."

"Don't drown." Jasher's voice followed me as I wandered slowly up the curved staircase leading to our rooms. "And don't forget to look for deer ticks."

I froze. "What?" I poked my head back into the hall.

Jasher was still sitting on the floor. He tilted his head back and gave me a sweet smile. "There are ticks in Scotland, especially in wooded areas. Do a thorough search before you go to bed."

"Eurgh." I let out a disgusted sigh. "I'm covered in midge bites, my toes and fingers feel like ice, and every shred of clothing on me is wet and stuck to my skin. Why not add a few ticks to the party?"

"And mud. You've got it all up the back of your legs," Jasher replied.

I let out another groan and ambled my way up the stairs.

Thankful that my room had a tub, even if it was pretty small, I started the hot water and added a generous dollop of both the complimentary bubble bath and the bath oils. The small bathroom soon filled with steam and the scent of eucalyptus. Stripping off my wet clothing and tying my hair up on top of my head, I let out a long moan of pleasure as I sank into the tub. Letting my eyes drift shut, I ruminated over the afternoon.

It had begun so well. Breaks in the clouds allowed filtered sunlight to breach the canopy with soft fingers. The ground was moist and tacky, but not muddy or slippery. It was perfect for combing the woods, until later in the afternoon when it began to rain gently. Although it misted prettily for a bit, we continued through it undeterred. But what began as a light drizzle thickened into a steady downpour. The ground turned greasy, and soon we were spending more time trying not to get stuck in the bogs than we were listening for drums and clues to the presence of a particular fae male. We'd gone far by the time we'd decided to give up and come home, and the wet forest did its best to keep us trapped, like someone didn't want us to leave. It took us twice as long to get back.

The search had been a failure. I was disappointed, but I could accept it now that I was up to my chin in fragrant bubbles.

When my fingers turned pruny, I let the water drain from the tub and turned the shower on to rinse the suds and wash my hair. I took extra care to inspect my scalp for telltale tiny lumps. When I was satisfied that no ticks had made their home in my skin anywhere, I got out and toweled off.

147

Turbaning my hair and worming into my bathrobe, I tied the belt tightly and opened the bathroom door to dry my hair before doing a faceplant into bed.

"Hello." Laec sat cross-legged on my bed, hair sticking up wildly in all directions, and eyes twinkling.

My heart bounced around my chest like a squash ball and I clamped my hand over my mouth to keep a scream in. Staggering backward, I hit the door to the bathroom.

"So easily frightened," Laec observed conversationally, his bright eyes roaming my be-robed form from my bare feet to the towel piled on top of my head. The muscles in his chest flexed and relaxed.

"What are you doing here?" I wheezed, my hand over my heart. It was still galloping around like a hare. "We spent hours looking for you!"

"We." He made a tsking sound and faked a pout. "That was your mistake."

My heart began to slide down my throat and settle into its normal place, slowly. I pinched my bathrobe shut with one shaky hand.

"Speaking of mistakes." My eyes narrowed. "Don't you know it's rude to come in without knocking?"

"Yes." He grinned wickedly then crossed his arms. "But it's you who sought me out. I felt like it would have been ruder not to appear when you'd spent so many miserable hours searching for me."

"You were watching?" I wanted to grab him by his throat and shake him.

"Of course." He got smoothly to his feet, leaving a dent in my pillow which should have been much deeper. He moved silently, elegantly, like a cat.

"You didn't come because of Jasher." I had been right, and now I felt dumb.

Laec nodded and the sympathetic look was back, his lower lip pooched out further.

"But he can see faeries."

Laec cocked his head, not taking his gaze from my face. It was unnerving because I hadn't yet seen him blink. I felt vulnerable, like he could see right through me.

"You mean the wee ones. There are a few without who can."

"As much as I'd like to continue this conversation, would you mind giving me a moment of privacy?" I hadn't moved from the bathroom door. "To dress."

"I do mind," Laec replied, coolly. "First, because you look delightfully ridiculous in that fuzzy thing. And second, I don't like waiting. Not for anyone. Not even a lost little Wise like you. I only came because I felt sorry for you."

I glared at him. "You're quite annoying."

I immediately regretted saying it. What was I doing being rude to this man? He had all the power because I didn't know what he was capable of. I wasn't sure what *I* was even capable of while this far off the ground.

To my surprise, Laec gave a low laugh and took a few steps toward me, his eyes still on my face. "You sound like Fyfa."

"Who is Fyfa?"

"A friend." He took another step closer, now he was at the foot of my bed. If we'd both reached out, we could have touched.

"Stay where you are, please." I swallowed, uncomfortably aware of the solid wood of the bathroom door at my back. My hands tingled.

There was a scratching sound at the window, followed by the squeak of hinges. Laec looked behind him to see tendrils of ivy--ivy responding to my command--curling around the edges of the open window frame, pushing the window open farther and crawling into the room like tentacles.

Laec looked at me again, this time with respect. "The little Wise makes a threat?"

"How do you know what I am?"

Surprise widened his eyes and for a moment he reminded me of an owl. "Is that an honest question?"

"Of course," I snapped back.

Those fae eyes roamed the terrain of my face and he didn't answer right away. He took another step closer.

I stiffened and the ivy tendrils crawled farther into the room, making the mortar between the stones crumble in places. There came the sound of dust sifting to the dresser. I really hoped he didn't make me ruin the castle walls. It would be tough to explain to the laird and lady.

His expression lost some of its flirtatious arrogance. "I'm not going to hurt you."

He closed the gap between us, moving so smoothly it was as if he was on wheels. He stopped and looked down at me, his face less than a foot from my own.

"Why were you looking for me today?" he asked, his gaze dropped from my eyes to my lips and back up again. His expression was like a curious animal.

"I...I." my words caught in my throat and I tried to swallow but my mouth was dry. "I was hoping you could help me help my friend, the girl who was missing. We found her, but she's in a coma."

He leaned an inch closer, nostrils flaring. I couldn't tell if he wanted to kiss me, bite me, or just smell my fear.

My fingers were clenching my bathrobe so tightly that I wasn't sure I'd be able to let go of the fabric.

"Evelyn," I added hoarsely.

My knees quivered as his scent swept over me: morning dew, leaves, tree oils, pine cones.

"Something immortal did this to her," I went on.

His eyes darkened and he cocked his head.

"I saw it in the residual. It's like a ghost, only not a ghost. It looked like it was made of black flames."

His lips parted and eyes widened a fraction. "*Na sheasamh gu hìosal.*"

"Excuse me?"

His gaze sharpened. "You are distracted by what is happening in front of you."

My mouth dropped open in confusion.

Swiftly, he lifted his hand between us. Pinched between his fingers was a rolled-up piece of newsprint.

When I took it, he stepped away. "Don't miss what is happening behind your back."

I looked down at the rolled-up paper. There was a puff of air against my face, no more than an exhale. When I looked up, Laec was gone. I let out a long, frustrated groan.

"I wish you'd stop doing that," I said loudly into my empty room.

The ivy tendrils began to withdraw, pulling the window closed behind them.

Hurriedly, I changed out of my wet robe and into my warmest pajamas. Crawling under the coverlet with the newsprint in my hand, I leaned my back against the pillow and unrolled it. It was an article. I gasped and bolted upright. It was dated for the day after tomorrow and the headline screamed:

Recently Discovered Medieval Mummy Missing from Morgue!

A thin tendril of smoke curled upward from the article and I squeaked and dropped it. With a fizzle of sparks sweeping across its surface, the article burned up and vanished with not so much a whiff of ash left behind.

CHAPTER SIXTEEN

"*L*ooking good, guys," I said as I emerged to where Will, Lachlan, and Jasher stood near the now framed up cottage, looking at a blueprint spread out on the table and talking about whatever was coming next.

"Morning, Georjie." Lachlan sent me a grin that warmed my entire body. "Nice to see you. We were beginning to think you weren't interested in the goings-on now that there wasn't a dead body in the walls." He winked.

I shot him a grin. "Yeah, you know me. Only interested in the morbid."

As much as I would have loved to hang around and flirt with Lachlan, I didn't have time for it. There was only one thing on my mind. I had to fight not to dance impatiently in place like a child wanting candy while standing in line at the grocery store.

As casually as possible, I said, "Jasher, could I speak to you for a minute?"

Jasher handed the plans to Will and looked up with interest. He had dark smudges under his eyes. My guess was that he'd lain awake all night thinking about Evelyn.

"Of course," he said.

I felt Lachlan's eyes on me as Jasher joined me on the path and we went back toward the garden maze.

"What's up?" he asked.

I turned him to face me, gripping his arms with both hands. I practically hissed the words. "He was in my room last night."

Jasher's brows shot up. "Laec? Are you serious?"

I nodded furiously. "I got out of the bathtub and he was sitting right there on my pillow!"

Jasher let out a huff and put his hands on his hips like an angry teacher. I was still nodding, thinking he was indignant about the fact that Laec had invaded my privacy, but he said, "After we spent all day looking for him? What a wanker."

I sent him a withering look. "Thanks for being concerned about my well being. There was a topless fae man in my room last night—aren't you even a little concerned?"

Jasher made a sound in the back of his throat. "You're standing here in one piece in front of me, Georjie, so no. Besides, of all the girls—sorry, women—I've met in the world, you're the one I worry about the least. You're a badass Wise."

"Whatever." But I couldn't help but smile.

"What did he want?" One dark eyebrow ratcheted up lasciviously. "A midnight tryst?"

"Don't be absurd. He said there was stuff going on behind our backs, gave me a newspaper article that said the body we found in the wall was stolen from the morgue."

Jasher put a hand up under his hat and scratched his forehead. "I'm confused. Someone stole the body?"

"Not yet." I shot him a meaningful look. "The newspaper was dated for *tomorrow*."

"Whoa, a prognostipaper?"

I stared at him. "You think you're clever, don't you?"

"I know I am."

"Okay, Mr. Clever, explain how the paper then spontaneously combusted. One moment I was holding it and reading it, the next it went up in sparks."

"You're unknowingly the main character in a *Mission: Impossible* film."

"Jasher, this is serious. What should we do?"

"That depends."

"On?"

"Do you think Laec is for real? If you think he's real and you trust that he wants to help us, then maybe this is an authentic look into the future. If you think he's somehow a fake, or that he's just messing with you, then wait and see what happens. Another twenty-four hours and you'll know if that paper he gave you was for real or not."

There was no question to me that Laec was real. There was no way anyone could vanish or do magic like that and not be real. "He's the real deal, Jasher. He helped me find Evelyn, so why would he toy with me now?"

Jasher spread his hands. "In that case, he probably gave you that information so you could stop it from happening."

"I should go to the funeral home and warn them." I turned away, rubbing at my forehead where a dull ache had been since I'd woken up this morning.

Jasher pulled me back. "Think that through for a second, Georjie. You said that Inspector Hamilton suspects you of something."

I rolled my eyes. "He totally acted like it."

"If you show up at the morgue, warn them that someone might want to steal that mummy," he blinked as if finally hearing his own words out loud. "Why on earth anyone would want to do that is beyond me, but let's go with it…"

I picked up Jasher's train of thought. "They'll know who I am, they might even call the police, and Inspector Hamilton will be wondering how I came by the information in the first place."

Jasher nodded. "It should be enough to call and just give them an anonymous tip. They'll put their guard up, make sure their cameras are rolling, give their security a little extra caffeine, and bish, bash, bosh. You've done a good deed for the week."

Sounded reasonable enough.

Will called Jasher from the clearing.

"Sorry, Georjie, I need to actually get something done since I missed time yesterday, and I want to see Evelyn before visiting hours are over."

I watched him go, noting the droop of his usually straight shoulders. Jasher was putting up a brave face, but he was hurting. I couldn't explain why my powers weren't enough to rouse Evelyn; I'd done a lot for other sick and injured people so easily, but Evelyn was out of my reach.

Blackmouth Castle had a small office down the hall from the kitchens where I was able to make free local phone calls. I sat at the wooden desk piled high with tourist pamphlets and aerial photographs of Blackmouth and looked up the number for the mortuary in Inverness. It rang for so long I wondered if it was closed, but eventually a man answered.

"Yes, hello," I said, giving a Scottish accent a try. My heart decided this would be a good time to start the pump running double time. I cleared my throat. How did people make anonymous tips? "I'd like to make an anonymous tip."

I pinched my eyes shut, feeling like an idiot.

"Oh." The man paused. "That's rather unusual. Go ahead, please."

So polite. "I understand you have a body there that was recovered from Blackmouth Castle."

"Ah. Yes. Our medieval Jane Doe. Remarkable find." He sounded cheerful.

"Is it?"

"I should say so, yes. It's not every day we get a four-hundred-year-old corpse to prepare for burial." I opened my mouth to continue when he hit me with, "Especially one for which the cause of death is the subject of some…conjecture."

My head came up. "They still haven't figured that out?"

"They can't seem to agree on it, at any rate. A number of causes have been put into the forms, but that's highly unusual. There could be many contributing factors toward a death, but there's always one that pulls the pin, shall we say. Not that I'm qualified to say, but I've never seen a team so divided over the fate of a victim."

Interesting. "What do they think it was?" I winced as I heard myself. When had I lost the fake Scottish accent?

He laughed. "Her documents read like a murder mystery. Poisoning, dehydration, suffocation, strangulation."

I pulled the hood of my sweater up over my head with one hand as a chill swept over me.

"But I'm getting carried away. You have a tip for us?"

"Yes, but I was first wondering when she was set to be buried. The story is a sad one. Whoever she was, she was taken from her family far too soon and in such an awful way. I wouldn't mind paying my respects." I sent a silent thought of gratitude to Jasher for suggesting this anonymous call, but my face was still red. I sounded like a total weirdo. Thankfully, the man on the other end of the phone didn't seem to notice or care.

"Oh, well you're in luck," he replied as though there was nothing strange at all about being attached to a three-hundred-year-old dead body. "She's not yet left the mortuary, but she's set to be transported to Blackmouth Cemetery tomorrow. I'm afraid I don't know the precise time. I'm not going to be here; I also work the home in the next town over."

"I see."

"As interesting as our Jane Doe is, I do have rather a lot of work to do, Miss…" he paused, waiting for my name.

"You should increase your security tonight," I blurted and then put a hand over my eyes and grimaced. I would have made a terrible spy. *Mission: Impossible* my arse. I tried to put the Scottish accent back on but knew it didn't sound right.

"Security? Uh." Bless his heart, he sounded like he was taking me seriously. "Well, we have very good locks on the doors. We've never had a break in before, at least not that I'm aware of. And this facility has been run by my family for thirty-two years."

"That's good," I replied, shifting uncomfortably in the chair.

"Why?"

"I'd rather not say how I know, but I have reason to believe someone might try to break in and steal the Jane Doe."

Silence stretched out for a full five seconds, then he said, "Gosh. I don't suppose you'd care to elaborate?"

"I can't, I'm sorry. Just notify your local police station and step up your security." My hand was still over my eyes and my cheeks burned with the heat of shame. Who says you can't embarrass yourself with no one else in the room?

"Well, I suppose I can turn on the CCTV," he said doubtfully. "We don't usually use it. If you could tell me a bit more about the threat? I understand you don't want to tell me much, but perhaps you could tell me who you're afraid of and…why they might want to steal an old corpse?"

I opened my mouth, but didn't know what else to say. The mortician was actually taking me seriously, which completely endeared him to me, which made me feel horrible that I was doing this anonymously. "Sorry, just, thanks for listening and keep an eye out," I mumbled one last time and hung up the phone.

I sat there staring at the phone for a full minute before thumping my forehead down on the pile of pamphlets in front of me.

* * *

Just before Jasher left for lunch, I caught him in the front parking lot as he was putting away the generator he'd rented for the job.

"It's done."

He nodded as he heaved the generator into the back of Gavin's work truck and threw a tarp over it. "Good."

"Just—" I grabbed the strings of my hood and began to twist them into knots.

Jasher eyed my hands. "What?"

"Should we..."

He got there without me having to finish. "What, stand watch? No, way, Georjie. You've just given an anonymous tip. What would you do if you were the mortician?"

"Call the police."

"Exactly. And who seems to have a problem with you lately?"

"Inspector Hamilton."

Jasher nodded. "Points for Georjie. Don't go making things worse for yourself than they already are." He slammed the tailgate up and fished the keys out of his pocket. "I don't even know what the inspector could possibly think you had to do with Evelyn's coma."

"He thinks it's weird that I knew exactly where to look."

"Well, it *is* weird." He hooked his fingers under the door handle. "But even if you were the one to find her, there's no reason for him to think you had anything to do with it. You're friends."

"He knows you and Evelyn are dating," I said.

"So, he knows Evie and I are dating, why should that implicate you?"

"He thinks that you and I dated also," I explained. "He suggested that I was jealous."

"That's..." Jasher blinked and took a moment before finishing his sentence. "...Insane."

"Tell me about it."

"We never even dated," Jasher sputtered, "and *why* would he think that we did?"

"Maybe Lachlan said something," I suggested, weakly.

"Lachlan? Why would he ..." a look of understanding dawned on his features, and he slid me a sideways look. "Ohhhhh. So you talked to Lachlan about me, and Lachlan mentioned it to his dad."

My cheeks were burning. I covered my eyes with my hands. "This is so humiliating."

"Don't worry, Georjie." Jasher's words took on a teasing tone. "Most women can't control themselves when they get close to these charms." He gestured to his face, his muscled torso.

I gaped at him with amused exasperation. "Who *are* you?"

The cocky smile drained from his face and I could see the scared little boy behind the bravado. "I'm not sure." He flashed me a smile but as quickly as it was there, it was gone again. "I felt like myself around Evie, I always have, since the moment I first met her."

"Really?" I leaned against the truck, hoping he'd go on. Jasher did not open up easily. This felt like the first time he'd done so since I'd gotten here.

"She's done something to my heart, Georjie." Jasher's eyes misted up and he covered them with his hand.

I pulled him into a hug and he squeezed me so tightly I felt like I might pass out. A sliver of jealousy that had nothing to do with romance pierced my gut. Jasher had warmed up to me once he saw some similarities between us, namely that we could both see the faeries that were hatching in his greenhouse, and we'd even shared some passionate kisses. But even so, he'd always seemed guarded. I guessed Evie had something special.

Jasher pulled back and looked down at me. The lines around his mouth deepened. "I'm worried sick about her." He took my hand. "You might be the only one who can help her. Promise me you'll keep trying?"

I swallowed hard and nodded. "Of course."

I could feel the weight of expectation and helplessness settling over my heart. And what if I couldn't help her?

CHAPTER SEVENTEEN

$\mathscr{I}$ had yet to finish my breakfast the following morning when Ainslie called to me from the hall outside the kitchen. Leaving my coffee and almond croissant sitting on the table, I made my way toward her voice at the front of the castle.

I paused as the front foyer came into view. Ainslie stood at the entrance with one of the broad doors swung wide. In the open doorway, and blocking most of it, was Inspector Hamilton. My stomach did a slow, nauseating forward roll. Keeping my expression neutral, I crossed the foyer and came to stand beside Ainslie. The housekeeper had question marks in her eyes.

"The Inspector would like a word."

"Good morning, Inspector," I said coolly. "What can I do for you?"

"Would you mind stepping outside with me for a moment, miss?" The inspector backed out of the doorway and stood to the side.

"Sure." I was wearing a thick woolen cardigan, which had become my morning staple. I loved it because it had pockets, but there were no buttons or anything to fasten it. I pulled it shut around me and crossed my arms to pin it closed. Stepping out onto the landing, I gave Ainslie a confident smile as she swung the door shut. I didn't miss the look that said, 'Don't be making trouble for us, I have enough on my plate.'

"I understand you made an anonymous phone call to the funeral home in Inverness yesterday?"

I felt like he'd hit me in the face with a polo mallet.

The inspector was waiting. "Was that you?"

I nodded, seeing no way around it. I'd mentioned Blackmouth Castle, I had a Canadian accent I didn't do a good job covering up. Why hadn't I gotten Jasher to call? Then again, he had an Irish accent, so...we might have ended up here anyway. I began to piece together a story, frantically, while hoping he couldn't hear my heart racing.

The inspector stared at me and the silence grew heavy.

"It was," I replied, lifting my head, my arms tightening around my torso. I wondered how it was that I could feel so incredibly uncomfortable in the presence of this man and yet feel so the opposite when I was with Lachlan. In this case, the apple fell extremely far from the tree.

"Could you please explain why?" The inspector asked. There was a twitch in one cheek just below his right eye and every so often, his upper lip twitched just beneath his left nostril, giving hints at a sneer. This man did not like me, and I was trying his patience further.

"Sure, just that some kids––teenagers––came by the castle asking if they could see the body that had been found in the walls. I told them they couldn't, that it was going to be buried. As they were leaving, I heard one of them say to his friends that they should break into the morgue so they could see her."

"Her?"

"The body."

"You know it's a her?"

"I ran into the osteoarcheologist in Inverness not long after the body was taken in for research." The 'I' in this case was intentional. I'd been with the inspector's son, but preferred to keep Lachlan out of things given that I didn't know how much Lachlan had told his father, and his father clearly mistrusted me. "He told me the body was female."

"I see. And these kids…" The inspector's gaze picked me apart. "Did anyone besides you see them?"

"I don't think so." I pulled myself up to my full height. The inspector and I stood eye to eye, though he was probably double my weight. I hadn't done anything wrong, and damned if I was going to allow him to intimidate me.

"Did they come here? To the front door?" he asked.

"No, just into the parking lot." I couldn't have imaginary teenagers knocking on the door. Ainslie almost always answered the front door and the inspector would most certainly be questioning her when he was done shredding me up.

"So how did you know they were here if they didn't come to the door?"

"I could see them from the window up there." I gestured to the second-story parlor. "I do my homework from there most mornings. I came out to see what they wanted because they were kind of loitering there."

"How many were there?"

"Two." I tried not to pause or shuffle awkwardly as I answered. What I really wanted to do was stare at the ground, mumble, and ask him if we could be done now.

"Both boys?"

"That's right."

"Did you get any names?"

"No."

The inspector clasped his hands behind his back. "Could you pick them out of a line up?"

"Sure, of course." I tried to exude some level of annoyance. "Inspector, may I ask what this is all about?"

He gave a cough, for the first time looking more uncomfortable than I felt. "The body is missing."

I gaped at him. This time there was no acting. Laec's article had predicted the truth. "Were the perpetrators caught on camera?"

"No," the inspector bit out in irritation, but I knew it wasn't me who was annoying him, for once. "No, even though you'd warned him, Mr. Brown still did not turn on his CCTV." Muscles in his jaw popped. "Regrettably."

I rubbed a hand across my forehead and let out a sigh. "There must be other evidence. How did they get the body out? And why would someone take an old mummified corpse?"

"I was hoping, Miss Sutherland, that you might be able to lend some insight where those questions are concerned. You're the one who warned Mr. Brown. You're the one who found Evelyn. You have to admit, your relationship to these events might appear more than coincidental." His deductive eyes bored into mine.

"Well, I can't. I have no idea why anyone would want to steal some old body." I gave him an apologetic smile. "I'm sorry I can't be more helpful. If you have any suspects, I'd be happy to look at their photographs."

That was never going to happen. There were no boys. I didn't know if the inspector knew it or not, but my lies were as thin as tissue paper. Whatever was going on here was supernatural, but he didn't want to hear that and I sure didn't want to say it.

"May I go inside, Inspector? It's chilly out here and I have work to do." *Chilly* was an understatement. It was freezing.

Our breath hung in front of our faces and my fingertips felt like little ice-cubes.

He waved a hand toward the door. "Certainly."

Ducking inside, I crossed the foyer at a brisk walk. Ainslie appeared and went to talk to the inspector herself. I smiled at her as we passed and got that same questioning look from her. I hoped my face said that everything was normal, everything was fine, but the moment I was out of sight, I bolted down the stairs and jammed my feet into my boots. I yanked on my coat and headed out the back door toward where Jasher and Lachlan would be working.

Crossing the yard at a forced walk so I didn't alarm anyone, I passed through the maze and made my way to the work site.

After saying good morning nonchalantly to the men, I asked Jasher if I could talk to him for a second. He put down his tools and followed me into the trees.

The moment we were out of sight and far enough away, I turned and grabbed his arm, panting. "The body's gone, just like the article said. There was a break-in last night. The inspector was just here, might even still be here questioning Ainslie. He was questioning me and man does he seem suspicious. I told him I overheard some teenagers talking about wanting to see the body." I let out a forced breath. "That guy does *not* like me. Considering how things look, I can't really blame him."

"Whoa, whoa, whoa, Georjie." Jasher put his hands on my shoulders. "Take a breather, love. You're talking so fast I can hardly understand you.

I nodded and sucked in a deep breath. "Sorry. Let me be clear. *The body is gone.*"

Jasher released my shoulders and let out a long, slow breath. "What now?"

I paused, processing. I'd been thinking about that as I

scampered around the castle and through the maze. "The only lead we have is what Lachlan found about that missing woman."

"Daracha?"

I nodded. "He said she went missing from the jail. If I can find the original location of the old jail, surely I'll be able to see something in a residual that might reveal an answer."

Jasher nodded. "Okay. Well, Mr. History can help you with that, too. He hardly ever shuts up about this place, not to mention his collection of books, articles, blah, blah, blah. I know more about highland battles and even medieval gossip than I ever wanted to. I'm sure he'll have an old map of this place."

I nodded. I hated the idea of bringing Lachlan into this mess. It would be a lot harder to lie to Lachlan than it was to lie to his father, but what choice did I have? Evelyn's life was at stake.

* * *

That evening after helping Ainslie with the dishes, I wrapped up and wandered toward town. Jasher had left already to spend the evening at Evelyn's bedside. He'd taken to reading her stories from her collection of Jane Austen novels. Having completed *Northanger Abbey*, he'd moved on to *Sense and Sensibility*. Just the fact that he was dedicating time to reading to Evie aloud in his evenings revealed a lot about his feelings for her. Jasher wasn't the type to sit and read; he was more the type to brood and play guitar.

The temperature was not so low for an East-coast Canadian, hovering just above zero, but the damp slowly worked its way through my layers and when it reached my skin I shivered and tightened my scarf around my neck. If Jasher had paused his international travels somewhere a little further south, we would have enjoyed a break from a brutal winter. The temperatures even so close as Edinburgh were a whole five degrees warmer.

By the time I reached Lachlan's cottage, I felt certain a thin layer of ice had formed across my face. Knocking on the door, I tucked my gloved hands into my armpits and pulled off my gloves. I lay my slightly less frozen hands on my cheeks to warm them.

That was how Lachlan found me when the door swung open.

He grinned and stepped aside. "Georjie! What a lovely surprise. Come on in."

"Sorry, I should have texted to let you know I was coming."

He waved away my apology. "I'm just happy I get to see you. You've been busy." He closed the door behind me and helped me out of my layers. "How's school?"

"Fine." Truthfully, I'd barely managed to skim a B on my last paper. Distractions had a price. "I was hoping I could get your help with something."

Lachlan hung my coat in the tiny closet behind the door and turned to me, straightening. "Anything."

"I'm curious about where the old jail of Blackmouth was, and I thought you might have old town plans in your collection of historical goodies." I rubbed my hands together to warm them.

"Sure, I do. Can I make you a cuppa?"

I nodded, blowing warm air onto my fingers.

While Lachlan made us tea, he prattled on about the build project and his latest obsession––the history of Stirling Castle, which was purported to be haunted by the ghost of Mary, Queen of Scots.

Blowing on our tea, we sat in Lachlan's cozy sitting room, where a tall bookcase jammed from top to bottom with spines was only the start of his collection. He got up to put a log on his fire before slipping into an adjacent room and returning with a few cylindrical cases.

"I've several maps of the Blackmouth." He selected one cylinder and lay the others on the coffee table in front of our knees. He tapped a finger on one of the discarded ones, neatly labeled with a small, handwritten sticker stating *C.1596.* "This is the oldest one I have, produced by a Dutchman named Mercator. There is an older one out there, but I've yet to get my hands on a copy." He flashed me another sweet grin, his eyes sparkling. "One of the many items on my wish list."

"You're either the easiest guy in the world to Christmas shop for, or the hardest," I said with a laugh. "Are those all copies?"

He nodded. "These are, but I have a couple originals, too. I keep them in a humidity controlled safe until I can find the right buyer for them." He popped the plastic cap off the cylinder.

"I didn't know you sold artifacts," I replied, catching a dizzying whiff of his scent, a mix of aftershave and cedar. "I thought you just collected them."

"I do collect them, but I try to sell the most important ones to museums so they can be enjoyed by the general public. I only ask for enough to cover my costs. Maps this old are far too important to be kept by a nobody like me."

"You're not a nobody."

He shrugged. "You know what I mean. A regular civilian." He upended the cylinder and a sheet of paper slid into his hand. Setting the cylinder aside, he unrolled the map and lay it on the table. I moved aside our mugs to make room.

To my untrained eye, the map was a mess. The notations were barely legible and the only real markings that clearly represented anything to me aside from the roads was the ocean on the east side, and a church marked with a cross. From the ocean, roadways fanned outward, meandering back and forth and crisscrossing over top of one another like a heap of spaghetti. Circular splotches and tiny drawings of what might have been buildings peppered the roadways and paths.

Lachlan squinted at the map, leaning over.

"Here's the castle." He pointed to a drawing on the north side of town, a spot beyond the rest, with doodles of trees surrounding it.

"That helps me orient a bit," I replied, "but the rest of it looks like something a five-year-old drew."

Lachlan chuckled, skimming the map intently. A moment later, he pointed. "Voila."

Squinting at the tiny smudge next to his fingernail, I could barely make out the word, *phrìsan*.

"Freesan?"

He threw back his head released a belt of laughter so genuine that it made me laugh, too.

"What?" I asked, still smiling.

He wiped his eyes. "Prison, Georjie. It's the Gaelic word for prison."

My face heated and I put a hand over my eyes. "Duh. I was looking for j-a-i-l. Blond moment."

"I get those all the time." But his grin was teasing enough for me to whack him on the bicep.

I cleared my throat and sent my attention back to the map. "But the original 'freeson' isn't there anymore, right?"

"Well, depends what you mean by 'original.' There is a jail here that's pretty damn old, mid-eighteenth century, but it's not the one Daracha would have been kept in because it was built well after her time." He tapped the little drawing marked prison on the map laid before us. "This would have been the one she'd've been kept in."

He didn't miss much. It was the first time Daracha's name had been mentioned, and I hadn't brought her up. "So, where was this one? I don't know Blackmouth well enough to make out that location in the modern-day town."

"For that, we'll need a newer map." Lachlan went to his bookcase and retrieved a more modern looking publication. Returning to the couch, he sat next to me and paged through what looked like a tourist information book.

"Blackmouth," he muttered, referring to the index and locating a page number. He flipped the book open to the chapter concerning Blackmouth and found a modern aerial view of the town, not unlike the ones Gavin had in his office. It was small, but the image was sharp. Laying the book flat on the coffee table next to the map, he scanned the two back and forth.

"Best bet is here." He pointed to a small green patch between two of the roads fanning out from the sea. Blackmouth's main roads hadn't changed much since the seventeenth-century, but there were a lot of residential streets now and it was difficult to make out which of the arteries on the old map were consistent with the profusion of throughways of today.

I stared for a long while at the two maps, switching back and forth and trying to overlay the new over the old in my imagination. "Are you sure?"

"Not one hundred percent," Lachlan admitted, "but if you use the castle as one main point, the main thoroughfare running north/south as another, and the water's edge as a third, it makes the most sense to me."

I triangulated the way he suggested and agreed; the location he'd chosen was the most likely.

"Thanks, Lachlan." I smiled at him before realizing I really had been a noob. "Shoot!"

"What's wrong?"

"I'm an idiot. I can't believe I forgot my cell phone. I could have taken a photograph of these."

"Oh, no problem. Just take them both," he offered.

"Are you sure?"

"Absolutely. I can also photograph them for you and text them to you, if you like."

"Actually, that would be great. I don't think I'll need to take these if the images are good enough."

Lachlan nodded, and I could now see the curiosity burgeoning in his eyes. "Can I ask what you're planning to do with this information?"

My lips parted, and my brain scrambled like a hamster on a squeaky wheel. "I…I'm just trying to paint a picture in my mind, you know?"

"Right." But Lachlan's gaze suggested that he didn't buy it. I wanted too much detail for simple curiosity's sake.

"Okay," I said as embarrassment once again heated my cheeks, "I've caught a mild case of your obsession with Blackmouth's history. I'm thinking of writing a paper for my history class on it."

His expression cleared and his face was taken over by a gleam of excitement. "Why didn't you just say so?"

But before I could answer properly, he was barreling forward. "I could help you with it, I've got more than the local museum even has. I could give you all sorts of fascinating points, the whole timeline." He made a sweeping gesture with his hand before getting up and going to his bookcase. "Half of this shelf alone is jammed with Blackmouth and Highland history…."

I let Lachlan go on for a while. It was mildly interesting, actually, but mostly I didn't have the heart to cut off his enthusiasm when he was on a roll. Before I left Lachlan's place I'd been informed of Blackmouth's place in Jacobite history, its main clans, how its residents had suffered over the years, and more than I'd ever need to know about the movement of common medieval commodities such as oatmeal and beef, and diseases that sprang from spoiled grain. My head was whirling as Lachlan led me to the front door.

"Sorry, I got a bit carried away," Lachlan said as he retrieved my coat from his front closet. "I've kept you up."

"Don't be silly, you've been so helpful," I replied, stifling a yawn.

"Let me drive you back to the castle."

"That's really sweet, but I love the walk."

"You're sure?"

I nodded. In truth, I was tired, and the big hill leading back up to Blackmouth Castle was daunting after a long day. But now that I had the location of the old jail, I wasn't planning to go straight home.

I took in Lachlan's profile, the shadow of a beard on his cheek, the soft lips, and my breath caught momentarily in my throat. He threw me another one of those megawatt smiles as he helped me with my coat.

I zipped up my coat and ignored the warm feeling growing in my belly.

Our gazes caught on one another's like burrs to wool and my mouth went dry. Seconds ticked by until I found my voice. "Thanks for your help."

His blue eyes softened. "It's my pleasure, Georjie. Really."

I almost stopped breathing when it occurred to me that I might get that kiss he'd threatened. Was I ready for that? Swiftly, I admitted that I was, but then he was holding the door open for me and the moment was over.

CHAPTER EIGHTEEN

I headed toward where the patch of green had been on the map, as it was only a little out of the way. Easy enough to swing out and loop back toward home. Twenty minutes later, I found it--more of a vacant lot than a park--sandwiched between a row of townhouses, a playground at the back, and the post office.

"Here goes nothing." I squatted and clawed out a nice chunk of dirt. "Show me the old jail on the night Daracha got out."

A grainy black and white image flickered to life, overlaying the view of the playground. I could barely make out the shapes of the swing set and monkey bars through the residual of the ugly stone building. It sat there like a toad, with bars on its narrow windows and a doorway I'd have to duck to enter. Definitely a medieval prison.

Two men stood at the entrance where the low wooden door stood ajar. Blackness yawned from within. The men were having a conversation I couldn't hear. One of them wore a tunic with the hood dropped back. A rudimentary belt around his waist held a ring of keys. So the jailer, then.

When I looked closely at the grainy image of the other man, I gave a start of recognition. He'd been the man who'd pushed the wheelbarrow.

The men made an exchange. A blurry lump passed from the wheelbarrow pusher into the jailer's hand, and something small enough to hide in the jailer's hand was passed back.

The jailer put his back to the wall and the other fellow slipped inside the building. For a while, nothing happened. The jailer leaned against the stone wall and waited.

After several minutes passed, the other man emerged carrying the limp body of a woman. There were stains on the light-colored fabric. So she'd already been unconscious before she'd left the jail, or dead; there was nothing to distinguish the two, other than I thought I could see the woman's bosom rise and fall, but the images were unclear so I couldn't say for sure. I squinted, trying to make out more details. I caught dark marks on the woman's neck as the man shifted her weight in his arms. Bruises?

Strangulation had been one of the causes of death the mortician had listed. I gave a shiver and shifted under my coat, trying to warm up.

I took a surprised leap backward when a wagon came trundling onto the scene, driven by the same woman I'd seen in the first residual. I recognized her easily from the way her shawl was tied. The wagon was pulled by a donkey, and a wheelbarrow tipped on its side lay in the cart.

The men exchanged words I couldn't hear. The body of the woman--I couldn't help but think of her as Daracha by now--was unceremoniously dumped into the back of the wagon before the man climbed up onto the rickety seat and took the reins. A moment later and they disappeared into the shadows.

The scene flickered and winked out before winking back

to the beginning with the two men standing at the door in conversation.

I dropped the earth, knowing what happened next.

As I made my way back to the castle, I barely noticed my surroundings. My mind was busy processing what I'd seen. So the jailer was part of the conspiracy. He'd probably been bought off, and since the woman was a supposed witch, he could claim she'd either bewitched him or she'd magicked her way out of the cell. Whatever embarrassment or humiliation he'd had to endure as a result of failing at his job would have been offset by whatever the man had given him, probably money.

But what about Daracha? Had the man killed her in the jail? If he had, why bother going to all the trouble of taking the body up the site of Blackmouth Castle and walling her up? Why not just leave her corpse for the law to deal with, or bury her in an unmarked grave? It was weird. I now understood what had happened, but not why.

I remembered Lachlan talking about Daracha Guthrie, and how the name was from farther south and that women didn't have much cause to travel in those days. So what had she been doing up here?

I was nearly home and felt bone-weary. Making my way to the side entrance, I deposited my boots and jacket in the closet and headed up the stairs toward my bedroom. Halfway down the hall, I heard a creak and stopped, listening.

After having spent several hours every day doing my schoolwork in the front parlor which overlooked the driveway, I recognized the sounds of its floor boards. Someone was in there. I passed my room and Jasher's room and poked my head into the large sitting room.

The dark silhouette of a man pacing across the room crossed one of the windows.

"Jasher?"

He had his head down and was rubbing both of his hands along the sides of his face in agitation. He looked up.

"Georjie!" He crossed to me immediately and pulled me into a hug. "I've been waiting for you to get home. Is everything okay?"

I heard his heart pounding beneath his chest.

"Everything is fine with me. What about you?"

He pulled me into the parlor and had me sit on one of the sofas beside him. His face was a visage full of shifting shadows.

"I came from the clinic. Visiting hours are over at nine. I was looking for you and calling you."

"I forgot my cell phone. I went to see Lachlan. Why?"

He took one of my hands between both of his own, like a sandwich, and pressed on it. "It's Evelyn. She's weaker, Georjie."

My heart dropped into my stomach and I closed my eyes.

"You have to help her, Georjie," Jasher pleaded, giving my hand a little shake.

"I tried to rouse her when I found her, but she didn't wake up."

"You said her heartbeat seemed stronger," he said in a rush, "and that some color returned to her cheeks."

"Yeah, she did seem a little better. But she never opened her eyes, never responded."

"Please try again. Whatever is wrong with her, it's not normal."

"By not normal, you mean it's supernatural."

Jasher nodded vigorously. "Exactly. The doctors don't know what to do. They're making phone calls and adjusting her IV, but they're clueless. Worse than that, they're scared. I can see it in their eyes." He released my hand and raked through his hair again.

"I'm sorry, Jash."

"I'm more sorry for her poor parents." He turned to face me again in the dark and it seemed his eyes were vast misty orbs of terror. "What if she dies?"

"She won't die." My voice was full of confidence, but how was I supposed to know what was going to happen?

Jasher took my other hand and began to speak again but stopped. He lifted my hand and peered at it. "Why are you so dirty?" He looked up, hopeful. "Did you see something new?"

I let out a long sigh. "Not really. I mean, I have one more piece of the puzzle, but no real answers."

"Tell me. Everything that's happening is connected." Hope was rising on his face like the first touch of dawn's light. "It has to do with that bloody shadow-man. I know it."

"Maybe, but he wasn't in the residual I saw tonight." I told Jasher what I'd seen and he listened without interrupting me. After I finished, the night's silence filled the parlor until Jasher spoke again.

"Still doesn't make much sense. Why would they bother walling her up?"

I stifled a yawn. "I don't know Jash, but I'm exhausted. Can we talk about this more in the morning?"

"Will you go to the clinic first thing? Visiting hours start at eight. I have to work, but you could go and check in on her? Try to help her again?" The hope on Jasher's face was like small blades slicing across my heart.

"Of course I will, Jasher."

Jasher let out a sigh and got to his feet. "Good," he whispered as we went through the door and into the hallway. "Because I think you might be the only one who can solve this, Georjie." He faced me in the dark and put a hand on my cheek. "You're a Wise. If you can't help her, no one can."

There it was again.

We said goodnight and Jasher slipped into his bedroom. The door closed with a light snick. I stood in the hall for a moment before heading to my own room. I could almost feel the weight of expectation and hope laying its dead weight over my shoulders. Jasher's words echoed in my mind as I got ready for bed and slipped beneath the coverlet.

If you can't help her, no one can.

I fell into a fitful sleep with those words repeating themselves over and over in my mind, echoing off the walls of my skull and filling all my empty spaces.

* * *

I arrived at the clinic shortly after breakfast and checked in at reception. The same woman who had been working the night I'd been interrogated in the waiting room was behind the desk.

"I don't suppose you can update me on Evelyn's condition?" I asked.

"No change, as you'll see for yourself."

I sighed and handed her clipboard back. "I was afraid of that. They wouldn't consider moving her to a larger center, would they? A facility with more doctors experienced with comas?" I was merely fishing with this question. I didn't want to show up for visiting hours one day (and maybe with some new idea of how to help Evelyn) only to find out they'd moved her to Inverness or Edinburgh.

"That's her parents' call," the receptionist answered, "and they want to keep their daughter close. There isn't anything a larger facility can do for her that we can't do here. She's sleeping, not cancerous or in need of some risky and complicated surgical procedure."

"And you've never seen a case like this one before?"

"I've seen comas before, if that's what you mean, but usually they're the result of head trauma or a stroke or an infection in the brain. But Evelyn hasn't suffered any of that."

Her look grew sly. "If anyone might be able to shed more light on what might have happened to her, it would be you, Miss Sutherland. You're the one who found her."

Eurgh. It was like a broken record. "She was asleep when I found her," I replied, fighting to keep the irritation out of my voice, "in the same state she's in now."

The receptionist shrugged. "In a grave hole, though. Why do you think that is?"

"I have no idea."

The receptionist nodded, but her look was calculating. "Well, at least she's got plenty of friends. No one else in this clinic gets visitors as frequently as she does. Go on back, she hasn't moved."

"Thanks." I made my way through the open double doors and took the first left, and then a right. Evelyn's room was at the end of a long hallway and positioned near a set of emergency doors leading to the back parking lot. Being on a dead end meant her room was quiet and didn't see much traffic.

Several people had left bouquets for her. A vase on her bedside table held a spray of daisies and sunflowers, while a glass bowl on the dresser underneath the wall-mounted television held a profusion of white and pale green roses. The room smelled like summer.

"Hi, Evie." I shed my hat and jacket, draping them over the seat near the door. Walking around her bed, I sat in a chair that looked like it had been part of the hospital fixtures since the forties.

Evelyn lay with her hands folded on her stomach. Her right arm had a shunt with an IV drip attached. Her dark curly hair splayed out on the white pillowcase and her skin was only a shade darker than the sheets. She looked thinner. I watched her chest rise and fall, noting her shallow breathing. Putting two fingers inside her wrist to feel for her pulse had me closing my eyes in dread. Jasher was right. She was getting weaker.

"I don't suppose you might feel like waking up and having a conversation with me today, would you?" I took one of her hands and gently massaged the palm. "There are a lot of people worried about you, Evie. I know your parents are here every day, beside themselves with worry. And I hear Jasher's been reading to you. I hope…" My voice cracked as I fought back tears. "I hope you know that he loves you."

I hung my head for a while, feeling her faint pulse and listening to her breath.

I reached for a tissue and dabbed at my eyes. "Listen, uh, I have some abilities…you could call them gifts, I guess. I've been able to help a few people to heal faster in the past, and while I did try to help you when I first found you, you still didn't wake up. I don't know what's wrong, but I'm going to try again. If you can hear me or feel my intentions, I want you to do your best to wake up. Okay? Work with me, Evie."

I felt stupid talking out loud like this, but what if she could hear me? What if, inside that peacefully sleeping exterior, she was screaming, struggling to wake up?

I closed my eyes and let my focus drift inside and then down, down, down, through the concrete layers beneath my feet and into the layers of earth and soil underneath that. Slowing my breathing, I called on all of the healing qualities I could find, drawing the positive energy through my own body and into Evelyn. It was like sucking something too thick through a straw, but the energy did flow, I could feel it warming my limbs and strengthening my resolve.

Wake up, Evie, I thought. *Please, wake up. Come back to us.*

Evelyn's skin warmed beneath my touch. Her breathing deepened.

Not breaking our connection, I opened my eyes and was

pleased to see a flush of color in her cheeks, her lips pinked up, even her hair seemed to thicken and grow a little.

"Evelyn?"

My eyes were glued to those dark lashes against that pale skin, willing them to flutter open, willing for her to animate, to look over at me and smile.

Nothing.

I released the flow of energy moving through me and let out a long sigh.

"What a happy coincidence," said a male voice from the doorway.

I looked up. "Lachlan! Hey."

He came into the room and took the chair on the other side of Evie's bed. "Any better? She's got some color in her cheeks today." His gaze skimmed Evelyn's still form. "Looks thinner though."

"Yeah. No change, I'm afraid. Unless it's to lose more weight."

Lachlan took Evie's other hand and let out a long breath. "I've known her since we were babies. She feels so close, yet so far away."

"I know. I'm sorry. This must be hell for you."

He nodded, his eyes misting. "Worse for her parents though. Her mom sits with her every day, her dad plays guitar for her. They're hoping that familiar things will help her get better."

I nodded. "Sure can't hurt."

Lachlan reached across Evelyn's body and took my hand. The three of us were connected now, a little ring of hope. "What happened that night, Georjie?" His voice was low, quiet. "You can tell me."

"I told your dad everything already, Lachlan." I held his gaze, not flinching as he probed for...whatever he was looking for. "Why? What do *you* think happened?"

Lachlan's gaze flickered with something. Suspicion? Curiosity? "I don't know, I just think something really strange is happening and it all started with that body we found." He counted off events on his fingers. "First, the body. Then the night the dogs went crazy, which was the night before the day we realized Evelyn went missing. Now, the body's actually been taken from the morgue. Did you know that?"

I nodded. "Your dad told me."

"Really?" He recoiled in surprise. "When did you see my dad?"

I really didn't want to have to feed Lachlan the same lies I'd told his father. "It doesn't matter, Lachlan," I said, giving him a reassuring smile. "I just know, and I agree with you. It is weird."

He didn't even know the half of it. Only Jasher and I knew about the eldritch thing. Oh, and Laec, for all the help he was being.

Lachlan gave me a small smile, his cheek dimpled, and my secrets almost burst out of me. "Sure. We don't have to talk about it."

We sat quietly together in our thoughts until Lachlan broke the silence again with, "You coming to the bonfire tonight?"

"Bonfire?"

"Yeah, every year towards the end of March, the town hosts a bonfire and this year it's today. You didn't see the posters around town?"

"I've been a little distracted." Welcome to the understatement of the year.

"Well, you should come. It'll take your mind off things for one night. They serve hot cider and haggis, give pony rides to the kids, there's a band and a dance, and of course a few big fires along the beach. Every year some stupid teenagers set off firecrackers and get the dogs barking and the old ladies swearing. It'll be fun."

"Sounds great." I laughed. "Old Scottish ladies swearing, wouldn't miss that for the world."

"Bring Jasher, too, if he's up for it. That guy is really taking this hard. He comes here multiple times a day some days. He puts on a brave face but I can tell he's bleeding. Gavin's a little concerned because he's not at the jobsite as much as he should be. I told him to cut the guy some slack. He looks like the walking dead some days. You know, no sleep, too much self-medicating."

Jasher's words from the night before began the echo-dance around in my head again. I squeezed Evelyn's hand gently and sent her silent words of comfort.

I'll find a way, Evie. Just don't go dying on us.

"Hang in there, Evie," Lachlan whispered, as if he could hear my thoughts. "We'll figure this out."

The 'we' in his utterance warmed my heart. Even if I was the one with the secret supernatural powers, it was nice not to be alone.

CHAPTER NINETEEN

*T*he bonfire was exactly what Lachlan had promised. It seemed like the entire town came out bundled up in woolen coats and hats and all randomly breaking into songs I couldn't really understand. Kids ran amok along the beach while the bonfire, piled high with wood dried indoors all year for the occasion (I was told every family in town contributed to the blaze) grew larger by the hour. There was something comforting about a big fire on the beach with clusters of people chatting and drinking from steaming mugs. Dogs played tug-of-war with driftwood while kids were organized to play games like potato-sack races, and showed off their skills with the bagpipe. I couldn't say much for their skills but there was nothing wrong with their enthusiasm. Collection points for various charities had been set up around the beach and the park. There was even a pot for Evelyn's family.

I'd never be able to look at fire without thinking of my friend Saxony, a fire mage with a small fire literally living inside of her. What I'd seen her do with flames was seared into my memory forever, pun intended. I was seated on a log near the fire, staring into the flames and enjoying the crackle and snap when Lachlan found me.

"You came." He stepped over the log and sat beside me. He wore a tartan hat with a red pompom on the top.

"I said I would." I looked over at him as he crossed his arms over his chest and stared into the fire. "Nice hat."

Lachlan dimpled. "Make fun if you wish, but this tam has been in my family for over fifty years." It was threadbare and patched. In spite of its shabby state and bright colors, it gave Lachlan a surprisingly masculine air.

"Looks older than that, like God wore it while he created the highlands," I teased.

"It's been through a lot. Sat on a lot of heads, passed through a lot of hands."

"But not a washing machine?"

Lachlan knocked the back of my own hat forward so it fell over my eyes. Laughing, I pushed it back into place and we stared into the fire in silence, listening to the kids laughing and screaming in the distance.

"Do you think Jasher will come?" Lachlan asked. "Guy needs a little fun in his life."

I shrugged. "He'll be at the clinic until visiting hours are over. Maybe he'll come when they kick him out. I did invite him."

"I think *everyone* invited him. The story of the Irish bloke in love with the comatose Scottish lassie has gone through town like the flu."

"I think it's nice," I murmured. "Romantic."

Lachlan glanced at me through lowered lashes. "Speaking of romantic, how about I bring you a nice mug of mulled wine? I'll even grab you an extra cinnamon stick."

"How gallant. Thank you." I shivered and tucked my chin

into the neck of my jacket. "The cold on the beach goes right through you, even with the fire. My front is burning but my backside is a popsicle."

Lachlan planted a kiss on my forehead so suddenly that it startled me. "I believe I can fix that." He got up and stalked toward the drinks kiosk on the other side of the park.

Gazing through the top of the firelight and into the trees beyond the beach and beyond the park, I caught a flash of white light. It was a strange place to see light. The cluster of trees to the northwest was a scrubby strip of forest that ran parallel to the coastline for a several kilometers before connecting to the queen's land. Thinking the firelight was playing with my eyesight, I stood up and squinted.

The white light brightened and glimmered, a blue-white glow in a vaguely diamond shape. It seemed to dance and flicker in a joyful way, like it wanted to join the party.

A spunkie. I smiled and thought of Evelyn.

It was like the light knew I recognized it and flashed brightly like a ship's storm light in a gale. As I watched, the diamond shape stretched out to the sides, thinning, as though growing arms.

"What the..."

One of the arms beckoned to me. I rubbed my eyes and looked around. Lachlan was standing in line at the drinks stand. Kids and adults were scattered everywhere. A few folks stood a short distance from the fire, chatting in small groups. No one appeared to have noticed the white light.

It flashed again, then bobbed up and down like a cartoon character eager to make friends. It beckoned to me again, then winked behind a tree. The top of the diamond appeared from behind the tree like it wanted to play peek-a-boo.

I left the fire and strode across the beach toward the cluster of trees. At first, I just wanted to get a better look. I had no intention of entering the trees or following it. Weren't there fairy tales that warned against following will-o-the-wisps? Then again, weren't will-o-the-wisps also known for helping lost people find their way out of the wilderness?

I approached the tree line, close to where I'd first seen the light. It was now farther in the trees, still winking, still beckoning. It projected a kind of innocent curiosity.

A thought ballooned in my mind: *What if it's trying to tell me something? What if it can help Evelyn?*

Just a few more steps into the trees, and if it kept drawing me farther and farther from the party, I'd leave. I wasn't interested in a wild goose chase. I stepped between the trees and went several yards into the woods. Gorse plucked at my pants and the ground made a sucking sound under my boots. The flickering light bobbed in what looked like appreciation and drifted farther into the trees.

"Okay, I'm here," I said. "What do you want?"

It flickered again, the white light turning a soft blue, like the light of a full moon on a cold winter's night. It drifted away.

"I'm not going any farther," I called. "You're lucky I came this far. What's up?"

A hand grabbed my elbow. With a cry of fright, I whirled, hands up and ready to defend myself. Responding to my magic, long, ropy vines of ivy unraveled from nearby trees, moving lightning fast. They whipped around in the air like bullwhips, snapping menacingly. But they halted when I saw…

"Laec?" I sputtered, my heart racing.

My vines curled in the air, making a loose cocoon around us, like they wanted to watch.

Laec's body was relaxed but his fae eyes darted around at

the vines and then found my face. "Remind me not to get on your bad side."

The vines retreated, drifting away to wind themselves around the tree trunks.

"You came to find me?" I put a hand over my thumping heart.

Laec's expression grew serious. "I'm here to tell you that there's only one thing that will help Evelyn, and you have to do it soon."

I grabbed his shoulders with a fierce energy, hope taking flight in my chest like a startled bird. "Anything."

"Listen." His hands cupped my elbows and he stepped close enough for me to see the flecks of green in his eyes. "Tomorrow night there's a party at the queen's residence. You have to steal the antidote."

"What?" I shot him a wild look. "Dude, the queen lives in London. What makes you think I can get into a party she's hosting without getting arrested, let alone steal something from her?"

Laec rolled his eyes. "Not your queen, *my* queen. Queen Elphame."

The name circled my head in the air like an insect. It was familiar but I couldn't quite remember where I'd heard it before. "Queen Elphame?"

"Meet me in the woods west of Blackmouth Castle tomorrow night at midnight. I'll help you."

There was the sound of a twig snapping behind Laec.

"Georjie?" It was Lachlan, and he was close.

"Don't be late," Laec hissed. He gripped my shoulders and traded places with me like we were doing a dance, before spinning me and shoving me toward the sound of Lachlan's voice.

I staggered forward, feeling annoyed again at the way he'd manhandled me. I turned around to give him a piece of my mind, but of course, he was already gone. I gave a groan.

"That's getting old, you know!" I cried into the darkness.

"What's getting old?" Lachlan came through the trees bearing two mugs of steaming mulled wine. Two cinnamon sticks protruded from one of the mugs.

"A man of his word," I said with a smile before taking the cup and bringing it to my lips. "Mmmm, that's delicious."

He wasn't sidetracked. "Who were you talking to?"

"A spunkie." I grinned and headed for the beach. My heart felt anxious, but light and hopeful. Laec was going to help after all. The thought of seeing Evelyn's eyes open made me feel like I was walking on air. I kept at bay my fears about breaking into some fae queen's castle; I'd deal with that when the time came. Laec wouldn't suggest such a thing if he didn't think it was possible...I hoped.

"You saw a spunkie?" Lachlan sounded so enthusiastic about this that I blinked at him in surprise. We emerged from the bushes and walked down the beach toward the party.

"You make it sound like I won the lottery. It's just swamp gas. Evelyn told me about them when I first got here. Now I've seen all the local attractions and can leave Scotland satisfied."

His happy expression faltered. "You're leaving?"

"I was just kidding."

"Oh." He looked relieved and wrapped an arm around my shoulders.

I stopped walking and turned to face him. The smell of his soap drifted into my nose.

"Good, because you're not allowed to leave until..." He pulled me close against him and surprised me with a kiss on the mouth.

His lips were warm and soft and my heart felt like melting butter sliding down my insides and pooling in my pelvis. As he deepened the kiss, my toes began to curl inside my boots.

Catcalls down the beach broke us apart and we looked to see a cluster of young people making kissing noises and whooping.

Lachlan smiled down at me, his arm tightening around my waist. I held my mug of wine away so I didn't spill it, while I wrapped my other arm around his neck.

"I was wondering when you were going to make good on that promise." I sounded breathless. His face was still so close to mine. My lips were tingling, my pulse racing.

"Kept you in suspense, did I?"

"A little," I admitted. "Come on, you can't tell a girl you plan to kiss her and then ghost on the promise like that."

"I'm sorry," he replied, and I saw from his expression that he really was.

I told him to shush and pulled him down for another kiss. The kids redoubled their whoops of delight and when I lifted a foot in the air behind me, they burst into laughter. When I released Lachlan, we were both out of breath. He put his forehead to mine and closed his eyes briefly, before we began walking again.

"I wanted to do it a long time ago, but with everything that's been happening...there was never a good time." He looked down at me as we approached the fire, the heat and light building on our faces. "If you don't mind me saying so, I think you know more than you let on." The words came out on a murmur.

My stomach lurched. "What makes you think that?"

He lifted a shoulder. "Just a feeling."

I opened my mouth to protest when he lifted a hand. "It's okay, Georjie. You don't *have* to tell me anything, but I want you to know that I'm here to help. I wish you'd let me. You don't need to go through whatever you're going through alone."

My vision blurred as my eyes misted. "Thanks, Lachlan. That means more than I can say."

He planted a kiss beside my nose and I turned my face up and offered my lips again.

CHAPTER TWENTY

"How do I look?" I stepped out from behind the thick foliage where I'd swapped my own clothes for the 'costume' Laec had brought for me. Standing before him in a glade flooded with moonlight, I held my arms out and my head straight. A sprightly drumbeat permeated the woods and I turned in time to the music, letting him observe my disguise.

Laec considered me thoughtfully, his eyes skimming me from head to toe. "You'll do. Just need to…"

He came to stand behind me, his bare feet silent on the fallen leaves and near-frozen earth of the forest. I suppressed a shiver when I felt his fingers in my hair, lifting, tying, fiddling. He stepped around me again and surveyed his handiwork from the front. His assessment concluded with my eyes, where his gaze locked with mine. Half his mouth lifted in a cocky smile.

"You'll fit right in, just don't talk to anyone. That accent." He shuddered.

I snorted. "Yours isn't exactly angels' music either." In truth, Laec's accent was lyrical and lovely, but I wasn't going to give him the satisfaction of letting him know that. Damn fae hunk was arrogant enough already.

I looked down at my getup, which included bare feet, and frowned. Not that I didn't like it, it was gorgeous. Laec had presented me with a gown the color of dawn. The hem, which hit at the ankle, was yellow. By my knees it had darkened to orange, at my waist it was a soft purple which transitioned into midnight blue at the chest, where it ended. No straps, and only a fine woven belt made of tree fibers kept it cinched above my breasts. A second belt hugged my waist. The gown was gauzy and as light as spider's silk.

I said, "I'm going to freeze in this."

"Are you freezing now?" Laec asked as he fiddled further with my hair.

"No." Huh. How about that. Winter in the Scottish Highlands and I was outdoors, barefoot, and wearing something suitable for the tropics, yet I felt perfectly comfortable.

"That's because you're in Stavarjak now."

My head snapped up. "I'm where?"

"Relax, you've been here before," he replied absently, eyes on whatever creation he was making on the top of my head. "When we first met."

I put my hands on Laec's cheeks and forced him to look at me. "Explain."

"Stavarjak is a fae province. You're here because you're with me and I don't have time to explain the politics or the physics. You have to focus." He made some final touch, then whacked both my shoulders like I was a soldier. After a nod of satisfaction, he turned and strode through the woods.

I stood there with my head cocked for a breath or two. When he'd whacked me, the pressure in my eardrums had increased subtly and there was now a smell in the air that hadn't been there before. Realizing Laec was nearly out of view, I dashed after him.

"Did you do something back there?"

Laec replied over his shoulder, "Keep up."

Trying not to be restricted by the tunic, I picked it up and bunched it at my hips with my hands to free my legs.

"Don't ruin the outfit, either." Laec didn't turn around when he said this, but it was as if he'd spoken the words to my face, so clearly could I hear them. "Fyfa wouldn't appreciate it. With any luck, I'll have those back in her closet and she'll be none the wiser."

"You took them without asking?"

"She's taller than you, but otherwise you're roughly the same."

I almost stopped walking. "She's *taller?*" There were some exceptionally tall women out there, but I'd never met any woman taller than myself.

"Try not to sweat or step in mud."

"Has anyone ever told you you're supremely annoying? How much taller? When can I meet her? Will she be at the party?

"And *I'm* the annoying one?"

I opened my mouth to retort when the rhythmic music drifting through the trees grew loud. Lights glimmered like fireflies in the distance. As the forest thinned, a bulky shape emerged, blacking out part of the starlit sky. I stopped walking altogether when a familiar castle came into view. Even Laec paused at the edge of the trees to let me take in what I was seeing.

"That's Blackmouth," I gasped. "But, not."

The lay of the land was nearly identical, the turrets and windows and features of the castle were the same but this version was something out of a fantasy. Flowering vines of species I didn't recognize hugged the corners and framed the windows. Colored faery lights flashed and swirled, darted and danced about, sometimes there and sometimes not. I hadn't seen fairies since I left Canada and the sight warmed my whole torso and raised gooseflesh on my arms.

"Faeries," I breathed.

My wonder expanded as my gaze swept the castle balconies, the terraces, the grounds. Tall, slender forms stood bathed in shadow and light, talking, laughing, sipping from cups and eating. Drums and flutes filled the air with haunting but heart-lifting music. A fat moon rose in the distance, unencumbered by the banks of clouds I'd become so accustomed to.

"How is this possible?"

"Think of the castle like a rivet." Laec's voice came next to my ear again, soft, nearly a whisper.

"A rivet."

"The without and the within exist on different planes, normally inaccessible to one another. But there are a few places in the world, Blackmouth Castle being one of them, where the mantle between our worlds overlaps. It becomes penetrable to some." He gestured toward the slender silhouettes of the partiers decorating the castle. "Like some of them." He looked at me. "And you."

I was so astounded I could only stand there and take in the view before me.

"The important thing is that you act as though you belong here. No one should bother you, though some will want to talk with you. Smile and move on. The vial you're looking for is kept in the queen's apartments on the top floor of the eastern-most turret."

"Gavin's library."

"The basic structure of the castle is the same, but once you're inside, you'll see how things are different. Try not to lose your way."

My gaze flew to his face in alarm. "I thought you were coming with me."

"I'll distract the queen's guards for you. You'll only have a few minutes. The vial should be easy to spot, it'll be the only one with clear liquid inside."

My heart had begun to pound hard as what we'd come to do began to sink in. "No, wait. This is crazy."

"Do you want to save your friend?"

"Of course, but…"

"Then you must. It's the only way."

"Why can't you get the vial?"

"Would *you* rather distract the guards?" Laec's tone had turned impatient.

My mouth felt like a desert, my tongue a roll of carpet. I shook my head. "I guess not."

"Okay then, let's go."

I felt his hand at my lower back and my legs locked up. "Wait, just wait a minute. I'm not ready."

Laec sighed audibly.

Ignoring him, I turned away and moved into the cover of the trees. Closing my eyes, I took deep breaths and visualized the interior of the castle. Going in through the back––the nearest entrance––meant passing through a wide, exposed foyer with very tall ceilings. A sweeping staircase leading to the second level went off to the left and to the right. I would have to take the right one, then make my way down four different corridors until I found the narrow door opening into a spiral staircase. At the top of the staircase, another narrow door opened into a circular room with windows overlooking the maze and the east gardens. Once there… well, I didn't know what would happen. Find the vial, take it, and get out.

"Georjie, the night isn't getting any younger."

I opened my eyes and took in the handsome, red-headed fae.

"I don't know whether to thank you or throttle you."

He gave a grim smile and swept his hand toward the party, adding a little bow. "You'll be in and out before anyone knows who the pretty blond is." He dropped his hand and cocked his head, eyes sweeping me again.

A hand at my lower back, which was not Laec's because he was standing where I could see him, shoved me forward. I gasped and glanced behind me but there was no one there. Laec hooked his arm through mine and I felt myself being dragged toward the castle.

Squeezing my eyes tightly shut, I thought, *for Evelyn.*

Fixing a serene expression on my features and listening as Laec began babbling in a language I'd never heard before, we approached the partiers in the garden.

It was impossible not to stare. Beautifully dressed fae gathered in clusters on the broad stone terrace that lay between the maze and the castle. They were tall, slender, and dressed in flowing clothing. I found it impossible not to rubberneck. Their hair came in every color of the rainbow, and their eyes were bright and too big for their faces, just like Laec's. Their ears were pointed, but varied wildly in size from tiny to long and sweeping out to the sides. Skin glimmered with a pearlescent sheen and clothing was minimal. There was no footwear, only some foot and ankle jewelry. The smell of flowers filled the air and I noticed exquisite blossoms around which tiny faery lights danced and from which little birds sucked nectar.

"Put your eyes back in their sockets," came Laec's voice beside my ear. His mouth continued to form those foreign words and his expression didn't falter. He appeared to be walking with a friend and discussing some pleasant topic or relaying some delightful story.

Fixing my eyes on the ground ahead of us and cocking my head slightly to show I was listening, I let Laec lead me through the party-goers and in through the open double doors. Avoiding eye contact with everyone we passed, I watched my feet as they stepped over the threshold and onto a fantastically colorful tile floor, which was nothing like the pale gray flagstone of Blackmouth.

Colors swirled, stripes and flowers, vine patterns and constellations of blossoms passed beneath us as Laec––my arm tightly looped through his––led me to the wide staircase. We began to ascend. Every stair was made of a different pattern of tile, it was a little like the hand-painted tiles Saxony had shown me when she'd returned from Italy. Only these were more elaborate, more colorful, more intricate. I wished I could go to my knees and look at them all more closely, as each one was its own unique piece of art.

Up, up, up the steps we went, passing clusters of seated fae partiers deep in conversation. In my periphery I caught a few glances but no eyes lingered on us too long; no one seemed suspicious. At the top of the steps, Laec released me.

"You know where to go." That voice near my ear again.

My hands and armpits had begun to sweat. My forehead and the back of my neck felt damp. My expression fixed, I turned down the long corridor, weaving through laughing partygoers. I overheard conversations in that foreign tongue Laec had used, but I also heard accented English words as I walked the hall like I had every right to be there.

The castle felt surreal. It was the same and yet not the same. I passed paintings, fountains, and sculptures I longed to stop and take in. Open doors drew my glance as I passed, where fae lounged and drank and conversed. It was a world I longed to explore, filled with creatures I longed to know. Some rooms had their own musicians, but the music within matched the music played elsewhere in the castle, never out of tune, always in key.

At the end of the corridor came the narrow doorway leading to the spiral staircase, and here I stopped, because there was no staircase. Poking my head into the circular tower and looking down, I saw a well-lit drop ending in a glimmering pool of blue water. It swirled and swirled, slowly and lazily, with what looked like colored petals drifting and turning in the current. Looking up revealed a clear view of the night sky and flashes of tiny colored fairies. Though I'd reached what appeared to be a dead end, the sight of the little fae made me smile. A tiny green light, half the size of my pinky fingernail, came to bob in front of my face. A feminine form was barely visible inside the light.

"Hello, little one." I held out my hand without expectation and was pleasantly surprised when the little green light landed on the pad of skin between the base of my thumb and my forefinger. Soft as a butterfly's touch and with a little glow of heat, the fairy landed and took off, landed and took off.

I was about to ask what her name was when she lifted off for the final time and drifted down toward the water. When she hit the level of my foot she stopped completely. Kneeling down and putting my hand out, I felt a solid but invisible surface.

Sweeping my hands slowly out before me, my fingertips crunched up against something hard. I traced the shape vertically until it flattened again.

"Stairs." I smiled at the little green light. "Thank you."

The fairy winked like a firefly, then fluttered out the door and down the hall behind me.

I continued up the invisible stairs, keeping my eyes on the walls and trying not to let vertigo overtake me. It was disconcerting to have a four-story drop visible below my feet. Arriving at the doorway, I stepped into a hall I could see, with a sigh of relief.

Pausing there, my heart leapt into my throat when I caught sight of two tall fae males standing on either side of the door leading to the queen's chamber. I almost turned around and went back down the stairs, cursing Laec under my breath, when the two guards shared a startled look and went running down the hall in the opposite direction. I hadn't heard or seen whatever the guards had seen, but I knew it wasn't a coincidence.

Heart pounding in my throat, I advanced on quiet feet and slipped inside the door the fae had left unguarded. The room before me had the same size and shape, the same windows and ceiling line as Gavin's library, but that was where the similarities ended. On one side, framed by two narrow windows, was a large bed dressed with bedding so light the fabric looked to be woven from clouds. More breezy looking textiles hung from the ceiling rafters on what had to be invisible wire, except that the reams of gauzy white rolled over lazily and drifted around as though they were actual clouds.

Opposite the bed was a wide dressing table with a mirror hovering above. Jewelry hung on invisible hooks, turning slowly like it was on display. Colored jewels sparkled subtly in the dim light, and rings orbited one another like tiny planets caught in one another's gravity. A shelf recessed in the paneling behind the dresser revealed a line of small vials, and it was toward these I went.

Had I not been terrified of getting caught, I would have explored every nook of the enchanted room, but already I could hear silvery voices in the hall. If they were the guards, there was no place to hide except for under the bed.

A vial in the middle caught my eye, as it contained a clear liquid. I reached for it but paused. Three vials down was another little diamond-shaped bottle with a crystalline liquid inside. Cursing Laec under my breath, my gaze darted between these two vials.

"Which one, Laec?" I whispered, hoping against hope that

he might hear me with his magic and his voice might appear beside my ear again.

"That depends," replied a soft voice that didn't belong to my fae assistant.

A shriek escaped my lips as I whirled around. I thrust my hands back against the dresser to prevent me from falling into it. My heart did a fantastic leap.

The statuesque fae woman standing in the open door-way——with one of the guards visible over her shoulder—— could not be anyone other than Queen Elphame herself.

Piles of glistening moon-colored hair made her even taller than she already was. A sparkling tiara as fine as spider's web perched on piles of soft curls. Her golden gown hugged every curve and gleamed where it swept over her breasts and hips. Her tapered fingers lay against her flat stomach, the nails long and white. Her eyes——naturally too large for her face and upturned at the outer corners——did not blink as she gazed at me without any expression. The irises were blue. A glint passed over them as if headlights had gone by and they darkened to violet.

I opened my mouth to say...I didn't know what, apologize, maybe. But she lifted a hand and passed it slowly, palm out, from one hip to the other. My mouth closed and my body stilled. Even my heart calmed and my eyelids felt heavy. I felt as though I'd had a little too much wine and I fought not to sag against the dresser.

She moved through the doorway and stepped aside, leaving room for the guard. He came to stand beside me and I felt a hand slip around my elbow. I stood there, helpless to do anything other than stare at the queen, as the guard held me and waited for orders.

I felt remarkably calm, considering I'd just been caught stealing red-handed from the queen's own bedroom. I wondered where Laec had gotten to and, almost without any feeling, wondered if perhaps he'd set a trap for me.

These fae had strong magic, magic I couldn't begin to understand. My own supernatural abilities were rooted in something I could wrap my mind around—soil, plants, trees. But to still my voice with a wave of her hand? That was something else entirely. I thought vaguely and without alarm, that I might never see my family or friends again.

"What were you after?" The queen's question slid past my eardrums like the warm furry body of a cat coming to lie beside you while you're mostly asleep.

The image of Evelyn rose in my mind, her pale face against her pillow, the dark circles pooling under her eyes. That glorious dark hair draped over the white fabric of her hospital sheets.

"My friend," I managed with great effort, the words coming out slowly and very calmly, almost in a monotone. "Evelyn...will...die."

I tried to lift my hand to point at the vials, but my hand only drifted up and slowed to a halt, as though trapped in cooling caramel.

The queen's amethyst eyes drifted around my face, then she slid aside as though standing on a moving platform.

"No one steals from Queen Elphame," she said, almost sweetly.

The guard's grip on my elbow tightened and I found myself being pulled toward the door. The edges of my vision darkened and everything grew soft. The ceiling drifted into view and something hooked me behind the knees.

I drifted, in some twilight zone, and watched with dull fascination as the ceilings of the castle floated by. A sensation of sinking slowly to the bottom of a deep lake overcame me. All became peaceful and I wanted nothing more than to sleep. So I let sleep take me.

CHAPTER TWENTY-ONE

*W*ith a gasp, I jolted awake, heart racing, eyes wide and searching. All of the fear and stress that I should have felt when I'd been caught stealing came rushing forward like a runaway train. Queen Elphame's magic had released me. My hands flew to my cheeks where my skin felt flushed and hot. My eyes pooled with unshed tears of humiliation, embarrassment, horror. Through a film of moisture, I looked around the room I'd woken in, felt the thin burlap mattress I'd woken upon.

I was in a cell and still dressed in the clothing Laec had loaned me. A bona fide stone prison cell with actual bars over the high, narrow window and crisscrossing the small square window in the middle of a thick-looking wooden door.

"This can't be happening." My voice was a whisper of terror. I couldn't be locked up in some fae prison.

But it was real. The stone was hard and cold, the mattress scratchy and rough against my skin. The air was cool and smelled of...actually, it smelled of moss and mulch and soil, a pleasant smell for a jail. The room was only large enough to accommodate the mattress, a bucket, and a few steps of space. The window was at least nine feet above the floor and through it a hint of morning light fell in a rectangle across the stones.

Getting to my feet, I crossed to the door and tried to peer through the small square window set in its middle. My view was another stone wall.

"Hello?" I called. "Is anyone there?"

Except for the distant sound of a bird cooing from well beyond the window, there was no reply. I tried a few more times and waited. Nothing. Grabbing the pail from the corner, I overturned it and stood on it, reaching for the window sill. My fingertips were still inches from the sill. I'd have to jump to catch it.

"Oh, this is a bad idea." I imagined missing the windowsill and landing crookedly on top of the pail, overturning it, and breaking an ankle.

I jumped anyway, hooking my fingers over the stone edge. Upper body strength had never been my strong suit. I was well acquainted with the embarrassment of never being able to do a single chin-up in gym class. My arms were too long and thin to pull my body weight up more than a few trembly inches. I never thought I'd mourn my decision to scorn weight lifting, leaving it to the shorter women who could easily gain the enviable firm curves of hard work. I had to admit, being able to do a few chin-ups would come in handy now.

Grunting and straining, I pulled with everything I had. True to form, my frame slid a few inches before my muscles refused to lift me any farther. Letting my arms go straight, I spread my legs apart so I wouldn't hit the pail and let myself drop. My kneecaps bashed against the wall, and I let out a few choice curses.

Pacing, I rubbed my temples as though a good old-fashioned massage would release the best ideas. I was an earth elemental, I had powers. There had to be a way out of this. And where was Laec? He'd gotten me into this mess, so I hoped he was trying to figure out a way to get me out of it. Did he even know I'd been caught? What had I been thinking? Of course I couldn't just sneak into some magic castle and steal whatever I wanted. Why had I let Laec convince me to try? I felt like an idiot.

My eye, attracted by morning light growing slowly brighter, caught on something small and green at the lip of the windowsill. A thin curl of vine––making its life where the seed had fallen––in the dirt between the stones.

I was about to rush forward and commune with the little plant when a rusty hinge squeaked somewhere beyond my cell. I went for the door instead.

"Hello? Is someone there? Please, I'd like to talk to Queen Elphame." Did that sound as ridiculous as I thought it sounded?

To my shock, her face slid into view. Those sparkling amethyst eyes locked on mine through the tiny square in the door.

"I'm so sorry, my…your majesty. I don't make a habit of stealing. I wouldn't have dreamed of doing it except that my friend is dying. Laec told me it was the only thing that could help her."

At the mention of Laec's name, those eyes widened a fraction, but her words weren't friendly. "Do you know what we do to thieves, here in Stavarjak?"

I swallowed. "I never even knew you existed."

"You say Laec put you up to this?"

"He said it was the only way. Please, please let me out so I can go home. I promise I'll never come back here."

At that the eyes did widen and something strange flickered in them just before they narrowed and grew cold. "We take even less kindly to liars than we do to thieves." She vanished from view.

"Wait! I'm not lying." Desperately, I wrapped my fingers around the bars and pulled my mouth to the window. "Please, I'm telling the truth!"

Hinges squeaked and a door slammed in answer.

I let out a groan and returned immediately to the tiny vine, possibly my only hope. Reaching for the slim green tendril, I bade it grow. It surged immediately in response, curling and stretching, its root thickening. Disturbed mortar dust sifted to the stone floor. The vine fattened. Buds poked out and grew into tight twists of leaves, which then burst open and spiraled outward.

The stones embracing the little vine shifted and more mortar crumbled. A crack shot down the wall, zigzagging between the bricks. The vine grew, and with it, my hope— but hope soon fizzled out when I sensed an impassable barrier had been struck at the outer wall. I knew I could use the vine to break a hole through my prison, plants were capable of incredible things when given a boost of energy from me. I'd held up an entire crumbling building with a single tree once, but this felt different. The barrier on the other side of this wall was magical, and there was no way my little vine was going to get through it. I could have it grow inward, as there was nothing stopping it from coming into my cell to join my imprisonment, but that wasn't helpful for escape.

When it was thicker than my wrist and strong enough to take my weight, I had it loop under my elbows and lift me to the window. Peering over the ledge, I saw a horizon of soft black forest and a lightening sky with soft rays of sun penetrating the tops of the trees. Flickers of colored light danced in the trees, flashing like fireflies.

Faeries.

"Help me, little fae," I whispered.

The colored lights paused simultaneously, then bobbed and weaved over the grounds toward the castle. Relief flooded me when I saw they were coming, but it was short-lived. The lights came to a halt several yards from the window. They bounced back and forth there like bugs hitting a window, then hovered, fluttering and waiting. They'd hit the barrier. I let out a long sigh.

"Thanks for trying. Got any ideas?"

In my mind was a distant echo, a name. A familiar one.

Fyfa, Fyfa, Fyfa. The little fae cries bounced around inside my skull. Then the colored lights drifted away. I hoped that meant they were going to get help.

I had the vine let me down to the floor and rubbed my arms and ribcage where it had been supporting my weight. The dawn was silent again, except for the calls of insects and birds. There wasn't even the sound of fae conversation; I guessed all the partiers had either gone home or fallen asleep.

Sitting on the mattress, I put my head in my hands and closed my eyes. I lost track of time and eventually reclined, staring at but not seeing the ceiling of my cell. I must have drifted off because when next I came to, proper daylight spilled through the narrow window. The sound of that squeaky hinge came through the bars of the door. I sat up just in time to see a plate of food shoved through the sliding doorway near the base of the door. The plate hovered there, as if waiting for me to take it. If the deliverer shoved the plate all the way through, the food would splat onto the floor. The plate shoved forward another inch and I darted forward to catch it before it fell.

"Thank you," I called.

No answer. Only the soft sounds of someone walking away.

Taking the plate back to the bed, I inspected the meal. A small green salad with little orange petals throughout, a dry potato with a crack down the middle letting steam escape, a brown bun, and a silvery gray sack I couldn't identify.

Balancing the plate on my knees, I picked up the sack. Its soft sides depressed as liquid sloshed inside. Using my thumbnail, I punctured the bag. A clear, odorless liquid trickled out. Water. I sucked at the bag greedily.

The meal was simple but it tasted good. I put the empty plate on the ground in front of the door and settled into wearing a circular track on the floor with thoughtful pacing.

Whoever this Fyfa person was, the faeries seemed to think that she was a good idea. How interesting that they hadn't recommended Laec, the one who'd gotten me into this bind in the first place.

Hours passed and I heard voices chatting distantly in the castle gardens. No one else came to visit or deliver food. I watched the patch of light travel across the floor and go dim before another plate of similar food and water was delivered and the other plate taken.

"Don't I get a phone call?" I asked the guard through the slot.

Not even a laugh. The guard left again on those light feet.

I sighed and returned to the mattress to watch the light leak out of my cell.

* * *

"Georjayna?"

I came awake with my muscles tense, my head lifted from the burlap, hovering as I listened. The cell was dark now save for a sliver of moonlight. Had I been dreaming?

"Georjie?"

A woman's voice drifted in through the window at the door.

Rolling off the mattress, I crossed the floor and peered into the dark hall. Light was blotted out by a face I couldn't make out well; only a set of eyes gleamed there.

"Fyfa?"

"Yes, I've come to get you out of here."

My heart gave a leap and my shoulders straightened as adrenalin flooded my system. "How?"

There was a jingle of metal and the sound of a key in a lock. "The old-fashioned way," she whispered as the door swung open.

I slipped into the hall beside my savior. A cool hand grasped mine and, without bothering to close the cell door, she pulled me down the hall. I wanted to ask her where the guards were and how she'd managed to get a set of keys, but saved the questions for later.

The hallway was too black even for shadows, but Fyfa led me through the passageway as confidently as a cat in dark.

Up ahead, a flickering yellow light came in the from the left. Turning through an arch, Fyfa led me up a spiral stairwell lit by torchlight. Through the doorway at the top of the steps––left open a crack––we were on a wooden landing where multiple hallways converged. A few more torchlit corridors with not a soul moving along them, and we slipped out through another door and into the fresh night air.

The moon drifted on flimsy clouds, skimming low over the trees.

I felt a grin crack my face as Fyfa dropped my hand but kept moving, through the gardens and into the line of trees not far from where Laec and I had emerged.

"I don't know how to thank you," I whispered.

Fyfa turned to face me, still a nondescript fae woman in the shadows of the trees where the moonlight was dim. She took my hand and I felt something small and cold pressed into it.

"How bad is your friend?"

"She's comatose."

"But she still looks like herself? She's still...beautiful?" Her eyes were urgent in the dark, her body tense.

"Yes, she's still beautiful." What a strange thing to ask. "Why?"

Fyfa closed her eyes and nodded with what I thought might be relief. "Listen well, because there's still time. But you have to act fast." She closed her hands around mine, enveloping what felt like a vial. "Take your friend far from civilization, as far as you can reasonably get. You'll need help for this, I know, but do it with no more than one other person if you can, two at most. Lay her on the ground under a hawthorn tree and pour half of this into her mouth. Then wait. If nothing happens, give her the rest."

"Wait for how long?" My hands were trembling.

"Just listen!" This was hissed impatiently, and I clamped my mouth shut. "Awakening her might attract the *ithe*."

"The ithe? Is that what you call the creature that burns like a black flame?"

She nodded.

"What is it?"

"If I ever see you again, I'll explain, but now there's no time." Fyfa's hands squeezed mine tightly, the corners of the vial almost cutting into my skin. "As soon as your friend is awake, return home as quickly as you can. Don't linger. If the ithe doesn't appear, the spell is broken and you've won."

"And if it does?"

Fyfa looked pained. "Don't speak to it, don't acknowledge it, don't tell it your name. It won't hurt you if it doesn't know what you are. You're not the target here; your friend is. Don't give it a reason to want you." She paused and looked down and back up. "Keep the dress."

I was shoved backward, almost violently. I tripped over a root and nearly stumbled. Of course by the time I'd recovered, Fyfa was gone.

I stood there blinking in the moonlight, then I realized the smell was different. It smelled like Scotland. And it was freezing. The sound of a car horn in the distance jolted me and I realized that Fyfa hadn't disappeared, she had shoved me back into my own reality——what Laec had called *the without*.

As I emerged from the forest, the lights of Blackmouth Castle as I knew it came glimmering through the darkness. Looking down in my hand, I saw the angular vial with the crystalline liquid inside.

Take your friend far away from civilization, she'd said.

But Evie was still in the hospital, and they weren't just going to let me take her. Like shuffling a deck, my mind flitted over my options.

One: let the hospital in on what had happened to me tonight and beg someone to help me try what Fyfa had recommended? And end up in the psychiatric ward myself. Two: wake up Jasher and ask him to help me break Evie out. He'd be more than up to the task, and he had the keys to Gavin's work trucks. We could figure out how to get Evie out of the hospital en route.

I looked up at Blackmouth Castle and aimed for the back door at a run, dress held up in my fists.

CHAPTER TWENTY-TWO

The moment I opened the door to Jasher's bedroom, I realized that he wasn't going to be the help I needed. The sound of heavy snoring was overshadowed only by the yeasty smell of stale beer. Frowning, I tiptoed into his room and opened the window to bring in some fresh air.

Jasher was a lump under his coverlet, dark hair poking out, pillow thrown on the floor, both feet sticking out. Given the smell, I thought I might find a few empty beer cans, but the room was relatively clean. So the smell was Jasher himself, then. My heart ached for him. He'd been so concerned about Evelyn and he'd been spending so much time at the hospital that I could only assume his present state was an effort to drown his sorrows.

I slipped from his room without waking him, changed rapidly into warm clothes, and headed out into the damp night in search of the only other person I might have a chance of recruiting.

A warm yellow glow through one of the small windows in Lachlan's living room lifted my heart a little.

He ushered me inside, pleased to see me. "Where have you been? Is everything okay?"

I took a bracing inhale. "I need to tell you something important, but there's a chance you won't believe me. Will you listen?"

Taking my coat, he hooked it on one of the pegs behind the door. "Of course I'll listen, Georjie." He took my hand and led me to his living room where books and magazines lay scattered about.

I wanted to ask him why he'd been up, but we didn't have time for chit chat. Sitting next to him on the couch where we'd been not so long ago, I faced him and began to talk. Everything came pouring out. I touched briefly on what had happened to me in Ireland before launching into more detail about Laec, his suggestion, and what it had led to.

Lachlan listened without saying anything. If I thought he was listening in disbelief I might have stopped talking altogether, my tongue in knots, but he gave no clue that he thought I was crazy. When I finished, I fell silent, my heart throbbing in the anticipation.

"I knew it," Lachlan whispered. His hand still held mine but his gaze was leveled at the hardwood floor, his expression muted.

"You knew it?" Relief flooded my limbs.

He looked up and I saw the light in his eyes, the excitement, the worry. "I *knew* it. It's the stuff I used to talk about as a kid until my father told me he didn't want to hear anything else about any fairytales. He couldn't abide anything that sounded remotely like nonsense."

"Did something happen to make you believe?" I searched his face.

"No, I never experienced anything myself, but this Queen Elphame you described, she's famous. Here." He released my hand and went to his library. Pulling down three books, he returned to the couch and laid them out on the table at our knees. I skimmed the titles.

"Scottish Fairy Belief: A History," I read aloud, pulling the velvet jacketed book toward me. "I know this book." I had skimmed through it while looking for any mention of Wise. I must have come across Queen Elphame's name and that was why she was familiar.

"She's mentioned in all of these books." Lachlan grabbed one and flipped open to the index where he ran a finger down the entries. "She's actually more of a lowland myth, but the fables rarely get it exactly right. Queen Elphame is also known as Queen of Elfland."

He flipped open to a page that included an illustration of a kneeling man in the woods, before him a blond woman in a billowy green dress. The caption read:

"I'm not the Queen of Heaven, Thomas,
 That name does not belong to me;
 I am but the Queen of fair Elphame
 Come out to hunt in my follie."

"She doesn't look anything like that," I said.

"That's just an artist's idea of her, but she's recorded in witch trial transcripts as having met with the accused." He braced the book on his knee and read aloud.

"The Queen of Elphame appeared in many witchcraft trials. For example, she was linked to one in 1597 when Andro Man was accused of practicing magic. During his confession, he claimed to have had an intimate relationship with the Queen of Elphame. According to his testimony, for more than thirty years he had been making love to and learning from the leader of the fairies. Andro Man said that he had several children with the queen and she had granted him with gifts of knowledge and healing. Moreover, according to a legend based on the previously described ballad of Thomas the Rhymer, he claimed that he was also kidnapped by the queen to have a sexual affair with her.

"This figure reportedly used to meet with women as well. It is said, for example, that she appeared in front of two women who were believed to be witches— Bessie Dunlap and Isobel Gowdie. Bessie claimed that the Queen of Elphame came to her for the first time when she was in labor. According to both women, the queen visited them many times. She reportedly taught them how to heal people and animals." He stopped and looked up. "I guess that's what she's doing for Evie."

"It wasn't Queen Elphame that gave me the vial, it was Fyfa. The queen was no help at all."

"Do you really think that Fyfa could have taken the vial and given it to you without the queen knowing?"

That gave me pause. "I don't know."

I realized then that an enormous weight had lifted from my shoulders. My eyes filmed over and Lachlan went blurry.

"Georjie?" I felt his hand on my knee.

A tear slipped down my cheek and I brushed at my eyes. "I never thought you'd react this way. It's such a relief to have told you everything and not to have been called crazy or thrown into the street."

He closed the space between us and pulled me into a hug. I let his warmth envelop me.

"I wish you'd told me sooner," he said gently. "I hate the idea of you going through this all alone, or worse, with some fae man who doesn't care what happens to you."

I drew back. "We don't have much time, Lachlan. We need to get Evie out of the hospital without alerting anyone."

"We'll need a distraction." He looked down at me, his face

close to mine, his expression serious. "This is a big deal, Georjie. A big risk. We're planning to essentially break a sick woman out of the hospital without her parents' or her doctors' permission, then take her far from civilization in the dead of night during the middle of winter, lay her on the frozen ground and give her some unknown substance that's supposed to heal her."

When he outlined it like that, my gut began to shrivel.

"What if it kills her? Or what if the journey kills her before we even get a chance to administer the potion to her? Do you trust these fae?" he asked.

I squeezed my eyes shut and pressed the palms of my hands into them, my mind and stomach churning.

I blinked up at him. "What's wrong with her is supernatural. What would Fyfa, Laec, or Queen Elphame gain from hurting Evie further? As far as I can see, this is our only hope."

Lachlan hesitated. "Fair enough, I mean, even the history books say that she was teaching people how to heal, but what if Evelyn isn't strong enough to make such a journey?"

"I think I can help a little, at least. When I found her, I used my own abilities to try and wake her up. Her heart got stronger and her color came back, I just couldn't rouse her. I'll bolster her until we can get her far enough from civilization to give the vial to her."

"Did she tell you why we had to take her out into the middle of nowhere?"

I shook my head. "There wasn't even time for me to ask anything, she just told me what to do and shoved me back into our world with this." I pulled the vial out of my pocket and held it on my open palm for Lachlan to see.

He gave a sharp intake of breath and stared at the vial, his complexion paling. He reached for it and I thought he was going to take it, but he only curled my own fingers around it.

"If I was more like my father, I would encourage you to call the authorities and tell them everything. Maybe they'd be willing to try—"

"You know they'd never believe it. It's not even worth discussing."

Lachlan let out a long sigh, his shoulders slumping. "No, you're right. But I wish there was another way."

I waited as he sat there stewing, his fingers working over one another.

He finally looked up and nodded. "Okay, let's do this, before Evie gets any weaker. God help us."

* * *

Lachlan parked in the small hospital parking lot and turned off the car. We sat in the dark for a minute, staring at the double doors. The Blackmouth hospital was not a big building, thankfully. There was a rear entrance near Evelyn's room, surely monitored by cameras. The front doors would be open and we could walk right in, but there would be a receptionist working, as well as…

"Any idea how many security guards they would have on watch right now?" I asked.

"I'd be surprised if they had more than two. Blackmouth is a small community, not much in the way of crime. No one will be on their guard. They rarely are. It's one my father's biggest complaints, although you can't blame the guards. Nothing much happens except maybe a few supplies get nicked here and there by patients and staff."

"We need a story." I pulled the hat off my head and scratched at my scalp where the wool itched. "What are we doing here in the middle of the night?"

"We could say one of us forgot our cell phone from an earlier visit, or something else equally important."

"And what if they escort us?"

A sharp rap on the back window was followed by the rear door opening. I clamped a hand over my mouth to stifle my gasp. Lachlan jerked around to look as Jasher slid into the back seat.

"Well, well, well." His eyes were fever-bright and his hair wild. "What are you two conspirators up to? Can't be having your midnight fun without me."

Lachlan looked like he wasn't sure whether to laugh or wring Jasher's neck. "Almost gave us a heart attack." He waved a hand in front of his nose. "You smell like a brewery."

Jasher laughed, a borderline mad sound. "Apologies. I thought I'd sleep it off and then come back to the hospital in time for visiting hours this morning." He let off a raspberry that sent a waft of hops by my nose. "Turns out, nope. Still drunk."

"Jasher, you need to go home," I said over the seat. "I did come to wake you but you were dead to the world and in no shape to help out. We don't have much time."

"You did wake me, I just had what you might call a delayed reaction." Jasher scooted forward on the back seat and put his arms over the seat. He hammered out a rhythm on the vinyl, looking from me to Lachlan and back again. "Don't have much time for what?"

"Jasher..." My patience was wearing thin.

Lachlan gave me a look, like he was having an idea. "Wait, this is perfect. Jasher already smells like a boozehound." He looked at Jasher. "Think you can act even more drunk than you currently feel? Like falling down, might need to have your stomach pumped kind of drunk?"

I brightened as his idea made the leap from his mind to mine. Unfortunately, it didn't make it as far as Jasher's.

"Why would I do that?" he asked.

I grabbed Jasher's hand. "We don't have time to explain,

but we can help Evelyn. We have to get her out of there, take her somewhere far from town and find a big hawthorn tree." I pulled the vial out of my pocket and showed him. "And we have to give her this."

Jasher's eyes widened so much he looked like he had those plastic googly eyes you find on kid's stickers. His voice went hushed with awe. "What's that?"

"It's from the faeries," I replied, saying the thing I thought would most get him to trust our crazy plan.

"They gave you a potion?" Jasher looked on the verge of disbelief, but I understood why.

"It's not from the little faeries, it's from the big ones."

"Laec gave it to you?"

"A friend of his. We don't have time to go into details. Will you help us to help Evie? This might be her only hope."

I saw Jasher's throat bob as he swallowed, then he nodded.

"Okay." Lachlan turned in his seat, body tense with energy. "Here's the plan."

CHAPTER TWENTY-THREE

The emergency entrance was a long set of double doors which slid open automatically. To the left was the waiting room where the inspector had grilled me, and to the right was a treatment room with all the bells and whistles. A nurse I'd never seen before stood just inside the doorway of the treatment area, holding a clipboard. She looked up as Lachlan and I half-dragged, half-carried Jasher between us. We stopped in the vestibule and the nurse opened the door to the treatment room and beckoned us in.

Most of Jasher's weight was on Lachlan. His head lolled to the side and his eyes were at half-mast. If I hadn't known he was faking it, I would have been convinced he was completely wasted.

The nurse gestured for us to set Jasher on a chair beside the door. We helped him down and there he swayed, mouth closed, eyes unfocused.

"A little too much to drink, I'm afraid," Lachlan explained to the nurse. "And he can't seem to open his mouth."

While she hadn't reacted to the drinking comment, her brows spiked at the other.

"His jaw is locked?"

She'd already set the clipboard down and was pulling on a pair of gloves. She bent to look at Jasher's face, peering into his eyes, fingers probing at the sides of his face. She frowned and straightened.

"I'll ring for the doc. One of you will have to give the receptionist his details." She gestured to the waiting area but her attention was on Jasher. "Go on."

Jasher didn't so much as nod or bat an eye as Lachlan and I left him there under the concerned nurse's care. Following Lachlan into the reception area, we were greeted by a woman with an explosion of dark hair on top of her head and a serious pair of cat-eye glasses. She handed us a clipboard and pen and bade us to fill out as much as we could about Jasher. There was no security guard in sight, but my stomach twisted with nerves at the security camera surveying the doors and waiting area. If this didn't work, we'd be in serious trouble––potentially manslaughter trouble. I refused to let the fear take root and shook my head. I wouldn't let anything bad happen to Evie.

I took the clipboard and shot a look at Lachlan. Slipping off to the side of the receptionist's desk, just barely in her peripheral vision, I took the pen and set to work on the forms, taking my time with the particulars.

Lachlan was already down the hall and around the corner. It seemed too easy, but then, how many kidnappings were there in small towns in the highlands? This staff wouldn't know what hit them.

Glancing at the receptionist, whose head was down and fingers were working over her keyboard, I sauntered over to a chair just out of her line of sight.

The moment I slipped out of her field of vision, I froze and waited, expecting her to address me. The sound of typing continued. I let out a quiet breath, set the clipboard silently on the chair, and followed Lachlan down the hall. As I rounded the second corner and hit Evie's hallway, I realized with a flood of relief that our crazy plan might actually work. Evelyn's door was open and I slipped inside, soundlessly.

Lachlan had already unhooked her IV and had Evie's sleeping form wrapped up in a blanket. He was just picking her up when I joined him. Evie's small pale face made my stomach twist into a coil of worry. If the antidote didn't work, I knew I would go after Laec and Fyfa and use every ability I had to make them pay. I squeezed my eyes shut, pushing the negative thoughts of vengeance away. Thinking bad things about anyone was dangerous. I never wanted to repeat the harm I'd done my mother by allowing negative emotions about her to run rampant. I slammed a lid on my doubts and focused on the fact that the fae I'd spoken with had nothing to gain by harming Evelyn.

Lachlan's face was beaded with sweat but he gave me a grim nod. I went to the door. Peeking out, I gave him a signal that all was clear. With Evelyn's bundled form in his arms–– she looked like a child––we headed for the staff entrance at the back of the building. I went in front of Lachlan, holding open a set of doors which separated intensive care from another wing of the hospital. We were nearly home free.

"Just what do you think you're doing?" A thickly accented and extremely surprised male voice froze us in our tracks.

We turned, Lachlan swinging slowly with Evelyn's body draped over the crooks of his elbows, her head lolling against his chest.

A portly security guard stood a few feet away, his expression wide with astonishment.

Without thinking about it, I went around Lachlan and approached the guard, a serene smile plastered on my face.

"I'm sorry about this." I reached up to touch his cheeks. A dose of belladonna flowed from my glowing fingertips. Spots lit up on his cheek like white Christmas lights beneath the surface. The guard slumped immediately and I wrapped my arms around him to break his fall. I let him drop gently to the floor, his head tipped back. His hat fell off and went rolling. I grabbed it and put it over his face.

"Come on." I left the guard there and went to the door, which I held open for Lachlan.

Lachlan was staring at me, waxy and sweating. "What did you do to him?"

A loud snore issued from beneath the guard's hat. "I put him to sleep. He'll be fine. Come on, we don't have all night and I don't want to have to put everyone to sleep in the bloody place!"

That got him moving. We made for Lachlan's car and I opened the back door for him to settle Evelyn in. When she was tucked in, Lachlan slid into the driver's seat while I ran around to the other side and got in next to Evelyn's head so I could keep her steady and monitor her.

"Let's go!" My body was vibrating from head to toe. Not in fear, not even with nerves, but with excitement. It was going to work!

Lachlan had just backed the car up and was preparing to turn when a figure came running around the side of the clinic, jacket flapping and sneakers slapping on the pavement. Lachlan waited until Jasher got into the passenger's side before driving away.

"Go, go! They'll be on the phone to the police by now." Jasher was panting after his sprint but he grinned like a wild man. He peered into the back at where I sat with Evie's head in my lap. "This is insane!" He said it in the same tone as someone shouting 'we won the lottery!' "It feels so good to be finally doing something! All the waiting around has been killing me."

"I wonder if they have my plates on video," Lachlan added in a much calmer tone.

"Why do you care? By the time they sort their heads from their asses, we'll be long gone. We might even be on our way back with a healthy Evelyn." Jasher's eyes were wild and still had that glassy look. He was desperately afraid for her; I could practically smell his fear, beneath the smell of beer. "This is going to work, right Georjie?"

"It will," I replied with conviction. "The fae won't let us down."

I never would have dreamed of trying such a crazy stunt if Evie's life hadn't been on the line. It would work. It had to, because the alternative was unthinkable.

"Just drive," I said. "Get us as far away as you can reasonably get us, Lachlan."

I looked down at Evie's sleeping face, so fragile in the dim light. She was a mere shadow of her former self.

The wheels turned and the miles slid by.

Lachlan turned the car off the main road and onto a side road which wound through the highlands like an endless serpent. I straightened in my seat when he turned the car again, this time down a single-track dirt road leading through a grove that was as black as the bottom of a well.

We passed through this dark tunnel very slowly, the vehicle rocking over the rough road. I held Evelyn with a hand on her shoulder and one on her forehead. From time to time I felt her pulse, which felt like the slow flutter of a butterfly's wing under her jaw. I sent a steady stream of earth energy into her, bolstering her strength.

"Where exactly are we?" Jasher muttered, speaking for the first time in well over an hour.

"I haven't been back here in years." Lachlan peered out through the windshield at the seemingly endless tube through the foliage ahead of us. "But I'm pretty sure there's an opening up here where we can park. I don't know how far out Fyfa was hoping we'd get, but this place is as remote as any."

"It'll have to do, because we're running out of time," I said.

Jasher peered back sharply over the seat, his eyes glittering coals in the dark. "What do you mean?"

"Her pulse has slowed even further, and…" I hesitated.

"And what?"

"I think she's…smaller. Is that possible?"

"If you said she's grown toadstools for ears, I'd believe you at this point," Lachlan said. "What do you say we stop this jalopy and get on with it?"

Jasher and I didn't have to say anything to agree with Lachlan; the tension in the vehicle was ratcheting up. My excitement at having broken Evelyn out of the hospital with relative ease had fizzled away and was replaced by nervous anticipation.

"Hang in there, sweetie," I said to the woman sleeping on my lap, who I was certain had lost mass in the short time we'd been in the car.

"Fyfa wanted hawthorn. I give you the biggest hawthorn I know of," Lachlan said as he pulled the car onto an open patch of earth. A soft rolling hill fell away and a large pasture opened up under the moon. A lonely tree stood sentinel in the middle, casting a shadow as the clouds broke and cold nighttime light poured over the hills.

The car's engine had barely died when both men were out of the car and had opened the back door nearest Evelyn. I cradled Evie's head as Lachlan pulled her form toward him. Jasher helped lift the sleeping woman up and settled her in Lachlan's arms. Jasher was still a little unsteady on his feet.

"We'll trade when you get tired, yeah?" Jasher said.

Lachlan nodded and we began to walk into the pasture toward the hawthorn.

CHAPTER TWENTY-FOUR

*L*achlan carried Evie across the spongy earth with sure steps. Jasher and I hovered close by in case he needed help, but he never faltered. A thick rind of moon cast its blue light over the rolling open hills, illuminating the landscape well enough to make out pockets of gorse. In the moon shadow of the hawthorn, Lachlan got to his knees and laid Evelyn carefully on the ground. I toed off my shoes, then pulled off my socks and tucked them inside my shoes. I didn't *need* skin to soil contact to help her, but the stronger my connection to the earth, the more powerful I felt. The ground was wet and cold. Moisture squeezed between my toes and soaked the knees of my jeans as I kneeled beside her. I pulled the vial out of my pocket and unscrewed the cap. Jasher knelt on Evie's other side and took her hand, while Lachlan squatted behind me and put a comforting hand on my shoulder.

Evelyn's face had changed so much since she'd first gone into the coma. The hollows under her cheekbones were pooled with shadow and her eyes seemed to rest too far back in her head. Her hands had always been thin, but now we could see the fine webbing of bones and veins threading over the backs of them. I remembered what Fyfa had asked, whether she was still beautiful or not. Evie was looking older now, and I was grateful we were so near to the end of the task.

Resting my thumb gently on her chin, I pulled her jaw down to open her mouth. Tilting the vial, I let half the contents trickle between her lips, slowly so as not to lose any of the precious liquid. Recapping the vial, I slipped it back into my pocket and put both of my hands on Evie's face.

Closing my eyes, I sent my focus into the ground, drawing on the earth's healing powers, pulling on plants up to a mile away. I could feel my hair moving on a supernatural wind. With a surge of power, the hawthorn tree's energy overflowed into me, spilling everywhere and making my whole body hum. I poured all of it into Evelyn, every muscle vibrating with it. Opening my eyes, I smiled as Evelyn's cheeks warmed and flushed with blood, her heartbeat grew stronger.

With a big inhale, her eyes flew open. A small cry escaped her lips as her gaze darted around the faces hovering over her.

I glanced around, eyes peeled for the eldritch thing. There was no sign of anything malignant and I felt the tension run out of my shoulders.

"Shh, you're all right." Jasher squeezed her hand and knelt low to kiss her cheek. "You're all right, Evelyn." A tear tracked down his cheek, glimmering in the moonlight. He brushed it away and smiled at me. "You did it. It worked." His voice cracked with emotion. "Thank God."

"Where am I?" Evelyn made as if to get up, but put her head back on the ground and closed her eyes. "I feel like a newborn. Why am I so weak?"

"You've been asleep for almost a week," I explained, brushing her hair back from her brow.

Her eyes misted up. "A week?"

"Don't talk right now and don't try to get up." Lachlan put a hand under the back of her neck. "Let me carry you, when you're ready."

Evelyn nodded, tears running from the corners of her eyes and into her hair. "My parents?"

"They're at home. They'll be the first people we tell once we get you back to the hospital. Don't worry." Jasher kissed her again, this time on the lips. "They've been worried sick. We all have."

"Where are we?" She looked beyond us, at the sky, the field, the hawthorn.

Jasher and I looked at Lachlan. "I don't actually know," I said with a laugh.

Lachlan's cheek dimpled deeply under the starlight. "We're in a vacant field owned by my uncle. We were instructed to take you far from civilization and this was the best I could do on short notice. Seems to have worked."

Evelyn blinked slowly. "I feel so tired. Don't talk anymore." Her voice became a whisper. "Tell me everything, after…"

"After get your strength back." Jasher nodded. "We will." He glanced up at me and saw my hesitation. "We'll tell you as much as we can."

When Evelyn was ready, Lachlan picked her up. She tucked her head under his chin and closed her eyes. Her color had improved as well as the strength of her heartbeat, but she looked almost as frail as she had before. As Lachlan led the way back to the car with Evie, Jasher pulled on my arm and kept me back a few steps.

"She still doesn't look like herself," he whispered, his dark eyes clouded with concern.

"She's awake, her pulse is strong and regular. I guess that was the best we could get. She just needs some time to recover, gain back what she lost."

His brow creased as we began to walk again, watching Lachlan's form with Evie's feet sticking out over his arm, her head just a mound of hair over his shoulder.

"I thought she'd go back to normal, you know. Be able to walk on her own." He gestured to the pair ahead of us. "Not this."

"Whatever was holding her was powerful, Jasher. So strong even my own magic wasn't able to help her without the potion Fyfa gave us. I think we're lucky that she didn't die."

Jasher nodded but still looked unhappy.

My own thoughts crowded in on me. I had also expected Evelyn to be returned to her former glory, so to speak. After all, it was a potion from a fae queen that we had given her, not over-the-counter drugs. Why hadn't it done more? I'd been hoping to be able to take Evelyn to her home, present her to her parents as whole and healthy once more. But though she was conscious now, she looked like a famine victim. She'd have to go back to the hospital.

I jumped when Jasher's fingers clamped over my forearm. "What's that?"

He didn't have to point. The edges of the field were now completely invisible, swallowed up in a gray fog so thick it was opaque. The fog rolled toward us, churning and swirling and swallowing up terrain like a hungry monster as it came. Jasher and I called to Lachlan, sprinting to catch up with him. He'd seen the fog too and stood there with Evelyn in his arms, gaping at the fog as he turned slowly.

"What is that?" His face was a pale circle with dark holes for eyes. The light was changing. The fog was not only closing in on us on all sides, but appeared to be steaming its way over top of us as well, slowly shutting out the stars.

"We need to get back to the car, now!" I put my hands against Lachlan's lower back and urged him forward.

He took a few steps. "I can't even *see* the car anymore."

The fog swept overhead, blocking out the stars and leaving us with only a few feet of visibility on any side. Lachlan's toe caught on a tussock and he nearly stumbled. Jasher caught him by the elbow.

Don't speak to it, don't tell it your name, Fyfa had warned. I reminded Lachlan and Jasher about the fae's warning and they nodded, looking frightened.

We were in a bubble now, the thick mist swirling and circling, billowing around us as if it was alive. Maybe it was.

"Keep going," I urged. "Even slowly. If we can make it to the car..."

"Except I'm not even sure which direction the car is parked in anymore." Lachlan spun slowly, squinting into the gray cloud.

"It's this way." Jasher took my hand and put his other hand under Lachlan's elbow, leading us in roughly the direction we'd been headed before we'd lost all visibility.

"I think a little more to the right," Lachlan replied, correcting the trajectory.

We took slow steps, moving together and warning one another about the little hazards coming out of the gloom—tree trunks and rotten logs half swallowed by gorse and grass.

"Smells like mothballs, or old moldy clothing," Jasher muttered as we plodded far too slowly for my comfort.

"Yeah, musty." Lachlan agreed.

"Like a grave." The words were so quiet the hair on the back of my neck stiffened. It was Evelyn who'd spoken. I let out a pent-up breath and felt my shoulders drop. *You'd know,* I thought.

"Who dares interrupt my awakening?"

The words stopped us in our tracks. It was a cold, slithery voice. It felt like the words slid past my skin and left a trail of slime.

"Evelyn, was that you?" I felt Jasher's hand tighten on my own.

"Don't answer." My warning came out sharp. "Keep going. Just ignore it."

"You can't ignore me." This time the words were an amused hiss. *"Tell me...who are you?"* Slow. Breathy. Seductive...and oh so cold.

I put a hand on Lachlan's back and encouraged him to go forward. He took a few steps and almost tripped again.

The voice snickered, wrapping itself around us and between us. The fog swirled faster when the voice spoke, and now it had a point of origin—behind us, and close.

Lachlan and Jasher both began to turn around. I tried to urge them onward, but when I saw their gazes both fixed on something behind us, I couldn't help but look.

A tunnel had begun to form in the fog. Grass and gorse and mulch became visible in a line leading away from us. The walls of the tunnel churned and puffed, boiling as if angry. The smell of death grew stronger. Jasher put a hand over his nose and mouth.

"Something is moving." Lachlan's voice was low and querulous. "Down there at the end."

"I see it." I couldn't tear my eyes from the end of the tunnel. In the dim light, a flickering shape with too many limbs appeared and disappeared in the swirling mist. Even before the fog pulled back, I knew it was the ithe. How did it have more limbs? I squinted, and saw that it didn't have more limbs...it was carrying something. Someone.

None of us had words for what we were seeing. The eldritch thing stepped from the fog carrying an emaciated woman in a fine dress the color of red wine. It stood there, the top of its head flickering like a black candle flame, its hands flickering from where they cradled the woman. They were the mirror image of Lachlan and Evie, only like something out of a nightmare.

"Daracha." Evelyn whispered the name, hoarsely.

I tore my eyes from the scene at the end of the tunnel. Evelyn's body had grown tense, her thin hand knotted in Lachlan's sweater, her pale face pinched and her eyes on the thing now standing less than fifty feet from us.

"Yes." The woman in the flickering thing's arms smiled, and it was like the grin of death's head. A skull shrink-wrapped with skin, and framed with startlingly long and lustrous hair. Her eyes were bright. She had glassy fingernails. Her skin seemed to thicken as we stared, smoothing over and plumping out. Her gown looked new and of a rich fabric.

Daracha patted the eldritch thing on its shoulder and it bent and set her on her feet. She straightened slowly, like an old person getting up from sitting for too long. She lifted her head and gazed at us. I could see the mummy's face in the face of the woman now standing before us.

Betrayal turned my spit to powder and my own foolish assumptions about the body in the wall turned my bones to lead.

Daracha had come back to life, and she'd used Evelyn to do it.

CHAPTER TWENTY-FIVE

*D*aracha took a few steps toward us. The ithe followed closely behind her.

"Stay back," I shouted, stepping forward to come between my friends and Daracha, my heart picking up speed.

"Who dared to close my wellspring?" Daracha said. "Name yourself!"

"Don't speak to her," I instructed quietly. Glancing back at them, my stomach gave a lurch at Lachlan's face. He was filmed with sweat and cords on his neck were standing out. He was getting tired; he'd carried Evie a lot tonight and was now just holding her, fear making his face pale and his eyes wide.

"What do we do?" I felt Jasher's hand on my lower back as he whispered. "She's advancing."

"I can't run," Lachlan said under his breath. His arms were trembling.

"Let me take her." Jasher stepped close to Lachlan and with a quick backward glance, he took Evelyn in his arms. Her eyes were just slits and her head lolled as though it was a little too heavy for her. Her lips were chapped. "Are you okay?" he asked Evie.

Her tongue darted out in an attempt to moisten her lips. "So thirsty."

A muttering from the end of the tunnel brought our attention back to Daracha, who'd come only a few feet toward us, I saw with some relief. She seemed to be speaking to the ithe in a foreign tongue.

Jasher didn't wait. He stepped into the fog as though he could see where he was going, heading roughly in the direction of the road. Lachlan grasped my hand and we watched Daracha as she came over the landscape. She walked like a woman of ninety, which––considering that she had been mummified for centuries––was terrifying. The ithe and she seemed to be in communion as she struggled to make her way forward.

"Come on." Lachlan squeezed my hand and tugged me backward. "We can move a lot faster than that, even if we can't see where we're going. At this rate, we'll reach the car before she's even halfway."

We faced forward and took a few steps. Jasher and Evelyn were lost from view, somewhere ahead of us and invisible.

"Where are you?" I called softly.

"Here." Jasher sounded a winded. "Follow my voice."

A glance over my shoulder sent a jolt of cold fear through me. Daracha and her pet were invisible too; the fog had closed in behind us. There was no longer any tunnel.

I put a hand on Lachlan's arm. "She's gone."

He glanced over his shoulder, his mouth pressed into an unhappy line. Sweat trickled down the side of his face in spite of the fact that he'd released his burden, in spite of the fact that it was a cold night. "That's even worse than seeing them."

I agreed. "Hello?"

"This way," Jasher replied from the darkness.

Lachlan and I corrected to continue to follow the sound of Jasher, trusting he knew where to go. We continued in this way, following Jasher's voice, which seemed farther and farther away from us with every call. The time between calls grew longer, then...

"Hey," I called.

No answer.

Lachlan stopped walking, his hand squeezed mine. "Listen."

We stood there banked by fog on all sides, looking at one another, panting and straining our ears. There was nothing. Not a footstep, not the call of an owl, not anyone breathing except for ourselves.

I called to Jasher again; again there was no answer. My mind raced, tripped, got up and raced again. If I could control the wind like Petra, I could blow all this blasted fog away so we could see what was happening. I couldn't control air, but maybe... maybe there was something else I could try.

I toed off my boots and ripped off my socks again, using Lachlan's hand for balance. He just watched and held me up, like he was afraid to make noise in the silence which had become so complete.

Planting the soles of my feet firmly against the cold ground, I closed my eyes and sent feelers through the earth like tentacles. My awareness raced outward, winding through complex root systems and deposits until I found the massive underground structures of the trees bordering the open space.

Leaves began to rustle as though a strong wind had blown up, only there was no wind, not yet. The whisper of moving leaves increased and became a loud whoosh, which escalated to the creak of branches rubbing against one another. Then the cracks and pops of thicker limbs came as they hit against each other. The sound had risen to a near-deafening cacophony, like a storm at sea.

The fog began to swirl and blow, and slowly grew thin.

"It's working." Lachlan had to yell over the sound. His eyes were bright and hopeful.

For all the swinging and swishing the trees were doing, they moved the air but a little. They were far away, and were like a small fan in a large room filled with smoke. The light wind lifted my hair and ruffled the locks at Lachlan's brow.

We saw the glittering eyes in the thinning fog at the same time, and we grabbed each other's hands. Lachlan let out a curse as the fog shifted, revealing the scene that had been hiding in the mist.

I gasped in horror.

Jasher was on the ground, Evelyn's body curled half over his stomach and half under his arm. Both of them were still. Standing over them was Daracha, and behind her towered the flickering thing.

She was taller now, straighter, and younger. Her face was filling out even as the mist diluted. Her hands, near skeleton hands only minutes ago, were now rounded out and strong. The hollows of her cheeks filled in as we stared.

"No!" I ran forward.

"He was just what I needed to be complete." Daracha said, unmoving. "Thank you."

Bare feet sliding on the wet grass, I sprinted to where they lay, so still, so pale. I fumbled in my pocket for the vial. Evelyn lay half conscious, cradled in Jasher's arms. She actually didn't look any worse, but Jasher…his skin was paler than I had ever seen it, his eyes closed. His lips were the color of chalk.

"You're too late," Daracha said softly.

Hands shaking, I unscrewed the cap and drained the rest of the liquid into Jasher's mouth. Tossing the vial aside, I planted my feet, pressed my fingertips to his cheeks and drew all the earth's energy I could manage, spilling it all into my friend.

The bones of his cheeks seemed too close to the surface, his skin too thin.

But his eyes drifted open and his heartbeat thickened. He took a breath. "Georjie?"

I felt Lachlan's hands on my shoulders, his legs against my back.

I glared up at Daracha. "I'm not too late."

But the words died in my throat.

Daracha was beautiful now. She was erect, her cheeks were rosy, her mouth a full rosebud. Her hair was long lustrous waves cascading over straight shoulders. A full, rounded bosom tapered into a tiny waist before flaring out into voluptuous hips. The sleeves of her gown were cut at three-quarter length, and her slender, pale arms ended in long-fingered, elegant hands—the kind of hands that any piano player would envy. She appeared to be no more than twenty-five.

Gooseflesh swept down my arms and across the back of my neck and I realized what she'd meant about being too late.

She was back. She was complete.

I put a hand on Lachlan's arm without taking my eyes off Daracha. "Get them to the car."

"What about you?" Lachlan bent to help Jasher rise, who was doing so under his own power, but he was slow, his movements weak.

"I'll be fine."

"We're not going to leave you here," he said.

"I'll be right behind you," I whispered. "Just get them out of here."

I got to my feet and stepped over Jasher and Evelyn,

putting myself between her and them. At my words, Daracha's fine dark eyebrow arched and her long slender arms crossed over her chest. Daracha wasn't fae; she didn't have the sharp-tipped ears. All witch, then?

"What are you?" I asked as I heard my friends make their way back to the car. The night sky was now visible, the fog nearly gone. The ithe wouldn't be far. If I could make Daracha talk for long enough, maybe my friends would get away.

"You know perfectly well what I am," Daracha replied with a laugh. "I'm not any different than you."

I couldn't hide my shock. "You're a Wise?"

Daracha's smile dissolved as quickly as it had come and she gazed at me with her beautiful eyes wide.

"Of course," she hissed slowly and her gaze turned hungry. "You're a Wise."

My hands curled into fists at my sides. She'd tricked me into giving away something about myself.

She uncrossed her arms. The movement put me on edge. "I can hardly believe my good fortune."

I didn't like the look on her face, the predatory ambition. She took a few steps toward me, heading to my left side. I took a few steps to the right. We circled one another like cats preparing to fight.

I didn't know what to expect. Would she attack? What kind of magic did she have? Should I run? All too late, I realized this was what Fyfa had been warning me about.

My senses reached into the earth beneath, stretching out to the ground Daracha was standing on, tasting, searching for some knowledge of her. My tendrils of energy snapped back the moment they sensed her acrid being. Her energy was like an impenetrable wall, a block of concrete, a dense mass of something still and cold and unforgiving.

Daracha was something altogether different. She wasn't

like any of my elemental friends, whose power ebbed and flowed in tandem with the earth's magnetic fields. This woman had an entirely different aura. She felt...wrong. She was a bottleneck, a place where energy stopped moving and died, where life withered. The power she had didn't come from the earth.

"What is your name, beautiful one?" Daracha asked, her voice oily. "I mean you no harm."

Distantly, I heard a car door shut and then another. The engine turned over and then idled. They were waiting for me.

With my pulse a steady throb in my ears, I turned to walk away, and almost ran straight into the ithe.

Gasping, I stepped back and stared up into its vacuous face. It was featureless, just a black hole. It looked like it wanted to suck me into itself, and once I disappeared inside, there would be no coming back. But it didn't touch me. It just stood there, its head tilted. Its long arms and the black flames on the ends of its hands flickered at its sides. They seemed to lick toward me, tasting me. I took another step back. I faced Daracha and crossed my arms.

"Let me pass, Daracha Goithra." Underneath my feet, unseen in the soil as it rolled beneath the surface, a tangle of twisted roots and threads of earth energy waited for my call. "You don't want to do this."

I didn't know what the witch and her tall fiend were capable of, but they didn't know what I was capable of either...I hoped.

Her lips parted. "You know my name. Let's not be rude. Come now. Your name, dear."

"My friends are waiting." Though I turned away and began to go around the ithe, my attention was in the soil beneath us, gathering power.

A few steps over the wet grass and I thought she might

actually let me go. Maybe she was afraid to test me. The witch had been dead a few centuries and had nearly sucked Evelyn dry in order to resurrect herself. I wasn't eager to see what else she could do. I just wanted to get out of there.

A black flame appeared in the grass ahead of me. It shot upward and formed the body of Daracha's minion, standing in my path.

I didn't stop walking, didn't alter my course. My hands and fingers curled, feeling the teeming power beneath my feet, flowing through my limbs. "Move."

It only lifted its arms as if to sweep me into a hug.

With a flick of my wrists, a gorse bush––dense with three-inch thorns––swallowed up the creature in the blink of an eye. All I could see of the ithe now was the flickering top of its head.

Stepping around the gorse, I began to run, leaping over tussocks and nearly turning my ankles on the uneven ground. Another ten seconds of sprinting and I'd be at the car. I could see Lachlan's face peering from the open window. He revved the engine. His expression was alight with joy to see me coming. He'd already turned the car around and was ready to hit the gas. Jasher cradled Evelyn in the back seat. Lachlan reached across the seat and opened the door.

"Come on!" His eyes were wide open and brows arched high. Then his pupils focused on something behind me and his brows pinched together. "No."

The ithe flickered into life in front of me. I had to slide in the wet grass to keep from running into it. It spread its arms wide again, as if to catch me in a hug of death. My bare feet slipped in the mud and I landed hard on my hip and elbow. Skidding another two feet, I came to a stop at the flickering feet of my enemy. My heart lurched into my throat as

Daracha appeared in my periphery, the fabric of her dress flowing around her on a wind I couldn't feel.

The sound of a car door opening preceded heavy foot-steps on the gravel as Lachlan came around the idling vehicle.

Daracha looked at Lachlan. "What a good friend you are. Look at you. You don't even know the danger you're in, do you?"

Lachlan didn't answer her and didn't stop walking until he was at my side, close enough to the ithe to have reached out and touched it. A strong hand curled under my armpit and lifted me back to my feet.

"We're leaving. Go back to whatever hell you came from," Lachlan snarled, and my heart gave a grateful pulse.

Lachlan curled an arm around my waist and turned toward the car, heading around the eldritch thing.

"I don't think so," replied Daracha, smoothly.

The ithe reached out a flickering hand and lay it on the top of Lachlan's head. His body stiffened.

I screamed and the ithe actually flinched at the sound.

Lachlan bent over and his breathing sounded heavy. "I'm okay."

"Are you?" Daracha asked.

"Shut up," I hissed and bent to look into Lachlan's face. Looking into his eyes was a blade in my heart. They were blank, no pupils, no irises.

"I can't see." Lachlan's voice was so calm and, in that moment, I thought I couldn't possibly love him more.

Rage filled me and I swung toward Daracha, my hands lifting, drawing the power that had gathered for me. Thorns shot from around her, wrapping around her dress, ripping the fabric, wrapping, entwining.

Purple lightning snapped between Daracha's fingers with

a crackling sound and the rising gorse drew back like it had been burned, the tips of its thorns smoking.

"Just you, that's all I want," the witch said as my gorse sizzled and withdrew.

"Give him his sight back," I snarled, "and let them go."

"No." I felt Lachlan grope for me. His hand found my lower back and he pulled me against him. I put my hand on his arm and squeezed.

Daracha ignored Lachlan. "You'll stay?"

"I'll stay."

I faced Lachlan and saw as he straightened that the gray was already fading from his eyes. But even as vision returned to his eyes, they filled with grief.

"Don't do this," he whispered.

I took his face in my hands. "Trust me, please?"

He shook his head and the quiver in his chin nearly undid me. Closing my eyes and drawing light from my connection to the earth, I pulled his lips to mine. Letting the earth's life run through my body and into him, I sent a message through the kiss.

She cannot hold me. Get them out of here. I'll follow as soon as I can.

I didn't know how much of my message he picked up. I wasn't telepathic like Petra, and I couldn't command anyone to do what I wanted with the power of my voice, like Targa, but maybe I could share what I wanted.

Lachlan's arms tightened around me and he kissed me back. I felt moisture on my face and knew he was crying. That was good; it meant he'd go.

Take them to safety, get Evelyn back to the hospital, I thought, letting the stream of white light continue to pour through me and into him, strengthening him, begging him to understand. I sent him one last thought before breaking the kiss. *I'll see you soon.*

He pulled back and looked down at me, eyelashes wet, but he gave me the smallest nod. Releasing me, he turned and made his way toward the car. The ithe watched him go, its invisible face turning on its neck.

"Hurry up," Jasher suddenly called, his voice rising with panic. "Evelyn... she's *shrinking* again!"

With a glance at Daracha and the satisfied look on her face, it hit me that this witch could not be trusted to uphold any part of a bargain.

"You're all out of medicine." Daracha's arms crossed casually over her stomach. "The goodbye kiss was sweet, but I don't have all night."

Lachlan ran toward the car and with a last desperate look in my direction, slid into the driver's seat and slammed the door. The car pulled away and was shortly nothing but taillights in the night and the sound of an engine growing distant.

"What do you want?" I faced her, hands at my sides and bare feet braced against the wet soil. Somewhere deep in my mind, a lot of lights were coming on, turning green. My body began to hum.

"You're precious, little Wise. You don't know just how precious you are." Daracha took a few steps toward me, and in her eyes, I saw red firelight flickering.

"You'll never leave my friends alone." She couldn't be trusted, and she had the power to blind or kill. She knew who my friends were now, what they looked like, even if she didn't know their names.

"Sure I will." Daracha took another step toward me. "When I'm done with you, I'll have no more need of them." She cocked her head and practically cooed the next words, like she was trying to comfort a baby. "It'll only hurt for a little while." A cold smile spread across her face. "Well, maybe for longer than a little while."

I had to destroy her. The realization swept through me like lightning. I actually had to kill this creature, not only to keep her from doing whatever awful thing to me that she had planned, but to protect my friends. I knew this as surely as I could feel the mud squeezing up between my toes. She would never stop.

I felt the presence of the ithe as it moved behind me, but I ignored it and closed my eyes, going inward and down. My spirit roots came easily and naturally, shooting out of the bottoms of my feet and deep into the ground. Power filled me, the earth's energies lifting me. I opened my eyes. Already, Daracha and the ithe were small figures at my feet and shrinking as my view changed to one from a great height. I could see my own small form far below, blond hair flying.

With a sound like thunder, the ground ripped open in front of Daracha. She stumbled back, purple sparks and electricity crackling at her fingertips. The ithe had vanished, perhaps he'd abandoned her? I felt a smile drift onto my face, slow and wide, as the Wise in me brought the power of the mighty trees to life.

Purple lightning shot from Daracha's fingers toward the place where I was rooted to the earth, but my connection to the earth was growing stronger and thicker with every moment that passed. Hot cinders of power stung my body but were little more than mosquito bites.

I swung an arm, sweeping it from the heavens toward the witch and hitting her body like she was a golf ball. Daracha flew through the air, her red dress fluttering in the wind. She twisted and spiraled, using the momentum, before landing on her feet in a crouch and then tumbling over and over with a cry. In a flash, she was up on her feet and running, skirts flying.

The split in the earth chased her. Rocks and rotting logs

fell into the gaping gorge as it zigzagged through the terrain. Daracha looked back over her shoulder and redoubled her efforts, leaping over the obstacles in the field like a gazelle. So fleet, so powerful and strong she was. She was fast, she was strong, but she couldn't outrun me.

With a sound like a thunderclap that shuddered the earth, the split raced toward Daracha, beneath her running feet. She lost her footing and slipped into the crevice, gripping at roots and scrambling to climb back onto the surface.

I caught a glimpse of her face and realized she was smiling—not just smiling, but laughing. She had to be insane.

With a flick of my hand, the earth she clung to shuddered like a horse's skin flicking off a biting insect. The roots slipped through her fingers.

For a moment I saw her splayed out and laughing as she fell, then I closed the crack in the earth over her with a thud and the wild laughter cut off abruptly.

With a snap, I returned to my body, the wind fluttering my hair and tugging my clothes.

A silence descended over the field so complete it was like the land had been covered with a swathe of velvet. Barefoot and filthy, I stood in the wet grass, listening. The ithe was nowhere to be seen.

I closed the earth so well and knitted its roots and rocks and layers back together so neatly, it was like nothing had ever happened. Scanning the dark line of trees, I found nothing out of place or unusual. An owl hooted, followed by the chirrups of insects. It was a peacefulness so surreal I might have been convinced that I'd imagined the whole battle.

I was crossing the field, heading for the road where Lachlan's car had been parked, when I tripped over something. Picking it up, I realized it was one of my boots, the sock still stuffed into the toe. With a little burst of power running out the end of my toes and across the length of my sole, I caused the mud and dirt stuck to me to fall to the ground. Pulling on my boot, I scanned the shadows until I found the other. I cleaned my other foot and pulled on my other boot. It was looking like a long walk home, or possibly a hitchhike, if there happened to be any travelers on the quiet country roads at this time of night.

With a shiver, I zipped my jacket up to my chin, pulled my hood over my head, and began a slow journey back to Blackmouth. My breath clouded in front of my face and I wished for mittens.

A little over an hour's hike in the darkest part of night and I arrived at the narrow paved road Lachlan had turned off. Drawing some energy from the earth, I turned and continued on down the shoulder.

A soft plum color was leeching into the horizon when a pair of headlights appeared in the distance. I watched them disappear into the dips and gullies and reappear over the gentle roll of the terrain, growing ever larger. When it was a hundred yards away I smiled, recognizing the shape of the lights. It was Lachlan.

The car slowed and he pulled alongside the shoulder, spraying loose rock into the ditch. Leaving the car to idle, Lachlan got out of the driver's side and came around to where I'd stopped in the ditch. I took a few steps to close the gap between us, but he covered the ground so fast that his hug took my breath away. He swept me into his arms and pulled me tight against his body. I could hear the relief in his voice.

"I came back as soon as I could," he whispered into my hair. "Leaving you there was the hardest thing I have ever had to do." He planted several kisses on my face, my cheeks, my forehead, my lips. "What happened?"

I gripped his hands with my own, feeling the tears that

wanted to well up and spill over my cheeks. I was safe, they were safe. Now I could fall apart if I wanted to. Lachlan was here to take care of me. But I found that I didn't want to fall apart. I felt a serene kind of sadness about what had happened, and a deep consolation that it was over.

"We won't have to worry about Daracha anymore." I gave him a brief explanation of what had happened after they'd left. "Where are Evelyn and Jasher?"

"Both of them are at the hospital, both have been given an IV. The police hadn't arrived before I turned around and left again, but I'm sure they're there by now."

"What's our story?"

"Well, neither of them is in any shape to talk. They're both exhausted, though it's amazing to see Evelyn actually conscious again. The clinic staff didn't know how to react when we walked in with her. You should have seen their faces." He put an arm around my waist and walked me to the passenger side door. When he opened it for me, I slid in, thankful for the heating.

Lachlan went around and got into the driver's seat. He turned the car around and began to drive home.

"Let me talk to my dad about it," Lachlan said after a few thoughtful moments of silence. "I'll handle him."

"What are you going to tell him?"

"A version of the truth, one that he can live with." He glanced over at me and took my hand. "I know my dad. He won't like the supernatural explanation, but the evidence will show that Evelyn is in much better condition than she was before we took her."

"Jasher isn't."

"No, but Jasher has his own story, his own reasons for not feeling his best."

"To do with drinking a little too much over the last few months?" I guessed.

"Something like that." With another glance, he released my hand and put both of his on the wheel. "I'll take you home. You must be exhausted."

"Can I…" I trailed off, losing my nerve.

"What?" Lachlan pulled to a stop at a crossroad and turned left onto a larger highway. "Tell me."

"Do you mind if I crash in your spare bedroom tonight?"

"Georjie, if you asked me to make you a crown out of wire and dew drops, I would do my best. Of course you can."

"Thanks. I just don't feel like being alone tonight."

"You feel alone at the castle?"

"With Jasher not in his room, and everyone else so far away and on different floors? Yeah, it does feel a bit lonely."

"Georjie, you're welcome to my spare bed for as long as you want it."

I thanked him and settled back into the seat, letting my thoughts roll over me as my eyelids drifted and the movement of the car lulled me.

By the time we arrived at Lachlan's cottage, I could barely stand because I was so tired. Lachlan showed me to his spare room and gave me a pair of cotton pajama bottoms and a t-shirt to wear to bed. I'd just crawled beneath the quilt and lay my head on the pillow when I heard a knock on the front door.

Lachlan answered and the rumbles of a low conversation between two men drifted to me under the door. I tried to listen, but my grip on the real world was too weak, and I slipped into the deep sleep of the overwrought.

CHAPTER TWENTY-SIX

I awoke to the feeling of my bed shifting under someone's weight. The frame creaked. Thinking it was Lachlan, perhaps coming to check on me in the night, I mumbled his name and rolled over. My eyes felt glued shut, but when he didn't answer, I rubbed them and sat up. My vision was blurry and I realized he was half naked, which sent my blood rocketing through my veins and startled me fully awake. But it wasn't Lachlan sitting on the end of my bed half naked.

"Laec!"

The fae was actually perched cross-legged on the edge of the footboard, like he weighed a pound, never mind that he appeared to weigh about two hundred pounds. His face caught a beam of light from the window and the lines and hollows of his face appeared deep and drawn. He looked serious.

I pushed myself up into sitting, pulling the coverlet against my chest. The fire of indignation swelled as I recalled what had happened the last time I'd seen him.

"I should string you up for abandoning me," I hissed. "Why do you keep showing up when it's clearly Fyfa who comes through when—"

"What have you done?" He interrupted me, and his look was so dark that it gave me pause.

"I killed the witch who was hurting Evelyn, no thanks to you," I replied. It was the first time I'd ever taken a life and I hoped it would be the last.

Laec dropped his face and let out a long-suffering breath before rubbing his eyes with both hands. I felt like a stupid child he was trying to teach a lesson to. Anger joined the irritation in my belly.

"Get out of here." My words were bitter. "I don't trust you. Tell Fyfa I'm coming to find her. I need answers." I glared at Laec. "From her, not from you. Don't let the door hit you on the ass on the way out."

"Elphame save me from stupid little Wise who don't know how to use their own gifts," Laec muttered under his breath.

"Excuse me?"

His hand came toward my face, palm out, fingers crooked and tense. "Try again, hollowhead," Laec intoned, "and this time...*listen.*"

What felt like a shower of hot sparks hit my forehead. I opened my mouth to reply, but was already falling back onto my pillow, eyes rolling up into my head.

My stomach lurched with the sensation of falling. I thought I was going to vomit when I landed on my feet in the clearing where Jasher had been building the cottage. Only there was no cottage—there was only the foundation with the beginnings of the original stone wall. The forest around me was thick and lush and full of the shadows of night.

"Laec?" My voice echoed around me like I was standing in a cave. *Laec...aec...aec...ec...ec.*

The sound of voices and the squeak of rusty metal came to my ears. Someone was coming; in fact, they were nearly upon me. The urge to run and hide was overpowering and I bolted toward the trees. Before I got there, the couple emerged from the thicket, the man pushing the wheelbarrow and its only wheel squeaking with each rotation. I was caught out in the open, but they didn't notice me. I was seeing the same residual I'd seen when I was with Jasher, only this time...*I could hear.*

My gaze fell to the body in the wheelbarrow, her limbs and the fabric of her dirty dress spilling over the side. Daracha's skin was pale in the moonlight, her lips full and dark, her cheeks full with the vitality of youth. Luscious hair tumbled from beneath her bonnet. My heart skipped a beat to see the witch again. How wrong I'd been to assume she was an innocent victim.

The man halted the wheelbarrow and with the woman's help, dragged Daracha's limp body unceremoniously toward her intended resting place.

"How long will the henbane last?" the woman asked in a thick highland brogue as they propped Daracha up and began to work on walling her up.

Henbane? So they poisoned her then.

"Long enough," replied the man. He sounded weary.

"What if it doesn't work?" The woman handed the man the trowel and put the bucket of mortar within reach.

"As long as she's kept off the ground, she canna come back. That's what she said."

My skin prickled and I stepped forward. "What did you say?"

Of course they ignored me and set to work building the wall around Daracha's form.

I paced in the clearing, watching and listening, but the

couple didn't talk again until the half-wall was built and the beam sat on top.

Impatiently, I spoke again. "What did you mean, as long as she's kept off the ground? Elaborate, would you?"

When the couple was done, they put the now empty mortar buckets and the trowel in the wheelbarrow and faced one another. The woman put her face against the man's chest. "What a nightmare." Her voice hitched and I knew she was crying.

He put his arms around her and held her, letting her cry. "Shhh, Mary. It's over now. She canna hurt anyone any longer."

"What if someone finds her?" Mary sniffed.

"They won't, at least not anytime soon. By the time this cottage can no longer stand, we'll be gone and it won't be our problem."

Mary looked up at her partner, misery etched on her face. "But, what if they bury her? She'll start all over again."

"Shhh." He put a finger on her lips. "Dinna think on it, Mary. You've been through enough, there's no use worrying about something that might not happen to people we'll never know. We've done the best we could against this... creature of darkness." He gestured toward the wall behind which Daracha lay dying. "She's been stopped for now. It will have to be enough."

My heart was pounding, and my whole body felt frozen in ice. I shook my head, wishing I could unhear all of this.

"No, no, no." I put my face in my hands as the couple began to walk away.

I looked through my fingers to see Mary look over her shoulder one last time with *that* look on her face, the one laced with so much emotion. I stood there aghast, horrified, confused. I knew what was coming next and dread filled me.

The ithe came slinking through the trees, sniffing around the wall where its master lay hidden.

"You know she's there. Why didn't you just unbury her?" I snarled at it. "Why did you leave her there for a few hundred years?"

The ithe ignored me, just moved in its flickery, dancing way. It stalked away, right through where I'd been standing when I'd seen the residual for the first time.

My face felt wet and I put my hands on my cheeks. When I pulled them away, I was sitting in bed. Laec wasn't there. Moonlight spilled in through the window and pooled where he'd been sitting. Tears were running down my face. Frustration and terror boiled in my gut, and anger that Laec had just vanished once again, leaving me to reel at what I'd learned. I was alone with my regret.

It wasn't over. Daracha would return. She'd return because of me, because I'd buried her, because I hadn't known any better. Her laughter as she fell into the earth echoed in my mind, making my skin crawl. It made sense now, that laughter. She wasn't mad, she'd just known it wasn't the end.

I didn't know how much time I had or what Daracha would want when she returned, but I knew without a doubt that she would return.

When she did, I had to be ready.

<<< >>>

End Book 1

Go directly to book 2

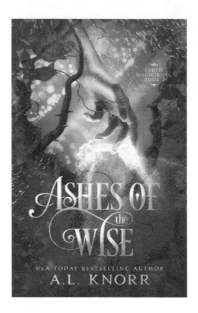

Her power has attracted the wrong kind of attention. Now a centuries-old witch wants to burn her at the stake...

Blackmouth, Scotland. After burying the vicious witch with her earth magic, Georjie is horrified to learn entombing the spellcaster in soil has enabled the dark woman to rise again...

Georjie and Lachlan travel to Dundee for clues to the fiend's power. But when the vengeful hag comes after her, Georjie narrowly escapes into the Fae realm. There, she's warned against returning to face the threat. But she can't let the monster roam free, even if it means risking her own life.

Can Georjie unlock her magic or will a sinister force claim her ashes?

Ashes of the Wise is the second book in the gripping Earth Magic Rises YA contemporary fantasy series. If you like wicked action, dark tales, and bold heroes, then you'll love A.L. Knorr's wild ride across realms.

Buy Ashes of the Wise to keep evil in the ground today!

Mira's Return Series

Returning

Falling

Surfacing

The Kacy Chronicles

Descendant

Ascendant

Combatant

Transcendent

Visit www.alknorrbooks.com to be kept informed of new releases and to get a free copy of Returning.

Made in the USA
Middletown, DE
31 January 2020

84009021R00156